Books by Brian Moore

The Lonely Passion of Judith Hearne
The Feast of Lupercal
The Luck of Ginger Coffey
An Answer from Limbo
Canada (with the editors of *Life*)
The Emperor of Ice-Cream
I Am Mary Dunne
Fergus
The Revolution Script
Catholics
The Great Victorian Collection
The Doctor's Wife

THE DOCTOR'S WIFE

BRIAN MOORE

A DELL BOOK

Published by
DELL PUBLISHING CO., INC.
1 Dag Hammarskjold Plaza
New York, N.Y. 10017

Dell ® TM 681510, Dell Publishing Co., Inc.

ISBN: 0-440-11931-6

Reprinted by arrangement with
Farrar, Straus and Giroux, Inc.

Printed in the United States of America
First Dell printing—September 1977

For Jean

The plane from Belfast arrived on time, but when the passengers disembarked there was a long wait for baggage. "This plane is full seven days a week," said a chap who stood beside Dr. Deane watching the first suitcases jiggle down the conveyor belt. "It's the best-paying run in the whole of the British Isles," the chap said. Dr. Deane nodded: he was not a great one for conversation with strangers. He saw his soft canvas bag come down the ramp looking a bit worn at the edges, and no wonder. It had been a wedding present from his fellow interns twenty years ago. He picked up the bag, went outside, and took the bus to Terminal II to catch the twelve o'clock flight to Paris. It was raining here in London. It had been very blustery when he left home this morning, but the weather forecast had predicted clear skies over the southeastern part of the British Isles. In the airport lounge, after being ticketed and cleared, he decided to have a small whiskey. It was early in the day, but he thought of the old Irish licensing law. A bona fide traveler is entitled to a drink outside normal hours.

On his way to the bar, Dr. Deane stopped at the newsstand and, after browsing, bought the *Guardian* and a copy of *Time* magazine. He then went and stood, a tall lonely figure, at the long modern bar. "John Jameson you said, sir?" the barman asked, and found the bottle. When Dr. Deane saw the amount of liquid poured in the glass, he remembered that he was in England. "Better make that a double," he said.

"A double, very good, sir."

He tasted the whiskey. Over the intercom a voice announced flights to Stockholm, Prague, and Moscow. He still found it odd to think that people could walk out of this lounge and get on planes for places which, to him, were just names in the newspaper. When he had finished his whiskey, he took two Gelusil tablets. He had ulcers, a family ailment, had had two bleeds over the years, and was supposed to be careful. Lately, he had been the opposite. Of course everyone at home drank more these days. It was to be expected.

When his flight was called, he was one of the first to board the bus that took the passengers out to the waiting aircraft. On the bus, he unbuttoned his fly-front raincoat, revealing a green tweed suit, a yellow shirt, and a green tie. The colors made his face seem failed and gray. His wife liked to choose his clothes for him. She had no taste. He knew this, but did not argue with her. He was fonder of peace then she.

Ahead, like wound-up toys, a line of planes crawled toward the takeoff point. Dr. Deane watched a huge American jet begin its lift-off into the rain-filled sky and wondered if he himself were taking off in the wrong direction. And then, with a rush of engines, his own plane was airborne and he was watching the English countryside below. If you could call it countryside. So many more houses and roads and people than at home. Fifty million on this island and less than five million in all of Ireland.

The plane came through rain and cloud to the clear skies predicted in that morning's forecast and, after a while, the stewardesses came around selling cigarettes and drinks. He ordered a Haig and noted that, duty free, it cost a quarter of what he had paid for the Jameson in the airport bar. Unbuckling his seat belt, he lifted the glass, looking at the pale yellow of the Scotch. His wife was dead against his making this trip, needle in a haystack, wild-goose chase, all the clichés she had in that head of hers. He had warned her to tell nobody, but perhaps that was asking more than she had in her. He looked down, saw that the plane was already over water, and craned his head back trying to catch a glimpse of the white cliffs of Dover. The stewardesses were coming up the aisle again, bringing trays of cold lunch. He thought of the letter that had turned up in Paris two days ago, a letter from the American, addressed to Sheila, in care of Peg Conway. His tachycardia began. It's just nerves, my heart's all right. I'm all right. I'm going over to see Peg and to talk to that priest. To see what I can find out.

The stewardess leaned in from the aisle holding a plastic tray on which were a plate of cold meat, a cream puff, and a green salad. "Are you having luncheon, sir?"

Dr. Deane did not feel hungry but there was his ulcer to be fed. He accepted the tray.

Peg Conway, a small woman, came in again from the front hall of her flat to stand like a child before Dr. Deane's lonely height. Old-fashioned, he had risen from the sofa as she re-entered the living room. "Please don't get up," she reassured him. "Here it is."

Dr. Deane turned the letter over in his hands, noting

the American airmail stamps, the address to which it
had been sent:

> MME SHEILA REDDEN
> C/O CONWAY
> 29 QUAI SAINT-MICHEL
> PARIS, 75005
> FRANCE
> *Faire suivre, s.v.p.—*
> *Urgent. Please forward*

And the address from which it had been sent:

> T. LOWRY
> PINE LODGE
> RUTLAND, VERMONT 05701
> U.S.A.

"You'll see that it was posted in Vermont on the
second. That's four days after they were supposed to
leave Paris."

Dr. Deane lowered himself back down on the worn
brown velvet sofa. He tapped the envelope on his knee.

"Why don't you open it?" Peg said.

He smiled nervously, and looked at the letter again.
"Ah, no, I don't think I should do that. It wouldn't be
right."

"It's an emergency, after all."

"I know."

"Look," Peg said. "She's supposed to be in America.
Well, *is* she? Look at the date on the envelope. If he
wrote her that letter, it means they're no longer together."

"Not necessarily." Dr. Deane lit a Gauloise from a

crumpled pack. "She might have got cold feet that night, then joined him later."

"After the letter was posted?"

"Exactly." He inhaled and blew smoke through his nose.

"I thought doctors didn't smoke nowadays."

"I backslid."

"So, what's your next move?"

"I was thinking," Dr. Deane said. "It's just possible she's with him now, at that address in Vermont. I might try ringing her up."

"You mean, ring up America? That Pine Lodge place?"

"Yes."

"You'd rather do that than open the letter?"

"Yes."

"Well, all right, then," Peg said. "It's an idea. Look, I'll go and get supper started. That way you won't be disturbed if you do reach Sheila. The phone's over there."

"I'll find out the charges on the call, of course."

"Don't worry about that."

He stood up as she left, then heard her shut the kitchen door with a loud noise, indicating that he would not be overheard. A big tabby cat came stalking in from the hall, arching its back, then leaning against his trouser leg. He looked again at the address on the envelope, and went to the desk where the phone was. Through Peg's French windows he could see the Seine far below, winding through the city; to his left, the floodlit spire of the Sainte-Chapelle behind the law courts, and, downriver, the awesome, sepulchral façade of Notre-Dame. To look out at a view like this, so different from any view at home, to pick up the telephone and speak words which would be carried by undersea cable to that huge continent he had never seen. It was as though he were not living his own life but acting in some film, a detective hunting for a missing person or, more likely, a criminal seeking to make amends to his victim. And now, dialing, and talking to an international operator, within a minute he heard a number ring, far away, clear and casual as though he were phoning someone just down the street.

"Pine Lodge," an American voice said.

"I have a person-to-person call from Paris, France," the operator said. "For a Mrs. Sheila Redden."

"I'm sorry, we don't have anyone registered by that name."

Dr. Deane cut in. "Do you have a Mr. Tom Lowry there?"

"Sir, hold on, do you want to make that person-to-person to Mr. Lowry instead?" his operator asked.

"Yes, please."

"Thank you. Hello, Vermont? Do you have a Mr. Tom Lowry there, please?"

"Okay, hold on," the American voice said. "Tom? Paris! Take it on two."

"Hello"—a voice, young, very excited.

"Mr. Lowry, I'm Sheila's brother and I'm calling from Peg Conway's flat in Paris. My name is Owen Deane."

"Oh." The voice went cold. "Yes?"

"I've been trying to get in touch with Sheila. I want to talk to her about some money I'm supposed to send her. Is she there?"

There was a moment's hesitation. "I'm sorry, I can't help you."

"I'm calling because there's a letter here from you, addressed to Sheila. We thought she was with you. Naturally, we're worried about her."

"I'm sorry."

"Well, look, if you know where she is, would you please pass a message on to her? Would you tell her to ring me collect in Paris at the Hôtel Angleterre? I'll give you the number."

"I'm sorry. Goodbye," the boy's voice said. The receiver clicked.

Dr. Deane stood, holding the phone, his heart starting up with the tachycardia that had affected him ever since this business had started. He put down the receiver, saw his pale face in the mirror, and, again, thought of what she had said to him that day: *Forget me. I'm like the man in the newspaper story, the ordinary man who goes down to the corner to buy cigarettes and is never heard from again.* To think it was only four weeks since she came here to Paris to start a perfectly ordinary summer holiday. She came to this flat, she stood in this very room. His eyes searched the mirror as though, behind him, his sister might reappear. But the mirror room gave him back only his own reflection, his Judas face.

Put your things in the spare room, Peg had written, and make yourself at home, because I won't be back till six. Sheila Redden let down her heavy suitcase and felt under the carpet runner on the top step of the stairs where Peg's letter said it would be. She pulled the key out, put it in the lock, and the door opened inward with a groan of its hinges. As she bent again to pick up the suitcase, a big tabby cat bounded past her, skipping into the flat. Would that be Peg's cat? Mrs. Redden went inside, calling "Puss, Puss," although Puss wouldn't mean much to a French cat, she supposed. Weren't French cats called Minou? She went into the front hall, still calling "Puss, Puss," damned cat, but then she saw it, very much at home, lapping water from a cat dish in the kitchen. So that was all right. She took off her coat.

It was quiet here: this far up, the street noises blurred to a distant monotone. In the living room, thinking of the great view there must be, she unlocked the middle set of French windows and stepped out onto the narrow balcony. Below her, the Seine wound among streets filled with history no Irish city ever knew and, as she looked down, from the shadowed underside of the Pont Saint-Michel a sightseeing boat slid into sunlight, tourists massed on its broad deck staring up in her direction. If they saw her, she would seem to them to be some rich French woman living here in luxury, right opposite the Ile Saint-Louis. The sightseeing boat slid sideways, as though it had lost its rudder, but then, righting itself, went off toward Notre-Dame in a churn of dirty brown water. Mrs. Redden leaned out over the iron railing to look down six floors to the street, where white-aproned waiters, tiny as the bridegroom figurines on a wedding cake, hurried in and out among sidewalk tables. Into her mind came the view from her living room at home. The garden: brick covered with English ivy, Belfast's mountain, Cave Hill, looming over the top of the garden wall, its promontories like the profile of a sleeping giant, face upward to the gray skies. Right opposite her house was the highest point of the mountain, the peak called Napoleon's Nose. She thought of that now, staring out at Napoleon's own city. L'Empereur on his white charger Marengo, riding into the Place des Invalides, triumphant after Austerlitz; clatter of hoofbeats on cobblestones, silken pennants, braided gold lanyards, fur shakos, the Old Guard. Napoleon's Nose. And this. She stepped inside again, closing the big windows, going to the front hall to get her suitcase. But then—it put the heart across her—heard someone moving about inside the flat.

Burglars. Or worse? Ever since the bomb in the Abercorn, anything at all made her jump. She stood mouse quiet, listening, until, oh, God, thank God, she saw who it was. A girl moving about in the spare room.

"Did I scare you?" the girl asked, discovering Mrs. Redden and the look on Mrs. Redden's face.

"No, not at all."

The girl, a Yank by the sound of her, had on blue jeans and a peasant blouse you could see through. A big backpack sat open in the middle of the spare room. The girl picked up a comb, a hairbrush, and some makeup things. "I was supposed to be out of here an hour ago, but I got tied up on the phone. You're Peg's friend from Belfast, right?"

"That's right, yes."

"I'm Debbie Rush."

"Sheila Redden," Mrs. Redden said, and there was one of those pauses.

"So," the girl said. "How are things in Belfast?"

"Oh, the usual."

"It must be rough, right? Are they ever going to settle that mess?"

Mrs. Redden smiled what she hoped was a friendly smile. Yanks. Kevin had an American aunt who was over on a visit from Boston last summer: she would wear you, that one. Of course, this girl probably worked with Peg. That would be it.

"I guess you've just got to get the British out of there," the girl said.

Mrs. Redden did not honor this with an answer. "Do you work in the office with Peg?" she asked.

"At Radio Free Europe?" The girl began to laugh. "No way. I'm a friend of Tom Lowry's. He's a friend of Peg's and, when there was a foul-up on my charter flight home, he spoke to her and—she's really nice—she let me crash here until you came."

At once Mrs. Redden felt guilty. "I'm putting you out, then?"

"No, no, it's all right. I'm going to a hotel tonight and tomorrow I get a flight, I hope." The girl hoisted the backpack, wrestling it onto her back. Her breasts stood out under the sheer blouse. Mrs. Redden helped straighten the backpack on the girl's shoulders.

"Oh, thanks," the girl said. "I'm glad I'm going downstairs, not up. How about those stairs?"

"Good for the figure," Mrs. Redden said.

"Yes, right." The girl, gripping her backpack straps, turned and marched like a soldier into the hall. Mrs. Redden hurried to open the front door. "Well, it was nice meeting you," the girl decided.

"I'm sorry to be putting you out like this."

"No, no, have a nice vacation. See you."

Mrs. Redden, holding the door open—she didn't want to close it until the girl had gone, it would seem rude—watched the blond head bobbing down and around and down and around, until the staircase was empty.

Four hours later, when Mrs. Redden and Peg Conway were celebrating their reunion with dinner at La Coupole, two homosexuals, coming through the restaurant, stopped, stared at Mrs. Redden, whispered to each other, then bowed to her in an elaborate manner.

"You don't know them, surely?" Peg asked.

"No, of course not."

"They must have taken you for someone else."

"Or maybe they think I'm a man dressed up in a frock."

Peg laughed. "You're mad, why would they think that?"

"On account of my height. The way I stick up out of this banquette."

"When are you going to get over that notion about your height?"

"You never get over it," Mrs. Redden said.

"Speaking of queers"—Peg Conway began to laugh again—"I wonder what ever happened to Fairy Rice?"

"Wasn't he the end?" They laughed together, remembering: he had been a fellow student at Queen's who wore a sweater as long as a short dress and sat in the front row at lectures, polishing his fingernails with a chamois nail buffer. "His old mum died," Mrs. Redden said. "I saw the death notice in the *Belfast Telegraph* a couple of years ago."

"Do you remember her haunting the Students' Union, waiting to give him his lunch in a picnic basket?"

They laughed.

"I heard he went to England," Mrs. Redden said.

"Fairy did?"

"I think so."

"Tell me," Peg said. "Have you and Kevin ever thought of emigrating?"

"Oh, Kevin would never leave Belfast."

"Why not?"

"It would mean starting all over, working up a new practice. Besides, he never wants to travel. It's taken me two years to get him to join me on this holiday in Villefranche."

"I remember he used to like a good time, though," Peg said. "The races, do you remember?" As she said it, she saw him, Sheila's big lump of a husband, standing in the members' enclosure at the Curragh, a reserved-stand tag in his buttonhole, lifting his field glasses to look down the track.

"Gosh, yes, that used to be great fun. Driving to Dublin, spending the night in Buswells Hotel, then all day Saturday at the races, and a grand meal before we drove home. But, he has no time now."

"A person should make time."

"It's hard for him, though," Mrs. Redden said. "I mean, with this group practice. And now he has an extra job as a surgical consultant to the British Army. They have him down to their H.Q. in Lisburn three or four times a week. It's too much work for one man. And it hasn't improved his disposition, I can tell you."

Peg Conway was not listening; she was watching the door. All evening she had been hoping Ivo would show up, but now it seemed unlikely. She said, "Talking of Villefranche, I spent a terrific, dirty weekend in the South of France recently."

Mrs. Redden was embarrassed. "Oh?"

"His name is Ivo Radic. He's a Yugoslav."

"A Yugoslav," Mrs. Redden said. So there *was* a new man.

"A refugee. He teaches English and German in a grotty little private school in the sixteenth arrondissement. At any rate, he's an improvement on Carlo."

"What happened to Carlo?"

"Don't ask. That wife of his can keep him. Ivo is divorced, at least."

"Ivo Radic," Mrs. Redden said, as though trying out the name.

"I met him by the merest fluke," Peg said. "Hugh Greer—you remember Hugh Greer?"

"Of course," Mrs. Redden said. Hugh Greer, a Trinity prof. Peg's big early love.

"Well, Hugh had this American student in Dublin, a boy called Tom Lowry. He asked Tom to look me up when he came to Paris this summer. So Tom did, and then he invited me around for a drink at his flat. And his roommate was Ivo. So, in an odd way, I met Ivo because of Hugh Greer."

"You still keep in touch with Hugh, then?"

"Yes. Poor old Hugh. He has cancer, did you know?"

"Oh, God. What kind?"

"Lung."

"How old is he?"

"About fifty. Listen, would you like to meet Ivo?"

Mrs. Redden thought: What could you say? "Yes, of course," she said.

"Good. I'll tell you what. We'll finish here and go to a café called the Atrium for coffee. Ivo and Tom's flat is just around the corner from there. I'll ring now and see if Ivo can join us," Peg said, getting up at once, very purposefully, to march off to the *cabinet de toilette* where the telephones were. Mrs. Redden watched her go, then, in her shy, furtive way, glanced at the people in the next booth, an aristocratic-looking old Frenchman and his young son, both eating Bélon oysters and sucking juice from the shells. She thought of the first time she had ever been in La Coupole, that summer she was a student at the Alliance Française. Her Uncle Dan showed up in Paris and took her to lunch here to meet a young man who was the Paris correspondent for the *Irish Times*. After lunch, they went on, all three of them, to a garden party at Fontainebleau, at the house of some Swedish countess who was a friend of Uncle Dan's. Uncle Dan knew everybody. Cancer, he died of. Hugh Greer has it now. On the day of Uncle Dan's funeral I traveled alone on the train to Dublin. Kevin had to stay behind to operate. Everybody who was anybody was at the funeral, the cardinal in his crimson silks, sitting in the episcopal chair at the side of the altar during the Mass, and at Glasnevin cemetery I saw De Valéra: he took his hat off and stood, holding it over his chest as the priest said the prayers for the dead. Lemass, the Prime Minister, was beside him and every other government minister as well, the whole of the diplomatic corps, everyone. When the Irish Army buglers sounded the Last Post after the prayers, I was sitting in a big rented Daimler with Aunt Meg. I wept, but she didn't, she just sat watching it all, her cane rammed between her knees as though that was what was keeping her up straight, and as soon as the bugles were lowered, she said, "Fruitcake, I forgot them. I ordered seven from Bewley's. Tell Mrs. O'Keefe to lay out five with the sherry and sandwiches. Sheila, are you listening?"

Mrs. Redden looked again at the old Frenchman and his son, who had now finished their oysters and were drinking Loire wine and mopping up the oyster shells with thin slices of buttered brown bread. She turned and saw Peg coming back through the huge room, giving a thumbs-up sign from afar. The Yugoslav must have said yes and so we'll end up at this Atrium place, the three of us. Mrs. Redden smiled at Peg, but into her mind came Uncle Dan's grave the last time she had visited it, alone, two years after his funeral, a stormy day with lightning and thunder, no cross on the grave, nothing about who he was, just a slab of gray Connemara marble laid flat like a door on the earth. His name: Daniel Deane. 1899–1966. She bought a few carnations in a shop beside the cemetery. Uncle Dan liked to wear a carnation. The cemetery attendant gave her a little blue glass vase. Red carnations in a blue glass vase, she left on his grave.

At the Atrium Peg chose a table with a good view of the Boulevard Saint-Germain. Mrs. Redden was again reminded of the French way of sitting, not really facing your table companions, but all of you turned around to watch the passersby. The Yugoslav had not yet shown up.

"I love just being here, just watching the people," Mrs. Redden said, staring at the parade on the pavement outside.

"Most of this lot would be better off at home studying, than lallygagging around in fancy dress," Peg said.

"Next week is end-of-term exams at the Sorbonne. Thank God, I'm not a French parent."

But Mrs. Redden wished *she* were. Here your children could go where they pleased, without your worrying about bombs, or their being stopped by an army patrol, or lifted in error by the police, or hit by a sniper's bullet. If Danny lingered at a school friend's house until after dark, usually he had to spend the night there.

The waiter came.

"Listen," Peg said. "If we want a cognac, let's order and pay for it before Ivo comes. Otherwise, poor lamb, he'll insist on standing treat."

"All right, but only if you'll let me pay," Mrs. Redden said. *"Deux cognacs et deux cafés, s'il vous plaît."*

"Bien, Madame," the waiter said.

Maybe it was the cognac, or maybe it was the prospect of Ivo's joining them, but there was now a noticeable heightening of Peg's spirits. "So, tomorrow night you'll be in Villefranche in the same hotel you were in on your honeymoon. It means one thing. You liked it the first time."

This annoyed Mrs. Redden, although she did not show it. At nearly forty years of age, you'd think Peg would have grown out of her schoolgirl mania for talking about sex all the time. But no fear.

"You're blushing," Peg said.

"Oh, stop it."

"Listen, Sheila, I envy you. I suppose you're one of the few people I know who's still happily married. Certainly you're the only one who's going off on a second honeymoon—how many years later?"

"Sixteen."

"God, is it that long?"

"Danny's fifteen. We were married in 1958."

"So, you're what? Thirty-eight. You don't look it."

"I am thirty-seven until next November," Mrs. Redden said, laughing.

"Ivo's four years younger than me. I suppose that
sounds really decadent."

"Oh, nonsense," Mrs. Redden said, but thought, *I*
couldn't do it, but then, I'm not Peg, she's done all the
things I never had guts to try, going on to London for
postgraduate work after getting her M.A., then the
U.N. in New York with the Irish delegation, and now
Paris, and this big money with the Americans. She
lives like a man, free, having affairs, traveling, always
in big cities, whereas, look at me, stuck all these years
at home, my M.A. a waste. I don't think I could even
support myself any more. "You know," she said to
Peg, "it's working and traveling that keep a person
young. It's sitting at home doing nothing that makes you
middle-aged in your mind. I was just thinking about
it the other day. It's as if the only part of my life I
look forward to now is my holidays. There's something
terribly wrong about that."

"I suppose," Peg said, but Mrs. Redden noticed that
she wasn't really listening. Someone had come into the
café and now Peg was signaling to him. Mrs. Redden
stared at the newcomer: four years younger than her,
who does she think she's kidding? Ten years is more
like it. The boy was very tall, with long dark hair and
a pale, bony face. He wore a brown crew-neck sweater,
brown corduroy trousers, and scuffed desert boots of
the sort Mrs. Redden's own son had bought last year.
He smiled as he came up, throwing his head back to
toss the long hair out of his eyes in a gesture once
used only by girls.

"Hello, Tom," Peg said.

So he was not the boy friend.

"Sheila, this is Tom Lowry. Sheila Redden."

"Hi," he said, then turned to Peg. "I'm the bringer of bad tidings, I'm afraid. Ivo's put his back out again."

"Oh no."

He sat down, casually, his legs astride the café chair, his arms resting on the chair back. He stared at Mrs. Redden, then said to Peg, "He was on his way up here to join you, but, a moment after he went out the door, I heard him yell and found him in the courtyard all seized up."

"He'll blame me," Peg said. "You'll see."

"No, no," the boy said, but as he spoke he was no longer looking at Peg, he was staring again at Mrs. Redden, making her wonder if there was something wrong with her. She looked down at her skirt, but it was not that. It's my face he's looking at.

"So what should we do?" Peg asked.

"Why not come around to the flat? Ivo would like to see you and I could give you a drink."

"I don't know," Peg said. "Well, maybe if we just pop in for a moment. Would that be all right with you, Sheila?"

"Yes, of course." What else could she say? And, wouldn't you know, the moment she agreed, Peg was up on her feet again, ignoring the cognacs, which were not even finished. "Wait," Mrs. Redden said. "I have to pay."

"Let me get it"—this Tom Lowry said.

"No, no." And so, after a fuss, Mrs. Redden paid, and they found themselves going down a dark side street behind the Marché Saint-Germain, Peg in hell's own hurry, forging on ahead, leaving her alone with the stranger. The first thing she thought about him was that he was taller than she, which was a relief, but still, from habit, she squinched down as she walked beside him. He seemed the quiet type. *The Quiet American,* by Graham Greene. But then she remembered that Quiet American was a sinister sort of character.

"You're from the North?" he asked.

"Yes."

"I thought I recognized a touch of Ulster. Are you on a holiday?"

Other Yanks said "vacation." He was different. "Yes."

"You're here alone?"

She glanced at him, under the light of the street lamp.

"I'm sorry," he said. "It was just that Peg told me something about you coming with your husband."

"Oh. He's joining me at Villefranche tomorrow."

"So you're only in Paris for one night?"

She nodded, and he did not speak again until they reached his building, where Peg waited impatiently outside the locked street door. As he took out his key to open it, Mrs. Redden saw him glance at her again, much as she herself looked at people when she was curious but didn't want them to see it.

"Wait till I get the light," he said, ushering them into a pitch-black courtyard, fumbling somewhere, until a light came on, a dim French contraption which only stayed lit long enough to let them hurry across the courtyard to the ground-floor flat where he lived. As he put the key in his own door, the light went out again. He unlocked in darkness, then, entering, let them into a brightly lit hall.

Very small, was her first impression of the flat. There was a tiny neat kitchen on the right, a little bathroom, one small bedroom in the back. A man's dark suit jacket was hung over the back of a chair in the hall, knife points of white handkerchief sticking up from its breast pocket. They went into the little sitting room where, lying on his back on the floor, was a very good-looking man formally dressed in dark suit trousers, white shirt, and red wool tie. Mrs. Redden thought of a dead person laid out for a funeral.

"Good evening." The man on the floor had a deep foreign voice. "Excuse me, receiving you like this."

"Oh, Ivo, dear," Peg said, at once going down on one knee beside him, running her fingers through his graying hair. That is not a man who likes to have his hair tossed, Mrs. Redden decided, as the man on the floor turned his head away from Peg.

"This is my friend Sheila Redden. Ivo Radic."

The handsome man smiled at her and said he was pleased to meet her. Tom Lowry came into the room with a bottle and four thimble glasses. "Ah," said Ivo. "Slivovitz. May we offer you ladies a *digestif?*"

"Darling," Peg said, "first let's get you up and onto your bed."

"I prefer the floor. It is therapy."

"Surely you'd be more comfortable sitting up?"

"If I do not lie flat, I will not be able to teach tomorrow. And if I do not report for work, then *le Docteur* Laporte will again underpay me at the end of the month."

"But you have a board in your bed. We'll put you on the bed and we'll all sit in the bedroom."

The handsome man laughed, unamused. "Your friend," he said to Mrs. Redden, "wants to run my life."

"Ivo, please," Peg said. "At least lie on the settee."

"The settee is too soft," Ivo said. He kept smiling at Mrs. Redden. "Did you have a pleasant journey from London, *Madame?*"

"I flew from Ireland, as a matter of fact."

"Ah, Ireland."

Tom Lowry began to hand around the thimble glasses. Peg had risen from her kneeling posture and still stared at the man on the floor, as though there were no other people in the room. "Are you trying to tell me something, darling?" she said. "Are you in a bad temper?"

"No, my darling, I am in a very good temper."

"Well then, do get up."

Tom Lowry, beckoning Mrs. Redden to a seat, smiled as though to reassure her not to heed this tiff.

"It's Sheila's one night in Paris," Peg went on. "It can't be much fun for her to sit here with you lying on the floor like that."

"Oh, don't worry about me," Mrs. Redden said, unwisely, and looked again at the Yugoslav: he had dark eyes; he really was handsome, she decided, but at the same time he was one of those men she was afraid of, the kind who looked as though they might be cruel to you. He turned back to her now, smiling at her, ignoring Peg, holding up his thimble glass of liqueur in a toast. *"Nasdrovie,"* he said to Mrs. Redden. "And welcome to Paris."

All watched as he tried the impossible: to bring the thimble glass to his lips and knock it back, without lifting his head from the carpet. At the last second, a little of the liquid trickled down the side of his mouth. Peg, who had retired to sit dejectedly by the small writing desk, rose up at once, opened her handbag, and took out a handkerchief, kneeling by him once more, dabbing at his chin.

"Please!" he said, turning his head away. But she insisted on finishing her task.

"How long have you had this flat?" Mrs. Redden asked Tom Lowry.

"Oh, it's Ivo's place, really. He just lets me sleep on the settee."

"Well, I must say the pair of you are very tidy."

"Ivo, get up!" Peg said suddenly.

Ivo smiled, but did not move.

"All right, then. If you can't receive visitors properly, Sheila and I had better go home."

Mrs. Redden looked at Ivo, saw the blood come up under his skin. Peg turned to her. "Ready, Sheila?"

Mrs. Redden stood, embarrassed.

"You are flying on to the Riviera tomorrow, *Madame?*" Ivo asked.

"Yes. To Nice."

"Ah, the land of sunshine. I cannot say as much for this city. Gray, gray every day. It is no wonder people here cannot keep their temper."

"I am not in a bad temper," Peg said. "But I'm going home. Good night, Tom."

"Thanks for the drink," Mrs. Redden said to both men.

"Not at all," said the face on the floor, then turned, basilisk, to Peg. "I apologize. You are in a *good* temper. It just pleases you to spoil my evening and perhaps this lady's evening as well."

"Good night," Peg said, turning and going out of the room. Mrs. Redden smiled awkwardly at the men and went to follow.

"I'll show you out," Tom Lowry said. "You'll need help with the courtyard light."

"Good night, *Madame,*" Ivo said. "Enjoy the sunshine."

Light flooded the courtyard as though it were some huge fish tank, revealing Peg hurrying, halfway across the open space, impatient to be gone. They caught up with her by the locked street door. "Listen," Tom said.

"Why don't you go back and have a word with him? I'll take Sheila home."

"No bloody fear. Sheila's only night here, and that selfish bastard has to put on an act."

"Peg, if you don't make up now, it will drag on for weeks. Please, go back in there."

The courtyard light went off. Tom Lowry disappeared to find the switch. When the light flashed on again, Mrs. Redden looked at Peg and saw she was wavering, so said, "Listen, go ahead. I'll walk down to the Atrium and wait for you there."

"You're sure you don't mind? Oh, he doesn't mean to be such a pain in the neck. The bloody man can't help himself. It's some sort of Yugoslav machismo nonsense."

"Of course I don't mind. Go on."

"I'll go with Sheila," Tom Lowry said. "That way you'll have privacy. We'll see you later at the Atrium."

Peg smiled. "You're both great."

And so, minutes later, Mrs. Redden was walking down a Paris street with this boy she had just met, the pair of them beginning to laugh, helplessly.

"Ivo, get up!" Mrs. Redden cried.

"The land of sunshine!" he said, and they laughed. She turned to him, seeing him toss his long dark hair, his eyes shining, his walk eager, as though he and she were hurrying off to some exciting rendezvous. And at once she was back in Paris in her student days, as though none of the intervening years had happened, those years of cooking meals, and buying Danny's school clothes, being nice to Kevin's mother, and having other doctors and their wives in for dinner parties, all that laundry list of events that had been her life since she married Kevin.

"What part of America do you live in?" she asked him.

"New York. Greenwich Village."

"That's the Left Bank part, isn't it?"

"Yes. I was born there, as a matter of fact. My father's on the staff at Saint Vincent's. It's the big hospital in the Village."

"He's a doctor, then?"

"Yes."

"My brother's a doctor," she said. She did not mention her husband.

At the Atrium, he led her to the rear of the café to tables used by the regulars. "Listen," he said, "it's your first day in Paris. Will you let me buy you some champagne?"

"Champagne? It's far too expensive."

"No, let me," he said. "I feel like it. Please?"

"Buy me a Pernod."

"Are you sure?"

"I'm certain."

He signaled the waiter. *"Deux Pernod."*

"Je suis désolé," the waiter said. *"Il n'y a pas de Pernod. Je n'ai que du Ricard."*

"Ricard, ça va," she said. *"Au fait, je le préfère."*

"Deux Ricard, alors," he told the waiter. And then said to her, "I don't know why I'm ordering. Your French is better than mine."

"It's what I did at university."

"Queen's?"

"Yes. You were at Trinity, weren't you? Under Hugh Greer."

"Yes, do you know him?"

"I did, years ago." She saw Hugh as she said it, stout, stammering, with trousers that always seemed too short for him. "Did you do Anglo-Irish Lit. with Hugh? His Joyce-Yeats show?"

"That's right."

"And what are you going to do now? Teach?"

"I don't know. I'm going to take a year off to think about it."

"A year off? You must be rich."

"No, there's a job. A friend of mine runs a small resort hotel in Vermont and he wants to go to Europe next year. I used to work for him summers, and now I'm going to manage his place for him while he's gone. It's a beautiful spot. Skiing in winter, a lake in summer."

"It sounds great."

"Why don't you come and visit me? As acting manager I can offer you a special rate."

She laughed. The waiter brought the Ricard and poured water in their glasses, turning the liquid from yellow to chalk. This boy, this stranger, picked up his glass and looked into her eyes.

"Sláinte," he said, using the Irish toast.

"Sláinte," she said, and, as they touched glasses, his hand touched hers, and she knew, at last, how it must be for the other person, for those men, over the years, who Kevin said had a crush on her. Now she shared it. In the past, so often, the crushes were a joke, like Pat Lawlor down at Mullen's Garage who, when she drove in for petrol, would pull a comb out of his overalls and arrange his hair over his bald spot. Or the young butcher at Kennedy & McCourt's who would bully his other customers to make up their minds so that he could get over to serve her. But there had been times when it wasn't funny. She always felt shy when she talked to a strange man, especially if the man was brainy. She would make an effort to be nice and men would respond, and, sometimes, they would get a look

in their eyes and begin to flirt with her. There had never seemed much harm to it, until, two years ago, suddenly Kevin accused her of "making eyes at men without even knowing you're doing it." "That's a rotten thing to say," she had replied. "And even if it were true, what's wrong with a little harmless flirtation?" "Harmless, my eye," Kevin said. "Brian Boland is a case in point. Anyone with an eye in their head can see the play you make for him the minute he comes into a room. Why, your voice even changes, you start aping his bloody Oxford accent. Poor Bridget Boland loathes your guts, and I don't blame her one bit. You make an absolute fool of yourself." "I do not," she said. "I like Brian, I *don't* imitate his accent but he *has* been abroad, he's interesting to talk to, he can talk about something else besides Paisley and the Provos. But if that's the way you feel about it, I won't even speak to him any more. The Bolands are supposed to be *your* friends, so if you're worried, just don't invite them." Beginning to cry as she said it, but Kevin kept after her, mimicking her, mimicking Brian's English accent, showing how she got excited when Brian talked about books, and then Kevin started to sing "Dancing in the Dark," making fun of her, and it was the most awful, hateful, hurtful row, malicious he was, he wouldn't stop. But afterward she lay awake in the night wondering if Kevin was right; was it true that what she thought of as just being nice was leading a man on? And, after that, she went out of her way to avoid Brian Boland, and if by any chance a man started flirting with her, she would at once make some excuse and move away. She did not want to give Kevin a chance to start in all over again.

But tonight was different. Tonight, for the first time, she realized what Kevin had been talking about. She felt her face flush and she stared into this boy's eyes. She knew she should not lead him on, but she wanted to do it. Besides, Kevin was hundreds of miles away tonight and tomorrow she would be hundreds of miles south of here. In the meantime, there was this excitement, this joy.

So they began to talk, animated, eager to know each other, and she asked him about his student days in Dublin and he told about digs and landladies and made it all fun, so that the time passed in no time until Peg walked in, looking a bit tossed and very pleased with herself, saying she was sorry to be so late. "What about a nightcap?" Tom asked. "No thanks," Peg said, and so all three of them went out of the café and stood for a moment, irresolute, on the street.

"Let me walk you both home," Tom Lowry said. "I'd like some fresh air."

"All right, then," Peg said, and suddenly he was between them, taking each of them by the arm, urging them forward along Boulevard Saint-Germain, where the crowds were queueing for a midnight film. As they passed the queue he released his grip on Peg's arm and eased her ahead on the crowded pavement, remaining behind himself, linked to Mrs. Redden. She noticed that. She felt elated. She noticed that he held tight to her all the way to the Place Saint-Michel, where, still talking eagerly to each other, they caught up with Peg and paused, all three, at the traffic light. In the square, four police wagons filled with French riot police sat, waiting for trouble. She thought of home.

And when at last they reached Peg's building, while Peg searched for the key to the street door, Tom Lowry moved close again and said in a voice that was almost a whisper, "Listen, if you'd like to go shopping tomorrow, maybe I could come along and carry parcels?"

"Oh, it's not serious shopping," she said and found herself whispering, too.

Peg had opened the street door and now turned to them, waiting.

"I could pick you up at ten," he said. "Maybe we can have a coffee?"

"All right. Ten."

And Peg heard her, for she said, "Are we going to have lunch together, Sheila?"

"Oh, Peg, I don't think we'd have time. My plane leaves at one-fifteen."

"Too bad," Peg said. "Tom, when's Debbie going home, is it tomorrow?"

"I think so."

"Because if she can't get a flight out, she can have the spare room again, once Sheila is gone."

"Oh, thanks. I'll tell her."

Debbie. Mrs. Redden saw the pretty girl in the see-through blouse. Why did I say yes to him about the coffee?

Together, she and Peg began the long climb up to the sixth floor. "I think you made a conquest," Peg said.

"Who?" She tried to look surprised.

"Tom."

"Don't be silly. I just didn't know what to say when he asked me about a coffee. Yanks are funny that way, aren't they?"

"I work with them," Peg reminded her. "And they're no different from other people. Actually, I always thought Tom was shy."

"I like him, he's very nice," Mrs. Redden said hurriedly and moved on ahead, not stopping until she reached the third-floor landing, where she waited for Peg, who followed more slowly. When Peg came abreast, Mrs. Redden, trying to sound amused, asked, "That girl with no bra, is she my rival, then?"

"Who?" Peg stopped, a little out of breath.

"Debbie."

"Who knows, with that generation," Peg said. "I don't think so, though."

And went on up to the top floor, taking out her keys again to open the apartment door. As she turned the key in the lock, both women heard the phone ring inside the flat.

"Is that your phone?"

"Yes, but I don't know who it could be at this hour of the night," Peg said, pushing the door open and hurrying down the hall. The ringing stopped just before she picked the receiver up. "Hello? Hello?" She listened, then replaced the receiver. "Too bad. I wonder, was that for you, Sheila?"

"I doubt it. Kevin wouldn't call this late," Mrs. Redden said, but there in the half-dark hall, her elation sank to a sudden fear. In her mind she saw the two Saracen armored cars barricading the lower end of Clifton Street, no one in the street, and just above the Army and Navy Club, Kevin's surgery. There was a blue van parked in front of the Army and Navy Club. *There was no one in the van.* You never left a vehicle unattended. A soldier in battle dress ran out (she had not noticed the soldiers) and beckoned hurriedly with his automatic rifle, ordering her into the shelter of a doorway. She saw, still as a painting, the empty street, rain wet on the pavement, the van *unattended.* Then, all at once, splinters in the air, the noise coming after the dust and smoke as the van blew itself up. She saw the huge dusty hole where the Army and Navy Club had been, the shattered windows and rubbled wall of Kevin's surgery. The soldiers had warned him in time. He and the patients had been moved out.

"Would you like a cup of tea before you go to bed?" Peg asked.

"Not unless you would."

"Well, let's go to sleep now and have an early breakfast before I go to work. Is a quarter to eight too soon for you?"

"No, no."

Peg moved toward her, her arms out, coming to kiss her good night, but now, in the half-dark hall, Mrs. Redden saw, not Peg, but that other woman, blonde, with dust on her hair, blood on her face, running out of the Queen's Arcade, shaking her fist. "Fucking Fenian gets!"

"You're shivery," Peg said, embracing her. "Are you cold?"

"No, no. I wonder who that was on the phone."

"Probably a wrong number."

Croissants, coffee, chatter, screams of laughter, two women in the ease of no child to get off to school, no husband to be fed, no boy friend to be watched for signs of a morning mood, talking, charting the movements and marriages of former friends, calling out anecdotes to each other as Peg hurried to do her hair and put on her suit, the chat so good and the time so quick and easy until the moment came when they kissed each other, hugged, promised to keep in touch, and then, suddenly, Peg was gone.

The hall door shut. Alone, Mrs. Redden felt the emptiness of being left behind. Turning, she went into the living room, opened the windows, and stepped out onto the balcony, craning down, hoping to catch sight of Peg below, on the street. She had hardly seen Peg, had hardly seen Paris; this part of the holiday was already ending.

Then, far below, Peg stepped out, hurrying along the edge of the pavement in her ice-cream suit, going to the corner to the Métro. "Peg?" Mrs. Redden called down, "Peg!" but it was foolish—with six floors and the noise of traffic, there was no chance. Peg was gone. Unaccountably she felt guilty about Peg, so decent and generous, and why didn't I stay over and have lunch with her, bad manners of me, because I wanted to see

Tom Lowry again, not Peg, but I should have done both, I should have taken a later flight.

The phone rang. She stood, irresolute, as its tone gonged through the empty flat. It might be Tom Lowry phoning to say he can't meet me. She went to answer, but the moment she picked up the receiver, she sensed it wasn't him.

Kevin's receptionist said, "Is Mrs. Redden there?"

"Speaking. Is that you, Maureen?"

"Yes, Mrs. Redden. Hold on, the doctor wants to talk to you."

"Hello, Sheila." His voice always sounded strange on the phone. "How are you getting on? Did you have a good flight?"

"Yes, lovely," she said. "How are things at home?"

"Well, that's why I'm ringing. John McSherry's mother-in-law died yesterday afternoon. The funeral's the day after tomorrow. It's a bloody nuisance."

McSherry was one of the doctors in his group. "But you don't have to go to the funeral of McSherry's mother-in-law," she said.

"Wait a minute." She heard the familiar irritation in his voice. "John's wife is laid up, she has a heart condition, you know. Anyway, I offered to hold on here for three more days to let him get things squared away at home."

"But why does it have to be you? What about Con Cullen, he could do McSherry's work, couldn't he?"

"I've already offered to do it."

"But why? They take advantage of you, time and time again. You're always the one who works extra days. Surely, just this once, they'll have the decency to let you get away in peace."

"Look, nobody forced me, it was my idea. And besides, it's just for two more days."

"But this is our holiday! We've been looking forward to it for ages."

"You have," he said.

"What's that supposed to mean?"

"It means, will you stop nagging me. I'll be in Villefranche on Friday. Just enjoy yourself and lie out in the sun. You don't need me for that."

"So you won't be coming before Friday, is that it?"

"Let's say Friday night. I'll give you a ring."

"Why bother?"

"What do you mean?"

"If you don't want to come on this holiday, then don't. You'll be far happier sitting at home, stuck into the telly."

"Oh, balls." He was shouting now. "We can't all live like you, ignoring the facts of life, dancing in the dark."

It was his oldest jibe. Dancing in the dark. "Suit yourself," she said.

"I'll be there on Friday night. Look, I'm sorry it turned out like this."

"You're not one bit sorry," she said, and hung up. But, of course, that was the worst thing she could have done. Now, if only she could ring back and apologize: but that wouldn't work, he would take it as a further insult, a false contrition. She never should have hung up. She turned and wandered, upset, through the flat, going back out onto the balcony, where, in search of self-justification, her mind replayed the conversation. What did he think a woman *did* alone in the South of France? Eating solitary meals in the dining room, going alone to the beach, dragging around the streets of Nice—what sort of holiday was that?—and not only that, he never mentioned Danny. And then, with shame, remembered that neither had she.

Far below, from under the Pont Saint-Michel a long black cargo boat slipped into view, a Dutch flag flying at its stern, a clothesline bunting of sheets and underwear flapping over its holds. A man in a German riverman's cap stood in the wheelhouse, the bowl of his pipe turned down. She looked at this passing barge, at this man who sailed his floating home through inland waterways to cities like Brussels, Amsterdam, and Hamburg, cities she had never seen, might never see. To sail away from all of the things that hold and bind me, to sail away, to start again in some city like Brussels or Amsterdam. Into her mind came the place Kevin always took them to for their summer holidays, a Connemara village with a fishing dock at the end of the single street, the fishermen's boat coming in from the sea at dusk, sailing into that postcard view of the sea bay under the Dolmen peaks of the Twelve Bens, a few summer visitors watching the boat dock, and, then, two red-faced fishermen in greasy Aran sweaters and black rubber Wellington boots coming up off the boat, walking along the quay carrying a flat wooden box filled with fish, she and Kevin and Danny following with the other summer visitors, going around to the back yard behind Cush's pub where the fish would be sold. And later, in Cush's, Kevin would stand pints for those same two fishermen, Michael Pat Lynch and Joe O'Malley. That's Kevin's idea of escape. That village is the only faraway place he ever wants to be.

The doorbell.

She went to answer, first thinking it was the cleaning woman Peg said might come, but then that it could be him. She saw herself in the mirror, hair blown about by standing out on the balcony, but no time to fix it, for the doorbell rang again. She opened.

This morning he was in a tweed jacket, a checked

shirt, and a tie, the dressed-up look of someone who normally doesn't think about what he puts on. She wished she had had time to fix her hair.

"Well, Tom," she said, smiling. "You're very punctual. Even early."

"Sorry. Too soon for you?"

"No, no, I'm ready."

"Where would you like to go?" he asked. "Rue Saint-Honoré?"

"Oh, I think the Galeries Lafayette is more in my line."

"All right, let's go there, then."

Poking around in a department store with him trailing after me, men are bored stiff by shopping. "Why don't we just go for a stroll? What about the Luxembourg Gardens?"

"That sounds good."

Later, going up the Boulevard Saint-Michel, she said, unwisely, "It doesn't change, does it? It's just the way I remember it from my student days."

"You studied in Paris?"

"Not really. I spent a summer here, ages ago, doing conversational French at the Alliance Française. I lived right in this quarter, as a matter of fact."

"Where?"

"A little place called the Hôtel des Balcons, near the Place de l'Odéon."

"I know it," he said. "Rue Casimir-Delavigne."

"That's right."

"Crazy," he said. "I stayed there last summer. When were you there, do you remember?"

"Oh." She did the sum in her head: twenty years. "Ages ago."

"The sixties?"

"Earlier sixties," she lied.

"Was it run down then?"

"It was my first time in Paris, so everything looked super to me. It was nice, though."

"So the *quartier* hasn't really changed?"

"Well," she said, and as she began to speak, she went back in her mind to that time, remembering the cafés she sat in, the Old Navy and the Mabillon, telling how Le Drugstore in those days was a big brasserie called Le Royal Saint-Germain, and about the Australian girl with red hair and white clown makeup who used to wander along the rue de Buci, always with two boy friends in tow. Trying to give him the sense of that summer, the excitement of coming from Belfast and Dublin to her first great foreign city. But not telling him the end of it, the sadness when the summer was over and she returned to Queen's for four years of study, locked up in Ulster for four more years of her life.

And so, walking beside him, she reached the Luxembourg Gardens and went down a gravelly avenue past kiosks unchanged since the time of Proust, old-fashioned wooden structures whose licensees sold old-fashioned balloons, children's wooden hoops, toy boats, tops, whips, and boiled sweets. From there they reached the *rond-point* and the octagonal basin and walked around the formal gardens and off down another avenue, in among trees and grassy lawns and the greening statues of poets she remembered from her Sundays, that summer long ago.

Talking to him: talking with an eagerness she had forgotten. At home, these last years, conversations seemed to fail. At home, if she would try for an hour of "general" talk, it was like floating on water. The moment you thought of sinking, you sank. Kevin would turn back to the television, she to a book. Lately, she read books the way some people drank. But now, with this stranger, the talk came easy as she told of the things that had happened here that summer; she and Edna Morrissey, what innocents they were, how they had lived two days on one *baguette* each, because Edna's mother had sent her allowance to the wrong address. She had been so wrong about Yanks, he was not at all like those desperate loud double knits who went around Ireland in tour buses. He was different.

At eleven, as the clock on the Palais chimed its slow announcement, he put his hand on her sleeve. "How about that cup of coffee?" And, later, sitting with her at a sidewalk table in the Café de Tournon, just below the entrance to the Sénat, where *flics* in white gloves directed traffic and Gardes Républicaines stood sentry outside their red-white-and-blue-striped boxes, he leaned across the table and again put his hand on her arm, as though unconsciously he could not help touching her. "What time are you meeting your husband this evening? Is he flying direct to Nice?"

"He's not coming today."

"Oh?"

So she explained about Kevin's being delayed until Friday. "Even then it's not sure. He's terribly busy just now."

"So he mightn't join you at all?"

"Oh, he'll probably manage it on Friday." She was angry with herself for having started this.

"But if he's not coming today, why not stay longer in Paris? You could sleep over at Peg's."

"Well, I've made arrangements with the hotel in Villefranche and my flight is booked and everything."

"You could change your flight, that's easy. And they'll hold the hotel room."

"No," she said nervously. "No, I couldn't, we have

demipension and I booked ahead. It's too complicated. Besides, Peg's busy, I wouldn't want to impose on her."

"Oh, come on, it's no problem. And I'm not busy, I'd love to show you around. First, let me buy you some lunch. Then I'll phone the airline. *And* the hotel. It's easy."

But it's not easy, she thought; easy for him, but I'm too nervous about things like that, I'm no Yank, I've already written to the hotel and paid my deposit and specially booked room 450, and got my tickets and left addresses and phone numbers with Mrs. Milligan. Besides, what if Kevin changes his mind and comes on to Villefranche tomorrow? "No," she said. "I'd love to, but I can't."

"Have lunch, at least. You can always take a later flight this afternoon."

But that would mean phoning British Airways and changing the flight, maybe being wait-listed on a later one, getting into Villefranche after dark, and besides, I wrote the hotel I'd be there early this afternoon. "No," she said. "I think I'll just stroll back to Peg's place and get my suitcase and make my way to the Invalides."

"You're sure?"

"Yes. I suppose I'm a real stick-in-the-mud."

He laughed. "Look, I'll come along with you and carry your bag. I'll ride out to the airport with you."

"What for? It's a long way out and back."

"*What for?*" he said, laughing again. "Does there have to be a reason?"

It was not very funny. Then what was she laughing at; what were they laughing at? She did not know. But there, sitting laughing in the Café de Tournon, she felt again as though she were a deserter from home. Again, she saw that woman in the Queen's Arcade after the Abercorn Café explosion, the dirt-matted

blond hair, the blood on the woman's cheek, the priest
kneeling on the pavement saying an act of contrition
over a dying old man, Mrs. Redden standing beside the
priest, holding the priest's hat for him, and, when the
woman ran out and saw this, her face became all hate
and she lifted her arm and struck the priest's hat out
of Mrs. Redden's grasp and hit Mrs. Redden in the
face, shouting, "Fucking Fenian gets!" as if Mrs. Redden and the priest and the dying old man had set the
bomb off and were not victims like herself.

She looked up at the clock on the Palais, then at the
flic in dark-blue uniform directing traffic, signaling with
his white-gloved hand, then wheeling like a robot to
beckon the opposing stream of cars. What about those
men you read about in newspaper stories who walk
out of their homes saying they are going down to the
corner to buy cigarettes and are never heard from
again? This is Paris. I am here. What if I never go
back?

Her flight had been called twice and now it was definitely the last call. There was no delaying it any longer, there was nothing to do but say goodbye, turn her back on him, and walk through the security check and onto the aircraft. An anxiety, the unreasoning anxiety of departure, came into her voice as she said, "Well, I *must* go this time."

He stared, his dark eyes all question, as though he waited for her to give him some sign.

"Goodbye, then," she said.

He did not speak.

"If you ever come back to Ireland you must look us up."

He moved toward her. She was sure he was going to kiss her, but, instead, he stopped and awkwardly held out his hand. For a moment she thought of kissing him on both cheeks in the French manner and making a joke of it, but her courage left her, and instead she shook his hand, then went up to the security people. A man and his wife were ahead of her in the check line, loaded down with cartons of gifts. She turned to look back. He was still standing there. She waved, he smiled and waved back. And then she entered the security checkpoint and, once through it, could no

longer see the departure lounge. When she entered the
aircraft, the seat-belt sign was already on, and as she
sat down in her allotted seat, a stewardess offered her
a choice of magazines. She took the first magazine off
the pile, hurriedly, because she wanted the stewardess
to move so that she could look across the aisle at the
window facing the terminal. But saw only the terminal
wall. No sign of him. The aircraft door shut and the
plane taxied out for takeoff. She sat, staring numbly at
the magazine cover.

L'EXPRESS
L'APRÈS
POMPIDOU

There was a photograph of the deceased President
and, under it, the caption:

GEORGES POMPIDOU
"L'avenir n'est interdit à personne." Gambetta

As the plane moved forward in the takeoff queue,
the quotation repeated itself in her head: *L'avenir n'est
interdit à personne*—the future is forbidden to no one.
The engines increased their thrust, the plane rushed
down the runway and lifted into the air. Outside the
window, great canyons of cloud opened and closed like
the corridors of heaven as the plane climbed up into
a bright-blue void. The seat-belt sign went off. On the
intercom, a female voice announced that drinks would
be offered and that luncheon would be served. She
remembered the fuss she had made in the British
Airways office in Belfast, two months ago, when the
clerk told her this luncheon flight was fully booked,
but that there was space on the later flight at three

o'clock. She had wait-listed herself on this flight because she didn't want to miss lunch. And if I hadn't done that, at this moment I would be having lunch with Tom Lowry in Paris. Why didn't I change my reservations this morning, why did I worry about the stupid old hotel? How did I get so bogged down in ordinariness that even this once I couldn't do the spontaneous thing, the thing I really wanted to do. The future is forbidden to no one. Unless we forbid it to ourselves.

Ninety minutes later, the plane began its approach to Nice, flying along the coastline over Saint-Raphaël and Cannes. Through the window she saw villas on cliff-sides, emerald swimming pools, white feathers of yacht sails scattered in the bays. When she had first looked down on this coast long ago on her honeymoon, she had turned in excitement, saying: "Oh, Kevin, wouldn't it be marvelous to be able to live here all the time?" only to have him take her literally and answer, "I suppose it would, if all I wanted to do was water-ski the rest of my life." She remembered that now, as the plane wheeled, pointing down toward land. Below her, cars moved, slow as treacle on the ribbon of seafront road. The plane skimmed the tops of a row of palm trees, came in over a cluster of white rectangular hangars to land with a jolt of its undercarriage and a sickening rear jet thrust.

The jitney bus which took her into Nice went along the Promenade des Anglais, then out on the Corniche road to Villefranche, under layer-cake terraces of luxury hotels, past villas set in high cliffs, hanging bougainvillea in walled gardens, a great sweep of bay curving out from smaller arcs of private beach. Again, she thought of herself and Kevin on that honeymoon flight, coming here to the direct opposite of the cold, rainy strands and bleak, limestone-fronted promenade boardinghouses of the seaside towns at home. And now, when the bus let her off at the top of the road above Villefranche and she took up her suitcase to walk down to the seafront, Villefranche was just as she remembered it. In those sixteen years, it was Ireland that had changed. Belfast bombed and barricaded, while in Dublin new flats and American banks had spoiled the Georgian calm around Saint Stephen's Green. And all over the country, in the smaller towns and villages, new housing estates and motor hotels. Cars everywhere: every farmer had his own car now, horses and donkeys were becoming a thing of the past; even in the villages of the west, the arrival of the morning bus was no longer the big moment of the day. Yet, paradoxically, here on the Riviera nothing had changed. It was as though, long ago, when this part of the coast had been built, house on house, terrace on terrace, winding street on winding street, nothing further could be added. Belfast, with its ruined houses and rubbled streets, was now, to her, the alien place. Here, as she came down into this small French town, she came home to the past, the remembered narrow, winding streets, the fountains and souvenir shops, the dusty orange customs building, the fishing boats lining the quay.

The Hôtel Welcome, too, was just as she recalled it, its rust-colored façade exactly as it had been in the *vue du port* paintings of Villefranche one hundred years ago. But when Mrs. Redden entered the hotel lobby and the porter came to take her suitcase, she saw that *something* had changed. Surely the residents' dining room was on this floor? She remembered those evenings when Monsieur Guy, the florid, courteous proprietor, would walk among the guests' tables at dinner-time, smiling, pointing to the pastel sky outside the windows, explaining to the new tourists that it was *l'heure bleu,* the twilight hour, for which, he said, *"la Côte est connue dans tous les pays du monde."*

"What happened to the dining room?" were her first words to the young girl at the desk. The girl looked surprised. "The restaurant is downstairs, *Madame.* On the quay," the girl said. "Do you wish a room?"

"My name is Redden and I've booked." And then she recognized the proprietor's wife, a sallow-skinned woman sitting in the little front office, going over bills. She spoke in French, to the proprietress, asking about the missing dining room. "Ah, that was a long time ago, *Madame,"* the proprietress said. "Now we have only one dining room for residents and non-residents alike. That's the restaurant below, on the quay. The dining room which was on this floor, the residents' dining room that you remember, is now the television room. What can you do? The clients want television, they have to have it. And I tell you, it is not at all good for business. Our bar is not what it used to be in the evening time. When were you last here, *Madame?"*

"Oh, years ago," Mrs. Redden said, thanking her, following the porter up to room 450, which had been reserved in advance. In the lift, she asked about Monsieur Guy and was told that he had died. It was on a Sunday, the porter said, in the height of the season, it was very awkward, the *direction* had decided not to mention it to the guests, people were on vacation after all, a death in the house is not gay. So Madame and the family just carried on and the funeral took place in private.

"How long have you worked here?" Mrs. Redden asked as the porter drew the shutters open, showing the familiar view of *la rade.*

"Ah," he said. "I am old in the service. Ten years, at least."

When she had tipped him and he had handed over the key and bowed his way out, Mrs. Redden walked about in the room. She had reserved it specially; it was the one they had had on their honeymoon and commanded the best view of any room in the hotel. The furniture was much as she remembered it; the bed would be different, but was no bigger than the one Kevin had fallen out of with such a thump that first afternoon, when they came back from the beach and made love. And there was the same sort of dressing table, and imitation green leather armchair and, out on the narrow balcony, the same little table and two iron café chairs where, their second morning, they had breakfasted *en terrasse,* taking their tray outside to find the couple from the room next door doing the same thing. Stiff with embarrassment in their honeymoon dressing gowns, they sat down in silence, aware that their neighbors were British. Then, on an inspiration, she spoke to Kevin in French and he grunted a reply, and the Brits nodded to them politely and left them alone. Afterward, in the bathroom, the door shut, she and Kevin shrieked with silly laughter. We laughed in those days: the fun we had.

Well, times change. She began to unpack her suitcase, first taking her toilet case into the bathroom, laying out her toilet things, making sure she had not forgotten to pack her diaphragm. Then she hung up her dresses in the bedroom, leaving plenty of closet space for Kevin's clothes. After Paris, she felt a bit lonely. She had brought some paperbacks, and unpacking them, she thought of taking a book and going down to the terrace to sit and read and watch the people stroll past on the quays.

When she finished unpacking, she lay, face down, on the bed. The hot sun came in at the open window; she could smell the sea and hear the slow stammer of a small boat's engine as a fisherman went out around the *rade*. Kevin was the one, whenever we'd come up to this room to change, the wine in us, the minute I'd take my dress off, he'd be pulling down my knickers, with a big cockstand on him, always wanting. We did more in this very room, and more often, than ever again. After Danny, it changed. As Kevin says, people are not really married until they have a child. I was lazy. The only job I was offered was teaching at Saint Mary's and that would have meant going on living at home with Kitty. Daddy dead, Eily married, Owen away doing an assistantship, my mother and I alone at home and always at each other. I married to get away, God forgive me.

It's true. I haven't had such a bad life, though. Nor such a great one, either. This morning, it was great. This morning I walked in the Luxembourg Gardens with someone I wanted to be with, and we laughed and it was exciting, he's someone I could have fallen for. But that's silly, it's over.

She got up, changed her dress, and did her face. I *could* send him a postcard from here. I could ring up Peg to thank her and offhandedly get his address.

There was no writing paper in the drawer by the bed table, no envelope either. I could go downstairs and buy a postcard, just to pass the time.

Later, wearing the good linen dress she had picked out the year before last at Donald Davies in Dublin, she came back slowly along the quay, past the four restaurants which faced on the port, having read the printed menus outside each and gone into all the shops at the end of the quay, having sat on the sea wall looking across to Saint-Jean-Cap-Ferrat, having inspected the yachts and small craft tied up along the lower quays, having selected four postcards and bought a tube of Nivea Solaire, Crème Bronzante, and even taking all that time, when she looked at her watch, not more than two hours had passed. If you were alone in a place, the time was very long.

She decided to sit outside the Welcome, have a coffee, and look at that novel by Muriel Spark. She would write the postcards later. She had read a good review of this book, but after a few pages she put it aside: these new novels were strange, not like the early ones, and besides, her mind went back to Tom Lowry walking her to the Atrium last night, and then this morning, in the Luxembourg Gardens, and at the airport, riding out on the bus with her. What an odd chance it had been, meeting him. If you lived in Belfast you never met anyone really new. She must phone Peg and get the address, then think of something funny to say on the card. Or say, in some subtle way, how she'd enjoyed their meeting. How she missed him. But could she say that without making a fool of herself? She decided to have her bath and think about it, then write the card here on the terrace while she had a leisurely drink before dinner.

In the lift, she was squeezed in with a French couple, a youngish man and his wife. The man looked up at her in that cold, appraising French way, and then dismissed her. Too tall. It was all done in a moment, familiarly, with no malice. She got out alone on her floor.

In the small bathroom, Mrs. Redden ran hot water, then went to the bedroom and took off her clothes. Naked, she looked at herself in the dresser mirror, thinking about a good tan. She was slim and her height made her seem more so; a girlish body with white milky skin that Kevin used to say made him think of sin. She liked hot baths, the hotter the better. She lay now in the water, letting the tub fill, her right hand resting on her stomach, her fingers riffling the wet bush of her pubic hair. Sometimes in the bath she would feel herself, touching and fondling her breasts, thighs, and stomach as though her body were not hers. Sometimes she would think of men and would drift off into a little story, an imagining, and, in the hot bath, would make herself come. She always felt lonely after that.

Now, lying in the bath, she thought of phoning home. Would he announce another delay? All of her life, it seemed, he had forced her to wait. He was the bread-winner: he made the plans, and he changed them. He rarely consulted her. He was the man, he paid the bills: he played on that. My God, how he played on it.

When she got out of the bath it was after six. Mrs. Milligan would be frying up some awful mess for sup-per while Kevin and Danny watched the television news. As she began to dry herself, she decided she would ring in half an hour's time. She must remember to ask Danny about his rugby match. But as she finished toweling her back, the phone rang in the bedroom. Naked, she ran from the bathroom to answer.

"*Il y a quelqu'un en bas pour vous, Madame.*"

"*Qui?*"

"*Un monsieur. Voulez-vous descendre?*"

Mrs. Redden did not answer. *What* gentleman?

"Will you come down," the voice repeated in En-glish, "or do you wish the gentleman to come up?"

"I'll come down." But I'm not dressed, my hair or face fixed. "In a few minutes," she added.

Dressing, she told herself it must be a mistake, or perhaps it was someone from British Airways, something to do with the airline tickets? If Kevin had changed his mind and was here, he would have come straight up to the room. Hurrying, she put on bra, pants, her Donald Davies dress, and sandals, a quick touch of lipstick, a comb through her damp hair, and out and down in the lift. When the lift reached the ground floor and paused for that little airbrake moment before it finally settled, all at once she knew. The lift door opened, showing the lobby, him standing there, throwing his head up at sight of her, very excited, smiling, awaiting her reaction. "Hello, Sheila. Mind if I join you?"

It was then she saw how nervous he was.

"But what on earth are you doing here?"

"I hate to be left behind at airports."

She stared at him. "When did you get here?"

"I just arrived. I got myself a room in a little place up the road. It's called Les Terrasses."

"You got a room?" she repeated stupidly.

"Look, you don't *have* to see me."

"Oh no." She felt herself blushing. "As a matter of fact, I was thinking about you. It's nice to see you again."

"I mean, you said you'd be alone till Friday. I thought you might like some company till then."

"As a matter of fact, I was just going to call home and find out if Kevin *is* coming on Friday."

"Oh," he said, embarrassed. "Well, don't let me interrupt. I mean, if you're going to ring now."

She glanced up at the hotel clock. "Look, I'll just go upstairs and make the call. And then let's have a drink together."

"Okay. Should I wait for you?"

She remembered her face and hair. "No, let's say I'll meet you here at seven. All right? In an hour?"

"Fine." He seemed disappointed.

As she went into the lift, she looked over her shoulder and he waved to her. It was, she thought, the unconfident gesture of someone who was afraid she might not come back.

Twenty minutes later, as she sat on the bed drying her hair with a hand drier, the call came through. *"Parlez, c'est Londres à la ligne."* London put her through to Belfast. She heard the phone ring at home and thought of the black receiver sitting on the worn whorled top of the monk's bench in the hall below the carved elephant tusks, which held an old brass dinner gong once owned by Kevin's grandfather. The phone rang and rang. But she knew they were there, sitting in the den at the back, stuck in with the damned telly.

"Double-four-one-double-five," said Mrs. Milligan, giving the number the way Kevin had taught her.

"Mrs. Milligan, this is Mrs. Redden."

"Is it yourself?" Mrs. Milligan said in her Donegal accent. "Are you all right, missus? Are you in France or where? Do you want me to get the doctor?"

"Yes, I'm grand. How's everything there?"

"They done Divis Street last night," Mrs. Milligan said. "A big bomb. They say it was the UDF. Anyway, there's two dead and a whole lot of people hurt. One family was patients of the doctor. The poor doctor, he was out half the night."

"Is he in now?"

"Aye, certainly, he's ate-ing his supper. Hold on now, I'll get him for you."

Kevin came on. "Sheila?"

"Yes, how are you?"

"Busy."

"Mrs. Milligan said you were out last night."

"Yes, a bomb in Divis Street, blew in the front of a house, patients of mine. The father, poor bastard, was killed and I have two of the kids up in the Mater now with their faces half blown off."

"Oh, God," she said, but she felt nothing. She had heard it so often, had felt sick so often.

"So, how are you?" he asked. "How's Villefranche, has it changed much?"

"Not one bit. Listen, what about Friday, do you think you'll still manage?"

He did not answer at once, pausing just long enough to let her know he hadn't thought about it. "I'm not sure. I have a patient going into emergency surgery on Thursday morning. It's one operation I really should do myself."

"Kevin, do you not want to come, is that it?"

"No, that's *not* it. It's just that a lot of things have happened all at once. I'm sorry. I wish I could be more definite."

"Well, don't worry about it." When she heard herself say that, it was as though some shocking stranger spoke inside her.

"Look, I'll give you a ring Thursday morning," he said. "You're having a good time, are you?"

"Yes, it's lovely here."

"Not too lonely?"

"No. It would be nice to see you, though."

"I know."

"Listen, is Danny there? Can I have a word with him? Is he all right?"

"Oh, he's in great form," Kevin said and there was a sudden cheerfulness in his voice, as though he had suddenly guessed that he might not have to come to France at all. "Trouble is," he said, "he's not here. I let him go off to spend the night with young Kearns."

"Oh, well. Tell him I was asking for him, will you."

"I'll do that, Shee."

Shee was his private name for her. He used it rarely. "Well, good night, Kevin," she said.

"Good night."

She hung up. If I put a few rollers in now, I can still be downstairs by seven. She sat again in front of the dressing-table mirror and saw that there was a special mirror light, which she switched on, the light coming on all around the edge of the glass, as though she were an actress in her dressing room. She began to sing, her voice small, wavering, reminiscent:

Dancing in the dark,
Till the tune ends, we're dancing in the dark . . .

She was on time at seven. The bar was crowded and waiters kept coming up to the counter to fill drink orders. "Why don't we go for a walk instead?" she said.

"Great."

But then she remembered her hair. She asked him to wait while she went upstairs to get a scarf. It was that time of day when the hotel guests were all coming down for dinner, so she had to wait a long time for the lift. When at last she reached her room, she took out the big flame-and-white Givenchy scarf that had been a Christmas present from Kevin's mother, and tied it, babushka fashion, around her head. It was all wrong. She retied it, but it was no better. There was another scarf, a yellow cotton one, but she had an awful time finding it, and when she tried it on, it was worse than the first scarf, and then her hair was mussed so she ran a comb through it and took the Givenchy scarf again and tied it another way and felt she could weep, why was it when you had more clothes than you ever used to have, nothing looked right? She tried a last time, wanting the mirror to be kind, but the mirror was not her friend. God, I look like the Queen at some gym-khana.

Going down again, with the lift stopping at every floor, squeezed in with four other people, she remembered the dark-blue sun hat she had bought, maybe she should run back up and get it? But if, after the walk, we go straight into dinner some place, what would I be doing wearing a sun hat?

In the hotel lobby there was a floor-length mirror which she could not pass but must stop in front of it for a last masochistic look. As she stared into the glass, she saw, reflected, the front doorway of the hotel and, just outside, Tom Lowry waiting for her. He was leaning against the iron railing, looking down at the people promenading on the quay below. Seen thus through the mirror, he seemed strange, a young conspirator waiting for his accomplice. Yet, at the same time, she felt an overwhelming urge to be seen with him, to go with him and leave everything else behind. She turned from the mirror and hurried out to meet him.

"I'm sorry. I had to wait ages for the lift."

"That's all right." He pointed to the sweep of the bay. "Is that a beach down there?"

"It is. A stony one."

"Let's walk that way."

And so they went down a flight of steps, walking side by side along the quay in the same direction she had taken that afternoon. The sky was fading to dark, the restaurants were filling up with people, and the strolling performers were out, just as she remembered them. There was the familiar type of trick cyclist, wheeling back and forth on a unicycle, wearing a frilly woman's hat. A swarthy young man sang Italian songs, cradling a monkey in the crook of his arm. The monkey, tiny and frail, was dressed in a tutu and clung to its owner like a frightened child. And there were new, less professional, entertainers, a trio of young Americans in jeans who drifted from restaurant to restaurant, playing guitars and singing rock songs in wispy, wistful voices.

Suddenly, as on a given signal, lights went on on each dining table in the restaurant they were passing and soon it was lights up, too, on the boats moored along the quay. Far out in the bay a huge luxury yacht flared in ostentatious display, a chain of colored bulbs illuminating its outline from rigging to deck, prow to stern. Within minutes, lights twinkled on from Villefranche to Cap Ferrat, as though the whole bay were a stage while, behind it, like some vast amphitheater, the sky went to black. Music came up loud, and Mrs. Redden, hearing the singing voices, seeing the constant parade of people, felt her eyes fill with pleasant tears. Walking with Tom Lowry down toward the stony beach, passing the entrances to the narrow back streets of the old town behind the seafront, she began to reminisce about Villefranche, telling him how, years ago, the U.S. Sixth Fleet used this town as a base port, how the Americans put up American street signs in these narrow Mediterranean alleys. She told him that the local nightclubs and bars presented Wild West songs and American music and how the tough Shore Patrol moved up and down the streets searching for drunken sailors. And how, that summer, the local hotel proprietors protested the way American naval wives went to the beach with their hair done up in plastic rollers. It ruined the tone of the resort.

Chat. But edited chat, for not once did she mention the year, or that she had been here on her honeymoon. He asked about the best place to eat and she told him Mère Germaine's, and when they went in, with that good luck which now attended on their every action, an elderly couple paid the bill and ceded them a table with a splendid view of the port. The waiter brought a local rosé wine and as Tom poured it Mrs. Redden realized that she was still wearing the ugly scarf around her head. Embarrassed, she unknotted it, pulling it into her lap, shaking out her hair, smiling at him. "Tell me," she asked, "do you often do things like this?"

"Like what?"

"Like picking up and coming five hundred miles when the notion strikes you."

"Never," he said. "I wanted to be with you. When we said goodbye there at the airport, I felt lonely. It was crazy. I never felt anything like it before."

"By the way," she said, "I talked to my husband on the phone. The trouble about being married to a doctor is that they can't plan anything in advance. He won't be here before Friday at the earliest, and I've got a feeling he may not come at all. He's going to ring me Thursday to let me know."

"He mightn't come *at all?*"

"No. He's very busy. Anyway, Kevin's not really keen on holidays abroad. He's quite content with the seaside at home."

"Well," he said, "the seaside in your part of Ireland *is* beautiful. That northern coast."

My part of Ireland. She looked at the colored lights on the millionaire's yacht out there in the bay. A day, long forgotten, came into her mind: her father, his green summer blazer slung over his shoulder, wearing white tennis shoes and cream flannels, walking with her along the promenade in Portstewart, her hand in his—she was twelve at the time—and on the other side, talking to Daddy, Chief Justice McGonigal, her father called him Johnny. "Oh, Johnny, Johnny," her father said, "I don't know. Dan's children were sent to English schools, they speak with English accents. Poor little West Britons he's made of them. I want my children to live here in the North, where they belong. Dan has had a great career, of course, the U.N., and Europe, and the trade treaties, he's done a lot, no doubt about it, but do you know, when I meet him now, my own brother, with his English accent, I feel a slight contempt for him. Poor Dan, he has lost himself. You and I, Johnny, we're still what we were, only older. But Dan is like an actor, always playing a part." And then her father turned and lifted her up in his arms and rubbed the tip of her nose with his bushy brown mustache, in the way that he had. "Take this little girl, now," her father said. "What happens to a child like Sheila when you remove her from her roots? Ah, no, no," her father said sentimentally. "Maybe I could have been a richer man and cut a finer dash if I'd gone off to London, long ago, when I got a first. But I wouldn't have had *this* child, do you see? I'd have some little Londoner here in my arms this minute, some little Samantha or Beryl, some dogsbody of an English-sounding name. Oh, darling," her father said, looking at her with his grave, hurt, hooded blue eyes. "Promise me you'll stay in Ireland, will you?"

"If I say yes, will you buy me a Mars bar?" she had answered and Justice McGonigal laughed and shouted out, "There you are, Tim, it's all economics, it's not patriotism, d'you see." And her father, laughing, put her down and gave her a shilling.

She looked back now at this eager stranger, this American boy, smiling at her, sipping his wine. "I don't know," she said. "Some people never want to go outside the place they were born in. And others seem to want to run away from the day they're old enough to walk."

"And which are you?"

"A runaway."

"But you didn't leave, did you?"

"No," she said. The singer with the monkey had come close to them. Wanting to show the monkey off, he took its paw and held up its long prehensile arm, trying to get the animal to stand up straight on his shoulder. But the monkey scampered down again and, shivering, clung to its owner's chest. "He's afraid," she said.

"What?"

"The monkey. He's afraid."

The waiter arrived with their first course, plates of tiny fried fish. The singer, ending his song, came around to collect, the monkey holding out a tin cup. Mrs. Redden put in a franc, and as the singer left the restaurant, the trick cyclist wheeled suddenly into the view of all the diners, going at breakneck speed toward the edge of the quay, pulling up miraculously short, then backpedaling in a sort of conga weave. Mrs. Redden found herself laughing and, laughing, turned to Tom. And there, in the middle of the music and the singing, found him watching her in the same eager, secret way she had spied on him an hour ago. Kevin and Danny are sitting at home, not knowing this thing that is happening. And then, suddenly, he said something and she laughed, her guilt gone, her mood back up on that high wire of excitement.

From then on, their evening sailed. They began to exchange silly jokes about their fellow diners, they finished the bottle of wine and ordered a second; they talked about books they had read, plays they had seen, talk she never had at home, and, still talking, excited, left the restaurant to begin a long stroll around the sea wall to Port Darse, where dozens of pleasure craft were moored. They idled on the quays, looking at sloops, sailing dinghies, and catamarans, at a sleek Chris-Craft riding at anchor, its owner sprawled aft on a deck chair, his cigar tip a tiny rosette in the velvet night. They climbed a steep pebbly slope to steps which led to the old town, where, under a lonely street lamp in a grassy alley, four local men played *pétanque,* the thud and click of the steel bowls strangely sinister at this late hour. Through narrow deserted streets, they came down again to the little square where the front door of the Welcome was still open, the lobby a harsh pool of light in the surrounding darkness, the night clerk dozing at his desk. In the public rooms two shut-off television sets stood, like surrogates for public speakers, surrounded by audiences of empty chairs. They took the lift down to the bar, where a few stragglers sat over a last drink, and moved to a table at the far end of the room. A waiter brought cognacs and Mrs. Redden showed her room key, telling the waiter to put it on her bill.

"What about tomorrow?"

She looked at him. "There's a sandy beach at Cap Ferrat. We could go over there by boat. I could get us a picnic lunch from the hotel here."

"Sounds great. What time?"

"Let's go right after breakfast," she said. "I want to get burned red."

"Why don't we have breakfast together. Say at eight, out there on the terrace?"

"All right."

And then, all at once, she felt she must be the one to do it. She stood and said, "I'm going up now. Thanks for a great evening."

"Do you have to go?"

"Yes," she said, and abruptly turned and walked to the lift. The lift cabin was already waiting, and as she went into it, she still felt that elation. She looked back through the little window of the lift and saw him standing by the table, watching her. Oh, God, I want to go back to him. She pressed the button and the lift went up, wiping out his image like a shutter click.

At seven next morning she woke and suddenly knew where she was and what had happened. She got up, excited, and went to the window to open the wooden shutters. There, in the cold morning sunlight, the millionaire's yacht rode at anchor in the bay. She stood in her cotton nightgown, her hand on the shutter latch, gripped by the mysterious silence of those decks. Once, in Galway, she and Kevin were walking in a narrow country road when a huge Rolls-Royce came up behind them, forcing them into the ditch as it inched past. At that moment she noticed an old woman peering out of a cottage door at the great silver motorcar and the thought came to her that the old woman's husband in all the years and all the labor of his life had probably earned less than the price of that Rolls. As now, she knew that Kevin in all his years of surgery and sutures and knives and blood had not earned as much as the price of that yacht. Why do some people lead such special lives? Remember Villa Cara, Groothaesebroekseweg, Wassenaar, Den Haag, Uncle Dan's splendid place, where Owen and I went on that holiday when we were children: the Italianate gardens, the chauffeured Mercedes, the menservants in white gloves? We children having lunch with Uncle Dan and Aunt Meg in the big dining room, white Dutch double tulips as the centerpiece: the first secretary, Brogan, so short that even at twelve I came up to his shoulder, arriving to play tennis with me. That Irish embassy in Holland, was it the closest I will ever be to the existence of the people on that yacht? Will they wake up this morning to a steward in white gloves bringing a breakfast tray on which sits one red rose? Will they order the captain to sail for Formentor after lunch? Imagine going down now to the quay, a private motorboat coming for us, taking Tom and me out to that yacht, the anchor up, stewards pouring champagne, us dancing on deck under the stars, sailing down to the Azores and on to the South Seas. Is there really a life like that?

The clock, which she thought she had set for seven, shrilled loud and late in the room. Hurrying, she pulled off her nightgown and sat naked at the dressing table, beginning a long, careful job of doing her face. Before leaving home she had consulted Madge Stewart at McElvey's. Madge had been trained at Elizabeth Arden in London, and now she put on the base in the way Madge had shown her and took out the new terra-cotta makeup Madge said would be just right in the sun. First she did her eyes, not too much eyeliner, trying for the natural look Madge talked about. She rubbed the blusher in high on her cheekbones, with a touch of it across her forehead along the hairline to give the beginnings of a tan. She was pleased with the result. She took out her yellow sundress, gave it a touch with the traveling iron, unpacked her blue swimsuit, put it with a towel and the suntan cream in her little traveling bag, adding the blue sun hat as an afterthought. Then went into the bathroom, still naked, and began to comb her hair. The sunglasses she mustn't forget, brand new with very big rims, all the rage in *Vogue* this year. At the last minute she put on lipstick and faced the mirror.

Awful. Too much. Why did I trust Madge, why didn't I have a trial run at home, the one day I want to look my best and it's awful, too much eyeliner, take a bit off, oh, God, I should have got up at six, too much blusher, put on powder, start all over, but it's too late, I must go down and order the picnics. She felt like weeping, but if she wept it would make her eyes even worse. She was shocked at herself for caring so much. But there it was. She did.

So, giving up, she put on her underthings and the yellow sundress and went down and managed to order the lunches and be on the terrace before nine. But he was there already: he must have come early. He jumped up, smiling at her. "Hey, you look terrific. Good morning."

"No, I don't."

"Yes, you do. What a great dress."

You would wait a long time before an Irishman would tell you you had on a great dress. "Thank you," she said.

At ten they caught the boat for Cap Ferrat. The beach there was sheltered, smart and private with real sand, brought in by truck and laid over the pebble stones. In the rear were a restaurant and changing rooms, and when the boat let them off at the small jetty, they paid their admissions and went straight up to change. A few minutes later Mrs. Redden emerged, wearing her blue sun hat and the big new sunglasses, feeling naked, white, and conspicuous in the swimsuit, which was also blue and new. As she came down the steps to the beach, instinctively she hunched her shoulders, trying to make herself smaller, peering out uncertainly at the blue-tinted world revealed through her new sunglasses.

Two teen-aged girls, sleek, tanned to an even cocoa brown, flashed by like a reproach. Then a man and his wife, wearing the most minimal of *cache-sexe,* both stringily muscled in a way that reminded her of race-horses, came parading past, as in a paddock. She moved a few awkward steps in the sand, pausing blindly before a platoon of beach mattresses.

Then she saw him coming toward her. He was wear-ing white swimming trunks. "I've got us two lilos," he said. "This way."

"Which way?" She stared into the sun.

As though it were the most natural thing in the world, he put his arm around her waist, his hand rest-ing on her hip. She hesitated, then went on down the beach, his arm still around her waist, walking in step with him.

When they came to the lilo mattresses, she put her traveling bag on one and sat, her legs tucked under her. "I look like a corpse in this crowd."

"You won't for long. That sun's very strong. Have you got some suntan oil?"

She nodded and took out the crème solaire bron-zante. "Great," he said. "You put some on my back, then I'll do yours."

He turned, presenting her his back. Obedient, she squeezed cream into her palm, and began to rub it across his shoulders, kneading it in. He had a long straight back and a deep chest, a boy's body, more like Danny's than Kevin's. She put more cream on her palm and began to rub it in just above the top of his swimming trunks.

"Good," he said. He turned, holding out his hand, and she squeezed cream into it. He rubbed the cream over his chest and forearms, then took the tube from her.

"Your turn. Lie down. Relax."

Careful of her makeup, she spread her towel on the lilo and lay with her head turned to one side, watching the quiet Mediterranean waves fold on the sand like the turning pages of a book, thinking of the wild bays of home, the long cold breakers, the deserted dunes, the rainy beauty of Gorteen strand. He began to knead her shoulders and neck, skillful and slow, his hands moving down her back to her waist, and up again. Mrs. Redden pressed her body into the mattress, aroused, the stranger behind her, his hands on her, strong, sure, caressing her. And then, all at once, he took his hands away.

"What about your legs?"

"Oh, I can do that myself," she said. She twisted around and sat up on the lilo. He had been kneeling by her mattress, and when she turned abruptly, he dropped his hands as though to hide his genitals. She felt her face go hot. She began to cream her legs, stretching her toes out toward the warm quiet waves. He said, "I wonder if Debbie got away yesterday. You met her, didn't you, that first day you arrived?"

It was as though he had slapped her. "How did you know I met her?"

"She mentioned it."

"Is she your girl?"

"Debbie?" He laughed. "God, no. She's my sister's friend."

"She's pretty."

"Do you think so? I think she's a pain. I have to be nice to her for Martha's sake, but she's heavy going, Debbie. Wow!"

"How old is your sister?"

"She's twenty-four." He pulled a wallet from the

waistband of his trunks and passed a snapshot over.
"That's her. Martha."

Mrs. Redden looked at a girl, dark-haired, carrying
a tennis racquet, smiling.

"My parents," he said, handing her a second snapshot. "At our summer place in Springs."

A man and a woman sitting in white wicker chairs
on the sundeck of a house, woods in the background,
the man in a rollneck sweater looked a little older than
Kevin; the woman, thank goodness, looked much older.
"Your father is young."

"He's in great shape. He's fifty-six, though."

She handed back the photograph. Twelve years older
than Kevin.

"My grandmother." An old lady in a curved, high-
backed chair, the sort of chair Mrs. Redden associated
with films about the South Seas. The old lady glared
at the camera; intent dark eyes like her grandson's.
"Gran's a disciple of Teddy Roosevelt. Speak softly
and carry a big stick."

"I never heard that expression."

"Didn't you? Well, her big stick is the purse strings.
Grandpa left money in a trust fund for our education
and Grandma administers it. A few years ago I had a
big run-in with her when she wanted me to become a
doctor like Dad. Which is why I wound up in Ireland
getting my Ph.D. at Trinity instead of some place like
Princeton."

"And who paid for your education?"

"Oh, my father paid the first two years. But then
Gran came around. Actually, she was nice about it. For
instance, this year when I got my degree she sent me
the rest of the trust money that was due to me from the
education fund. Just gave it to me as a gift."

Behind, in the beach restaurant, a girl began to sing

in Spanish, accompanying herself on a guitar. "What about you?" he asked. "Were you a big family?"

"No. Four. My oldest brother, Ned, is a dentist in Cork. I have a brother, Owen, who's a doctor in Belfast, and a sister, Eily, who's married to an engineer and lives near Dublin."

"And your parents, are they both alive?"

"No, my father died years ago. My mother died just last spring."

"I suppose you still miss her?"

"I don't know. We fought a lot. She once called me a born liar. I don't think I ever forgave her for that."

He laughed. "Why did she say it?"

"Oh, when I was small I was always making up stories about myself. That I was an explorer's daughter, or related to some famous person. Anything but the truth—that I was Sheila Deane of 18 Chichester Terrace, Belfast, a very ordinary little girl."

"And for that she called you a born liar?"

"Yes. I suppose she wasn't too bad, really. Poor Kitty. Funny, when I think of her now, it's always with a cigarette in her mouth, the cigarette bobbing up and down as she talks. She was a great storyteller and people loved to hear her yarns. Trouble was, she'd do anything to get a laugh. Even if it meant telling a story against us, or even against herself. She died of cancer."

"The cigarettes?"

"I suppose. There's a lot of cancer in our family. Both sides. My father's brother died of it, too."

They lay for a while without talking. In the warm sun she began to feel drowsy. She thought of home. I left a big cooked ham for Mrs. Milligan and told her to make sure they eat lettuce and lots of vegetables and to buy a roast next week, but will she? All she knows how to cook is fried stuff. Danny and his father will live off fried stuff and cake until I'm home again. Well, at least Kevin gets a good lunch at the hospital three days a week.

Kitty dead. And my father, long ago. I remember that morning, Owen coming into our room in his pajamas to tell Eily and me to go downstairs to the big bedroom. Kitty weeping, Daddy dead in the bed: he died in his sleep in the middle of the night, Kitty asleep beside him. That was one time I was sorry for you, poor Mama, to wake like that in the morning and find your man cold beside you.

The Spanish guitar music stopped, and behind them, the girl started to sing a song; the lyric was French and familiar, yet Mrs. Redden could not remember the song's title. She turned to Tom to ask if he knew, but he was not there. She sat up, alarmed.

There he was down by the water's edge, talking to the boat boys. She called his name. He turned and beckoned her to join him.

"I rented a *pédalo*," he said. "Come on, let's try it out."

She laughed. Kevin would never have done that.

Leaning back, bicycling, their legs moved the absurd little boating machine out into the bay, chuffering along under the rose and white façades of the big villas up on the cliffs, the smell of the sea in their nostrils, lolling under an azure sky, seeing small sailboats, the distant frieze of seafront at Villefranche and, farther down, a haze of heat over Nice. She no longer thought of her makeup, or even that she was getting red. She offered her face to the sun, as to a host on an altar, this boy beside her, holiday, holiday, holiday, never end.

And, later, after she had gone back to the changing room, showered, and put on her yellow sundress, she joined him, carrying the picnic basket the hotel had made up. He waited at a table under a Cinzano umbrella of bright red, white, and blue stripes, a bottle of local white wine in an ice bucket beside him. Kevin would have ordered beer. She opened the waxed-paper picnic packages and laid it out, all colors—white chicken breasts, two kinds of yellow cheese, fresh black figs, dull-red tomatoes, green grapes, and brown crusty bread—and they ate it all up like greedy children and drank off all the wine, which went to her head.

"Let's go for a swim," he suggested.

"So soon after eating?"

"It will cool us off."

In the sea he swam, and swam well. She lingered in the shallows, not wanting to wet her hair. Afterward, they lay on the lilos under a cloudless sky. The beach was quieter now, as most of the bathers had gone home for lunch. In the stillness she turned her head to look at him. His eyes were closed, and so, cautiously, she raised herself up and, leaning on one elbow, examined his face. Asleep, he looked so young. He opened his eyes and smiled at her. She lay back on the lilo and, after a while, felt him take her hand. She pulled her hand away.

"What's wrong?"

"Nothing."

He tried to take her hand again.

"Don't." Embarrassed, she sat up, hugging her knees. "Listen, let's go up to the restaurant and get a cup of coffee."

On the restaurant terrace they passed the stringily muscled couple, who sat at a corner table sipping orangeade and staring at a strange board with little black and white stones on it. Tom said it was a Japanese game called go. Now that they were no longer on dangerous ground, Mrs. Redden became lighthearted again.

"What should we do tonight? What about going into Nice and wandering around and having dinner some place?"

"Fine," he said. They ordered coffee, and for a moment she felt tense when he leaned across the table and touched his fingers to her cheek. "Your face is burned," he said. "You've had too much sun. How do you feel?"

"All right."

But, later in the changing room, she felt a stinging pain along the top of her shoulders. Her face was hot, and with the sun, the sea air, and the wine, she felt sleepy as they waited on the jetty for the boat to take them back to Villefranche, a sleepiness that increased as the boat crossed the bay and let them off on the dock, directly below her hotel. She thought of taking a shower, to wake her up. "What should we do?" she asked. "Should we meet here again around five and take a bus into Nice?"

"All right." He was looking up at the façade of the Welcome. "Which is your room, by the way?"

"It's on the fourth floor. I think it's the third from the left over there."

"You have a balcony?"

"Yes."

He walked her up to the front entrance. "I think I'll go for a stroll," he said. "I don't feel like sitting in my cell."

"It's that bad, is it?"

"It's no hell. Listen, do you have anything to read?"

"I have some paperbacks."

"What kind?"

"Some mysteries, and a Muriel Spark and a Doris Lessing. Look, I'll bring them down and you can take your pick."

"Good."

When they entered the hotel lobby, there was no clerk at the desk, so she took her own key down from the rack. Tom had already pressed the lift button.

"Should I go up with you?" he asked, and she saw he was embarrassed as soon as he'd said it.

"No, it's all right, I won't be a moment." She heard the lift coming. The hotel seemed empty: most of the guests were probably still out at the beach. I could let him come up to my floor, at least. Nobody's seen us together. I could bring out the books and let him pick one. It would save having to make two trips up and down.

The lift came, but she said nothing. He opened the door. "Should I ride up in the elevator with you?" he asked.

And what could she say? She nodded and they went into the small lift, facing each other, going up. When the lift stopped on the fourth floor, the corridor was empty. She began to go toward her room, he walking a step or two behind her. As she unlocked the room door, she thought of the mess she had left that morning. "I don't want you to see how untidy I am," she said apologetically. He smiled and remained in the corridor while she went inside. But the maid had been, the bed was made, things had been put away, the shutters were open to the view. She took out her half dozen paperbacks, Penguins and Panthers, and turned around to see that the door had swung open. He stood, waiting, in the corridor.

"Terrific view," he said.

"Yes, it is, you can see the whole port." And suddenly it seemed silly to make a thing of keeping him out of the room, so she said, "Come in and have a look. The place is tidy, thank goodness."

So he came in and stepped out onto the little balcony

to look down at the Gare Maritime and the chapel. "That chapel," she said, "was a fishermen's chapel. Then it was done over by Jean Cocteau."

He looked at it, then turned to her. "Terrific view," he said again. He went back into the room and picked a book off the bed. "This looks good. Kingsley Amis. Is it a sort of thriller?"

"I haven't read it yet," she told him. So it was all right. She was glad she had asked him in.

"All right, then, I'll see you at five," he said, and walked past her, going toward the open door to the corridor. In that moment their bodies touched briefly and she put her hand on his arm, detaining him. "I had a lovely day, Tom. Really."

As she said it, she was not quite sure what happened, but, clumsily, as though he had bumped into her, he put his cheek against hers and then, still holding the Penguin, put his arm around her waist, drawing her toward him. She felt herself tremble. She let him hold her, his cheek touching hers. As though this were a dream she was dreaming, she drew back, looked at him, then kissed him on the lips, her mouth partly open, a slow, soft kiss which filled her with a sensation as though she were about to faint.

They drew apart. She turned and pushed the room door shut. She sat down on the edge of the bed and he sat beside her, kissing her awkwardly, his hand moving down on her thigh, his fingers touching the bare skin inside her sundress. She turned her head away.

"Close the shutters," she told him.

He rose to obey. She stood, went quickly into the bathroom, unbuttoning the yellow sundress, quickly unhooking her bra, pulling her pants down over her hips. She faced the mirror, saw the white vertical line of her Caesarian scar, and, for a moment, put her hand protectively over it. Then, hiding nothing, turned and walked back naked into the bedroom.

When he saw her come in like that, he seemed startled, but, at once, as though he must instantly put himself in the same condition, unbuttoned his shirt, pulled it off, unbuckled his belt, and dropped his trousers. He wore white jockey shorts and as he lowered them and kicked his leg free of them, she saw his penis. He had a huge erection. As he came toward her, his penis dangled in front of him, bobbing up and down with each step. He put his hands on her shoulders and kissed her in the hollow of her neck, and, as he did, she took hold of that huge penis and felt its stiffness. Then, slowly, she knelt on the floor and put the length of it against her cheek. She kissed its tip. He watched her kiss his penis and then, gently, took her head in his hands and, bending down, kissed her brow. He knelt, facing her on the floor, kissed the hollow of her neck, laid her down on the rug, and lay down beside her. They kissed on the lips, a slow, gentle, open-mouthed kiss, and again she felt faint. As he had that morning he began to massage her, his hands kneading her back, moving around to caress her belly, his fingers searching between her legs. They kissed again and, in unspoken agreement, stood up, and she pulled down the bedspread, revealing white sheets. He lay beside her on the bed, facing her, his hands stroking her breasts, the tip of his throbbing penis beating like a pulse against her belly, just below her navel. Again, she took hold of it and squeezed it. He turned her around, urgently, making her kneel on the bed. He was behind her now, and when she looked around she saw it, red-tipped and throbbing, waving in the air at her back. Then he took hold of her hips and she felt him put his penis in the furrow between the cheeks of her bottom. She had never done this before and for a moment was afraid that he was trying to put it into her anus. But then, slowly, massively, she felt it enter her vagina. She leaned forward, pressing against the pillow, her face half buried, feeling him bear down on her and in her. And then, driving, urgent, young, he began to push it in and out, his hands reaching up her body to take and caress her nipples. Her eyes shut, her mind's eye filled with that memory of his huge penis and his flat boy's belly, that penis now driving inside her, her hand reached down to touch herself, exciting herself further. She had never done it this way, never with the man behind her like this, and now with her breasts tingling and his penis in her, she began to make small sounds of pleasure. "Now," his voice said, behind her, and as she began to come, she felt him come too, his hands suddenly gripping her hips, holding her, holding himself, thrusting in her.

She cried out.

Afterward, hot, yet shivering from her sunburn, feeling the wetness inside her, she lay, holding him, hearing his heart beat in his chest, a stranger with whom she had almost fainted with pleasure as never with Kevin, a man whose penis she now began to kiss and knead, feeling it come up, growing stiff in her hands, sure that here, in this heat, behind closed shutters on this bed, they were going to do it again, and that excited her; she knelt now, leaning over him, kissing his eyes, his neck, kissing his penis, kissing him with no shame, greedy; herself become someone she did not know could feel this way. His hands gripped her, lifting her up. She straddled him, looking down at him, lowering herself until she felt him, again, enter her.

* * *

He left her at six to go back to his room. At seven
they met again at the sidewalk tables outside the Welcome. He held her hand under the table, but they did
not discuss what had happened. "Do you want to go
into Nice?" he asked.

"No, let's just stay here. Let's eat here. We can put
it on my bill."

"That could be awkward for you. I'll pay."

A young man in a black suit (she had seen him
earlier, upstairs in the main lobby) came through the
bar and out to the terrace, looking for someone. To her
surprise, he came up to her.

"Mrs. Redden?"

"Yes."

"Telephone for you. Iar-land. You can take it one
floor up, in the *cabine.*"

"That will be my husband," she said to Tom. "Wait
here. I won't be long."

As she followed the hotel clerk to the lift, she felt
panic: it was kin to that feeling of blank fear that came
on her in her schooldays on the morning of an examination, when she would enter the hall, see the invigi-
lators come down the aisles, handing out question
books, and all answers would flee from her mind. The
clerk went to the switchboard, picked up his ear-
phones, then motioned her to go into the kiosk. The
phone shrilled twice. She picked up the receiver.

"Hello?" I must try to sound normal.

"Shee? Hello?" It meant he was in good form, calling her Shee. Or that he wanted something.

"Yes, Kevin, how are you?"

"How are *you?* How's the weather?"

"Super, I've just had a lovely day on the beach."

"Good. Listen, Shee, I know this is awful, but Martin Dempsey, who was to stand in for me next week, is down with the flu. Would you believe it?"

"Oh, God."

"Now, listen. I'm trying to arrange with McSherry to work things out. He'll know by Friday. Could you believe so many things would go wrong in one week?"

She thought: he has no notion of coming.

"Shee, did you hear me? Are you cross?"

"Of course not. Look, would you rather I came home?"

There was a pause at the other end. She could imagine him putting his head on one side and narrowing his eyes in the way he did when he thought about a question. Finally, he said. "Do you *want* to come home?"

"Not particularly. As I said, I had a good time today."

"Then why not stay? No sense spoiling both our holidays, is there? And maybe I'll manage to get away by Saturday."

"All right then. How's Danny doing?"

"Oh, busy. Rugby, mostly."

"Well, make sure he eats proper meals, will you?"

"Yes, I will."

"I suppose I'd better ring off now."

"All right. Good night, Shee. I'll let you know on Friday."

"All right. Good night, Kevin."

When she came out of the kiosk, the desk clerk smiled and waved to her. She waved back. *"Merci bien."*

"De rien, Madame."

She rang for the lift to take her downstairs again. He's not coming, *he's not coming,* we'll have all week together. She came out through the bar, almost running, hurrying to the table.

"He's not coming. He won't be here before Saturday, if he comes at all."

"You're kidding!"

"No, it's true. Aren't we lucky?"

And then, like children who have played a joke, they both began to laugh, laughter like a weeping spell, a release which must run its course. They laughed, caught their breath, then laughed again until, she sat silent, downed in an afterwave of guilt.

"I'm terrible."

"You're not," he said.

"I never did anything like this before in my whole life. I know you won't believe that."

"I believe it."

"I mean, never."

He nodded. "I know. It's the same with me. When I followed you down here I was scared stiff you wouldn't even speak to me. I love you."

Suddenly she could not look at him. She lowered her head. "You're far too young for me."

"Nonsense. That doesn't matter."

"Doesn't it? How old are you?"

"Twenty-six."

"I'm thirty-seven." Tears came into her eyes.

"Oh, darling, don't think about it. We're perfect for each other."

She reached into her handbag, wadded a Kleenex into her weeping eyes, and stood up. "Please. Let's go up to my room."

"Now?"

"Yes."

The lift was waiting at the back of the bar. They were alone in it, going up. In the fourth-floor corridor she fumbled with her key, dropping it on the carpet. He picked it up and, moving ahead of her, unlocked the room door, going in to the unmade bed, the open shutters. Mrs. Redden, catching sight of herself in the mirror, her eyes smudged from tears, began to cry again. He put his arms around her and sat her down on the edge of the bed and she turned to him as though in panic, kissed him open-mouthed and urgent, slipping her fingers inside his shirt. There, under the glare of her dressing-table lamp, he began to undress her, she helping him until she was naked. He put his hand out and ran the tips of his fingers over her nipples, which stood up, hard. She began to undo his trousers, then pulled them down over his hips, kneeling to pull down his shorts, taking his stiff penis in her hands, watching it as he reared up over her. He lifted her up, entering her, moving in her, she beginning to move with him, so excited she felt she would come at once, she could hardly stand it, it was so great, oh, God, she cried to herself, let this go on, let it go on.

Later, she lay on her back, the light out, looking through the bedroom window at the night sky, hearing the hum of talk from people dining at the sidewalk tables below on the quay. We should go down and eat. My hair is a mess.

"I'm hungry," she said.

He sat up. "Me too. Let's eat."

"I'm a mess."

"You're great, you're fine."

He went into the bathroom. The bathroom light switched on and fell like a flag across the bed in the darkened bedroom. She lifted her left hand and looked at the wedding ring Kevin had picked out for her at Samuels', a gold band and a platinum band, fused and intertwined. She examined it as though it were someone else's ring, then eased it a little off her finger. There was a white circle where it had been. She slipped it back in place.

"Come on, lazy," he called out. "Let's go down. I want to drink a lot of wine."

She sat up and saw herself in the dressing-table mirror. "I should do my face."

"No, no, you're fine as you are."

But she did her face.

When Miss Purdue came down late for dinner, Mr. Balcer was sitting over a coffee, watching the new couple whom Ahmed, the waiter, had just seated at a nearby table. Mr. Balcer rose to draw out Miss Purdue's chair. "Did you have a nice day?"

"Lovely," Miss Purdue said. "And you?"

"I went into Nice this afternoon," Mr. Balcer said. "I got two good ones."

"Who?" Miss Purdue sounded annoyed.

"Willy Brandt, coming out of the Négresco and driving off with a police motorcycle escort. And, about an hour ago, Caroline Kennedy."

"Where?"

"In the Place Masséna. I didn't recognize her at first. I had to ask the paparazzi who were following her."

Miss Purdue was dashed. She and Mr. Balcer had begun this game about a week ago. Each day they spied out celebrities and reported their finds to each other over dinner. Today had been a bad day for Miss Purdue. "I went to a flick around five," she said. "So I wasn't really in competition." She accepted a menu from Ahmed and then glanced around the restaurant.

"New couple?"

"Interesting," Mr. Balcer said. "They're residents. Or at least she is."

"How do you know?"

"See the room key sitting by her purse?"

"Something odd about them," Miss Purdue said, and both she and Mr. Balcer stared, unabashed, wisely certain that the couple's interest was held by the trick cyclist, as he sawed back and forth on his unicycle, inches from the quay's edge.

"Wedding ring," Miss Purdue said. "Husband and wife?"

"He's not her husband," Mr. Balcer decided. "How old would you say she is?"

"Forty?"

"Oh, come on. Trust a woman. I'd say mid-thirties."

But Miss Purdue was listening in. "She's Irish."

"Are you sure?"

"If you lived in London, you'd be sure. Not only are we inundated with them, we hear nothing else but their awful accent on telly every time their bombs go off."

"He's American," Mr. Balcer said. "Or he could be Canadian." Mr. Balcer was Canadian.

"One would have expected it to be the other way around," Miss Purdue said. "She should be the American. I mean, if it's a dirty weekend—which it certainly appears to be."

Miss Purdue picked up the menu and signaled Ahmed. Mr. Balcer continued to watch the couple, although the sight of them made him vaguely angry. Nothing like that had ever happened to him in all his sixty years. No one had ever stared at him with such a loving look. He watched them holding hands under the table, heard their laughter and their happy voices, watched them toast each other, touching wineglasses.

Mr. Balcer picked up his coffee cup. The dregs were cold.

When they had finished eating, Mrs. Redden suggested another stroll along the quay. He took her arm but she disengaged it and, instead, put her arm around his waist as they moved past the bobbing lights of the pleasure craft moored at the water's edge. "I was thinking," he said. "If your husband comes on Saturday, we have only two more days."

"He may not come."

"But if he does come?"

"Let's not think about that."

"We have to think about it." He tossed his head back angrily. "Christ, I hate this undercover stuff. I never was mixed up with anyone who was married."

"You don't have to be. I didn't invite you."

"I'm sorry." At once he put his arm around her. "I *am* sorry, Sheila. Listen, can I stay with you tonight? I could creep in and leave before anyone's up in the morning."

She did not answer.

"Or you could come to my room in Les Terrasses."

"What if Kevin rings me up in the middle of the night?"

"Would he?"

"He might. I don't know."

"Look, don't worry about it," he said. "I'll come to your room, but nobody will see me. I promise."

"All right."

But, later, going up to her room ahead of him, ostentatiously alone, she felt as she had when she was a child and some other kid had got her into something. People in love have no sense, she told herself. She went into the bedroom, put on the light, and tidied the bed, remembering how, that first time, she had come out naked from the bathroom. He must have thought she'd done it dozens of times with dozens of men. And then she remembered the diaphragm. She had tucked it away that first afternoon, under her cardigan in the bottom drawer of the bedroom dresser. I didn't use it, not then, not later. Oh, God, what if I'm pregnant by him? She opened the drawer, felt under the cardigan, and took it out in its plastic case. The Caesarian, the two miscarriages, the awful guilty feeling of first using it on Kevin's advice. Once it had seemed so sinful; now, so safe. Oh, God, how could I have forgotten it?

She heard him knock. "Just a moment," she called. Quickly she ran into the bathroom, pulled down her panty hose, and put it in. Then, flushed and nervous, she went out to the bedroom, unlocked the door, and admitted him.

"Didn't meet *anyone*," he whispered and hugged her. She relocked the door. Suddenly, as in a silent film, he began to strip off his clothes at a great rate. She smiled at him, then began to imitate him, but the wine she had drunk made her unsteady, and when she kicked her panty hose free of her ankle, she overbalanced and fell. She got up, saw him naked, and then he switched the overhead light off. In the dark, the shutters drawn to close out the Mediterranean moonlight, she moved down in the bed, found his penis, and put it in her mouth, sucking on it until she felt him contract his thigh muscles, his hands on her head, pushing her away. "No, I don't want it too soon, wait." She felt his mouth on her nipples, felt his hands moving over her stomach. His mouth went down: Kevin had never done that to her; she had read about it but now was ashamed that Tom was doing it to her, until she felt

his tongue inside her and, oh, God, she had to delay
him as he had delayed her.

In the dark he moved away and then lifted her up
in the bed, positioning her with her back to him, his
hands holding her waist. She heard the bed, the rotten
bed, grinding and jiggling so loud there was no question the people in the rooms on either side must hear it
too. But in her joy she forgot that, she heard nothing,
and soon she had to make him wait, hold still, hold still,
and then there must have been all the noise in the world
as she let him start again inside her, driving to the
climax, how many times today, there is no past, there is
this, just this.

Later, she slept. In her dream, Kevin waited for her
in the Great Northern Railway Station, standing at the
end of the platform under signs advertising the *Daily
Express* and the *Belfast Telegraph*. There was something familiar and threatening in this waiting, something
which told her it had happened before. The station was
very dirty and smelled of cigarette smoke, and on the
deserted platform lay dozens of crushed empty cartons which had once held fish and chips. She wore
black: she was coming home from Uncle Dan's funeral
in Dublin, and as she came up to the ticket barrier she
thought she had lost her ticket and was hunting through
her purse for it. Kevin would be angry if she had lost
her ticket again. When she could not find it, the guard
at the gate smacked his chrome ticket punch irritatedly
into the palm of his hand, then motioned her aside to
let other passengers pass in front of her. She found
money and paid again to replace her lost ticket. She
hoped Kevin didn't see her pay. She went out to him
and kissed him, but Kevin, looking strange, said, "I
heard you were not coming back." Who could have
told him that? "I heard you were off dancing in the

dark in France." "I'm home," she said. "Then it's over, let's go home," he said. They got into Kevin's new Audi and drove away from the railway station. It was raining, it was always raining. They were coming up Duncairn Gardens and a Jock soldier stopped them, signaling to them to pull over. The patrol was not doing a search; they were in an awful hurry, shouting in their Scots voices. And then, as Kevin pulled the car in to the curb, the car shook and she saw a big gray cloud of dust or smoke up ahead. It was the Swan pub that had been bombed: she knew the people who owned it, one of the daughters had gone to Glenarm convent with her, years ago, Nan Gallery, a red-haired girl, but her picture in the *Irish News* next day was black and white. In the black and white picture she did not look a bit like herself. PUBLICAN AND TWO DAUGHTERS KILLED IN EXPLOSION

It was a dream, she was dreaming it, she had dreamed different parts of it again and again since the bomb in the Swan and the picture in the paper. And now, in her dream, she was on a road in a bus, all alone, no Kevin or Danny, she was coming up to a barrier, it wasn't a police barrier, it was the Irish border, customs men came out and did not look at her but waved the bus on. She had no ticket. Then there was an English soldier up ahead in the middle of the road. The bus slowed and stopped, with an airbrake noise. The soldier came onto the bus and pointed his rifle at her, ordering her out. She screamed.

She woke in a dark room. She did not know if she had screamed out loud. She turned on her right side, expecting to see the phosphorescence on Kevin's alarm clock, but felt her body touch a naked body. There was no clock.

He was asleep, one arm across his chest as though

he were about to draw an invisible sword. In the pre-dawn light coming through the shutters she saw outlines of the dressing table and the imitation green leather armchair. She looked at him again. Asleep, he looked so young. If some English soldier came into the room now with his gun pointing at us, I would throw myself across the bed to protect him. Soon he will slip away and go to his own hotel. And when he does, I'll get up and wash my hair.

But she fell asleep. When she woke it was eight-fifteen and he was long gone. She rose, no time for hair washing. She must hurry to get ready to meet him for breakfast.

As usual, he was first at the table. He stood up when she came through the bar and made as if he would kiss her. But she saw other guests looking at them and shook her head. It was, she knew at once, a stupid thing to have done, so when they sat down she reached across the table and took his hand. "I'm sorry. That was silly of me. When did you go out this morning?"

"Six-thirty. No one saw me."

"Are you cross because I wouldn't let you kiss me?"

"Of course not."

"And so, what will we do today?"

He looked at her. "Let's go some place you've never been before."

"What sort of place?"

"A beach. Somewhere we can be without you remembering you were there with your husband."

"We could go to the public beach," she said. "It's pretty bad, but it's only fifteen minutes' walk."

"And you weren't there with him?"

"Never. He wouldn't go. He hates a stony beach."

"Okay."

* * *

That afternoon, when they had picnicked and sunned, and been several times in the water, Tom lay, blissful, on the stony beach, his arms around her. "Isn't this great?" he said. "This is just what I wanted."

"Stones and all?"

"Stones and all. I'm sorry I said that about you and your husband this morning. It's only natural, you'd talk about when you were here before."

"I'm not going to do it any more. I'm going to reform."

"Oh?"

"Yes. And from now on we're officially lovers. You can come to my room, kiss me in public, do anything you want."

"You mean it?"

"Yes."

"Isn't this a nice beach? Let's come here tomorrow."

Mr. Balcer did not care for the beach. He did not sunbathe, neither did he swim. Still, every day of his vacation he would walk along the quay after lunch until he reached the public beach, where, slowing his pace, moving along the promenade overlooking the pebbly shoreline, he would observe the sunbathers below. Girls were the interest, and sometimes, the French being what they were (and the Scandinavians more so), he would see a girl in monokini, her breasts bare, or, better, a couple up to something. Although, usually, this did not happen on the main beach but in the rocky coves.

In this way, on Friday, about three o'clock in the afternoon, he rediscovered the loving twosome from the Welcome. Miss Purdue had commented on them last evening, pointing to the empty table, deciding they must have checked out. Mr. Balcer disagreed: the table was set for two and still bore the same room number. And now, when Mr. Balcer rediscovered the couple in a rocky nook, screened from all but his eyes, he did not at first recognize them. This was because he was not looking at their faces but at what they were doing. In particular at what she was doing. He advanced on them quietly, at first seeing only a man and a woman lying side by side on a big white towel; then he stepped up on a rock, pretending to be looking at a sailboat in the bay. They were too busy to notice him. As he watched, the woman reached out and touched the boy's crotch outside his swimming trunks. Then, slowly, she began rubbing her hand up and down. Mr. Balcer felt almost as much agitation as though this were happening to him. He could see the growing bulge under the boy's white trunks. His breath became short. He hoped they would go on doing what they were doing and not notice him. The boy put his hand inside the bra of her blue swimsuit, pulling it down to expose her breast. Then they turned to face each other, and exchanged a long, open-mouthed kiss as Mr. Balcer with all his might willed the boy to pull down her pants. But the boy did not oblige. It was at that moment, with a shock, that Mr. Balcer saw the woman's face, and realized these people were his table neighbors at the Welcome. At once he became alarmed and, retreating to the safety of the promenade wall, climbed over it, to regain the pavement. Flushed, he continued his walk.

That evening when, as usual, he joined Miss Purdue at dinner, he did not bring up the incident. The lovers' table remained unoccupied, although the restaurant was full and there was a line of non-residents waiting to be seated. A little after nine, Ahmed came by, reset the table for four, then seated four waiting non-residents at it. Miss Purdue ordered coffee. When Ahmed came, she asked, "Number 450. Has that couple left?" "No, *Madame*," Ahmed said. "Office tell me they have booking for two weeks. But they did not come in this evening. If they come later I will give them a table in the bar."

"How very odd," Miss Purdue said to Mr. Balcer. "Imagine paying pension rate and not taking advantage of it. I'm afraid I'm much too parsimonious ever to do a thing like that. It does seem so wasteful. So American."

"By the way, have you read who's supposed to be in Nice today?" Mr. Balcer said. "Cary Grant."

"Cary Grant? Oh, he should be worth at least three points. I hope I bag him."

"I hope I see him too," Mr. Balcer said. "I remember him in *Notorious*."

"Do you?" Miss Purdue said. "It must be thirty years since that film."

When he had finished his coffee and said good evening to Miss Purdue, Mr. Balcer set off on an after-dinner stroll. The doctor had told him to walk as much as possible; it was good for his heart. But unless a walk had a purpose (like the girls on the beach), Mr. Balcer found the exercise boring. Halfway across the square, he decided to go up to the top of the town to see if those Brazilian cigars were in yet at the cigar shop on the main Nice-Monaco road. Normally, he found the climb too steep. But tonight, with a goal in mind, he set off at a good pace, navigating a flight of steps which came out on a square midway through the old town. As he crossed this square, passing a café on the ground floor of a small hotel called Les Terrasses, he experienced the thrill of a hunter who comes on sitting game. There they were, holding hands and talking, over the remains of a meal. The Irish lady wore a white dress and a red carnation pinned to her right breast, that breast Mr. Balcer had earlier seen nice and round and nude. She was very good-looking, he decided, but too tall, must be five ten or eleven; she and the boy towered over the other diners. Mr. Balcer eyed her figure. I wouldn't mind fucking her myself. I'd like to have her put her hand inside my pants and rub my prick. It was more exciting, somehow, when you thought of some nice-looking respectable lady doing things like that to you. Stiff in his pants, slower than before, Mr. Balcer resumed his walk, going all the way up to the Corniche road. The shop was still out of Brazilians, so he bought himself a nice Schimmelpenninck Corona instead, then went back down again, recrossing the square. Their table at Les Terrasses was empty now, a wine bottle upended in the ice bucket. As he went by, a light came on, on the first floor of the hotel above, and from habit, he glanced up. The window was open, tulle curtains floating out, and there in the lighted window was the Irish lady with the boy behind her, both of them looking down at the lights of the port. For a moment he was puzzled: what were they doing up there, when she had a room at the Welcome? Ah! This must be the boy's hotel. He walked on. He must tell that to Miss Purdue tomorrow. When he reached the Welcome, the TV was over for the night, the public rooms deserted. He took up an old *Paris-Match* and sat in the TV lounge to finish his cigar before going to his room. There, all alone in the quiet, he heard someone's footsteps in the lobby. A woman's voice.

"Were there any messages for me?"

"No, *Madame*."

"No phone calls?"

"No, *Madame*. I have been here all evening. No calls."

"Thank you."

Mr. Balcer, rising from his chair, saw her in the lobby, the white dress, the red carnation pinned on her breast.

"Do you wish your key, *Madame*?"

"Yes, you may as well give it to me now. I'm just going out again for a breath of air before I go up."

"*Alors, bonsoir, Madame.*"

"Bonsoir."

Going out again, was she? Off for more fucking? Intrigued, Mr. Balcer came from the TV room and passed by her, as though going out for a stroll himself. And, sure enough, outside in the shadows, waiting like a prowler, was the boy. Mr. Balcer, puffing on his Schimmelpenninck, strolled across the square and soon heard the light, rapid sound of her footsteps as she hurried past him to rejoin her lover. Mr. Balcer slackened his pace and drew on his cigar, pretending to savor its aroma. He watched the young man emerge from the shadows.

"All right?"

She nodded. "No calls."

"So he's not coming tomorrow."

"Looks like it. He might phone in the morning, though."

"Are you worried about him calling during the night?"

"No," she said. She kissed the boy's cheek. "Let's go back to your room."

Mr. Balcer, tonguing the tip of his cigar to glue the wrapping leaf which had loosened, watched them climb up the steps toward the square. He thought again of her fingers rubbing the boy's prick outside his pants. He touched his hand to his own and felt it grow stiff. Turning, he went back into the Welcome.

The bed in Les Terrasses was small, its mattress worn and hollowed by thousands of previous occupants. To get out of it without disturbing her fellow sleeper seemed impossible. She eased herself up carefully, hearing the bedsprings groan as she stood. Moonlight came through the tulle curtains, lighting his face. He did not wake. She negotiated the armchair and bidet which, with the shower, was on the left of the bed, and went to the window to look out at the deserted square. Beyond its rooftops she could see the moonlit bay and the millionaire's yacht at anchor. For hours she had been unable to sleep, her state one of excitement and a concomitant unease. In a few days all this would end. It could end the moment Kevin phones to say he's coming. Oh, please, God, let him not come.

She had thought "God." The word usually came to her lips these days as a meaningless ejaculation. She no longer prayed. She remembered when all that had changed, at the time of Pope John. It had begun when people lost their fear of hell and damnation. If you no longer feared damnation, you no longer had to believe in heaven. It was, she sometimes thought, a bad joke that when the people at home no longer believed in their religion, or went to church as they once did, the religious fighting was worse than ever.

She remembered what had happened two years ago: Danny noticed that his father no longer went to Mass, and one Sunday he suddenly refused to get dressed for church. "Daddy doesn't have to go, so why should I?" And when Kevin laughed and was not angry at Danny, she said to herself, They're both right, why do we keep on with this compulsory church attendance, when was the last time I knelt in a church and actually prayed? We don't believe, any of us. We don't have to go to Mass or communion, or any of it. And so they all slid out of it, and now never put their feet inside a church door except on great occasions like a wedding or a funeral. Just like Protestants. Of course, she had to lie and make excuses to the parish priest when he came around a couple of times a year with his hints and veiled reproaches about not seeing them at church functions. And of course, if anyone asked her, she would still say

she was a Catholic. In Ulster today, to declare that you
were no longer a Catholic was to risk being thought a
turncoat. But she did not think of herself as a Catholic.
Not any more.

Yet tonight, having said "Please, God" to herself,
she remembered how, once, she had asked God's help
in everything. She thought of her old fears, her familiar
sins, and thought how, long ago when she was a schoolgirl, she would feel a special happiness after making
her confession. And how, the next Sunday after Holy
Communion, she would walk down the aisle to her seat
knowing that if she died at that moment she would go
to heaven, her sins confessed and forgiven, her soul
purged and in a state of grace. It seemed like another
life, that long-ago time of rules and rewards, when
prayer and sin were real. Yet tonight, in the quiet of
this moonlit room, that feeling came back to her, that
pure Sunday communion peace. It filled her, shocking
her, for wasn't *this* sin, here in this room, committing
adultery with this boy, how could this be that same
state, that pure feeling of peace? Yet it filled her, it
possessed her totally. It was as though wrong were right.
Her former life, her marriage, all that had gone before,
now seemed to be her sin. These few days with Tom
were her state of grace. She turned, went back to bed,
and lay down beside him, holding him in her arms,
pressing against his warm body. She closed her eyes.
I am in grace. In my state of grace.

Next morning, after breakfast, they went down to the Welcome, ordered a picnic lunch, and, at the desk clerk's suggestion, walked across the peninsula of Cap Ferrat to explore the public beach at Beaulieu. Again, they drank a whole bottle of wine with their lunch and afterward a Belgian boy came up and asked if they wanted to play catch. Soon, they stood, all three, in a triangle, tossing the ball, absorbed as children. She felt careless and content, tossing the bright-pink ball in the air. She knew she must be putting on weight, eating these big lunches and drinking so much wine, but she didn't care, and now Tom, unexpectedly reversing the order of throwing, threw the ball not to the Belgian, but back to her. Determined not to be the first to miss a catch, she ran, splashing into the shallows to make the save. Both males applauded. She stood, small waves lapping her calves, wondering which one to throw to. Both began to signal, vying for her attention, so she feinted, pretending to throw the ball back to Tom, but instead hurled it hard in the direction of the Belgian boy, who caught it stylishly, using only one hand. He did not throw it back but hesitated, then asked what time it was. Tom said it was after three. The Belgian boy smiled and shook hands with both of them, saying his parents were waiting for him in town. Arm-in-arm, they watched him run off up the beach.

"Shall we start back ourselves?" she asked. "Let's go to your hotel today."

"Okay. But I guess we'd better check at the Welcome on the way."

She looked at him. "Have you been worrying all day about a message?"

"Sort of. Haven't you?"

"No. I've stopped." She kissed his cheek. "It's easier that way."

An hour later, having walked back across the peninsula, they came along the quay at Villefranche toward the entrance of the Welcome. "Wait here," she said. "I won't take a minute."

In the lobby, the desk clerk was talking on the telephone. She looked at her pigeonhole, but there were no messages in it.

"Anything for me? Room 450?"

"No, *Madame*."

"No telephone call?"

"No, *Madame*."

She went out of the hotel and waved in a victory sign.

"Nothing?"

"Nothing."

"Okay," he said. "Let's go to my room and change."

"You mean go to bed," she said. They laughed.

At five, somewhere in the narrow streets behind Les Terrasses, a church bell tolled the hour. Lying in the deep declivity of his single bed, knowing he was asleep, she moved slightly, turning to face the window and the tulle curtains floating outward in the evening sun. I am the one who must make the choices: he knows that. That's why he gets angry and talks about never being with a married person before.

She lay, her eyes open. The church bell tolled the half hour. I should get up and wash my hair. I'll set it, then iron the chiffon dress I'm wearing tonight. We'll go into Nice and have dinner. I'll get up now and leave him a note.

Decided, she slipped out of the bed. His hand caught her wrist. "Where are you going?"

"To the Welcome, to wash my hair."

"Wash it here."

"Can't. Besides, I want to change."

"Come back to bed."

"No. I'll see you at seven. Let's go to Nice for dinner."

"Why Nice? What is this, a farewell dinner? Our last night?"

"It's not our last night," she said.

At the Welcome the proprietress greeted her with the usual question about dinner and, on hearing she would not be dining in the hotel, again brought up the matter of pension.

"I know. Just bill me for pension. That's all right."

"Bien, Madame. Comme vous voulez."

Upstairs in her room, the neat bed reproached her absence. Unused room, uneaten meals, wasted money. She took out the chiffon dress and laid it full-length, like a person, on the bed. You be my substitute. She matched shoes to it, deciding on her blue sandals, then took a shower and washed and dried her hair. Later, she sat at the mirror dressed, making up her face. He dreams me and I dream him, we dream each other as perfect. And, mirror, never my friend, you can't deny that suntan, the look in those eyes. She smiled at the mirror. This chiffon dress is pretty. I look pretty. This is grace, the state of grace.

At a quarter to seven, humming to herself, swinging her evening bag up and down in an unladylike manner, she went along the corridor to the lift, where two older women, waiting, watched her jaunty approach, then exchanged looks as though she were drunk. She smiled at them as they all got into the lift and kept on smiling until, grudgingly, they nodded to her. "Good evening," she said. "Lovely day, wasn't it?" and, uneasily, they agreed. On the ground floor, smiling, humming, swinging her purse, she went across the lobby and handed her key to the clerk. As she went to go out of the hotel door, the proprietress came from her little office holding a gray envelope. *"Ce télégramme vient d'arriver, Madame. J'ai téléphoné à votre chambre toute à l'heure, mais vous étiez en train de descendre."*

"Merci, Madame." She took the envelope, stuffed it in her handbag, and went outside. Parked cars lined the pavement and jammed the center of the little square, so that, crossing to the opposite side, she had to dodge around, as in a parking lot. She did not open her bag until she reached the flight of steps which went up in the direction of Les Terrasses, then slashed the envelope flap with her fingernail and saw the typewritten message on the telegram form.

RANG TWICE BUT NO ANSWER.
ARRIVE A.F. FLIGHT 42 SUNDAY
AFTERNOON. LOVE KEVIN

After reading it twice, she put it back in her bag and started up the staircase slowly, as though distracted.

Halfway up the steps she stopped, turned around, and came down in a run, hurrying among the parked vehicles in the square, re-entering the Welcome, where, in rapid French, she ordered a call to be placed to her home number in Belfast. She said she would take the call in her room, and as she unlocked her room door on the fourth floor, the phone was already ringing. She sat on the bed, listening as the English exchange cleared the call through.

"Double-four-one-double-five," Danny's voice said.

"Hold on, please. Overseas call for you. Go ahead, caller."

"Danny?"

"Mum, is that you? How are you? How's the weather?"

"Fine. How are *you*? Are you eating vegetables the way you promised?"

"Yes," he said, irritated. "Do you want to speak to Dad?"

"Yes, please."

"Well, he's out."

"Where?"

"He went on a call. He said he'd be back very soon."

"Have you had your supper?"

"Not yet. I'm waiting for Dad."

"Well, listen, Danny, will you ask your father to ring me here at the Hotel Welcome—the Hotel Welcome—the minute he comes in. Tell him it's important."

"The Welcome. Does he have the number?"

"Yes. Are you playing rugby this week?"

"We have a game on Tuesday with the Inst. team."

"How's Neil?"

"Oh, fine. His father's giving him a ten-speed for his birthday."

"Lucky him. Well, don't forget to ask Daddy to ring. I'll be waiting here for his call."

"Yes, okay. Hey, can you hold on a minute, Mum?"

"Danny, this is a trunk call."

"But, Mum, I heard a car."

"All right, go and look."

She waited. She shivered suddenly, as though she had a chill. She heard Danny's footsteps running in the hall as he went to the back of the house to see if his father's car had come into the driveway. She heard voices, Kevin, it must be; yes, it was. His voice asked, "Is she still on the phone?"

She felt herself begin to tremble. There was a loud sound as Kevin picked up the receiver, pulling it by its cord along the polished black wood of the monk's bench in the front hall.

"Hello?"

"Kevin?"

"Sheila, how are you? Did you get my telegram?"

"Yes, I did."

"I've been trying to reach you on the phone, I rang at nine and then later around four."

"I was at the beach," she said.

"Yes, that's what I guessed, that's why I wired. What's up? Danny said it's urgent."

"Yes, in a way. Listen, do you really want to come on this holiday? Tell me the truth, now."

"Well, everything's fixed up. McSherry's standing in for me."

"Kevin, you didn't answer me. Do you *want* to come or would you rather stay at home until I get back?"

"No, I'll come."

"Because, listen," she said, and as she began to say it, she heard the tremor in her voice and wondered if he heard it, too. "I just wanted to say that if you'd rather not come, it doesn't matter to me. I mean, I've been half thinking if you don't come, I'll go back up to Paris for the rest of my holiday and pal around with Peg. I'd be quite happy doing that. Honestly."

"You mean you don't care if I come or not?" he said, enunciating the sentence very precisely.

"Look, it's not that, it's just that I know how busy you are. And I think it's silly your coming now, unless you really want to."

"But it's all arranged. I'd feel like a fool, canceling it now."

Then she knew. He didn't know what to say to Mc-Sherry, after asking for the favor. "Listen," she said. "You could tell McSherry I'm going to Paris and that I want to shop, and that you think you'll wait and have your holiday later on this summer in Connemara. Listen, he'll be delighted, won't he?"

Silence again. In the background she heard Danny call to Mrs. Milligan, "What's for pudding?"

"Besides, I really want to go to Paris," she said. "I was there for only one night. I feel I had no time to see anything."

"What about the booking in Villefranche?"

"Oh, they're very nice here. There'll be no trouble. They have a waiting list for the rooms."

"Well, this is sudden."

"Yes, but I think it makes good sense."

"When would you go back to Paris?"

"Oh, tomorrow, or Monday at the latest. I can bunk in with Peg. Listen, why don't we do it this way?"

"Hmm," he said. "I suppose I *could* call McSherry tonight. He was going to do an appendectomy for me tomorrow at nine. All right, then, if that's what you want."

"Listen, Kevin, I was scared to ask you, but really,

I'd rather be in Paris than here. I'd like to see the shops.
And that's not your cup of tea, is it?"

"No. And your pal Peg Conway isn't my cup of tea
either, come to think of it. By the way, who's the boy
friend at the moment?"

She felt herself tremble. And then realized what he
meant. "Oh, a Yugoslav," she said.

"God help us."

"So, it's settled, then. I'll go to Paris and you hold the
fort at home."

"Right. But one thing. Next year, I don't want to hear
any old guff about how we've got to go to the South of
France because I missed it this year. Promise?"

"Promise."

"Well," he said, and laughed. "When I think of the
knock-down-drag-out rows you staged to get me to
France this year."

"I know."

"Okay, then I'll cancel my flight. And don't be
spending a whole lot of money in Paris, do you hear?"

"I won't."

"Oh, by the way, what *about* money? What about
the bill there? Do you have enough?"

"Yes. I'm all right."

"Maybe I'd better wire some money to Paris. I'll send
it to Peg's address."

"No, no, I'll be all right," she said. Now it seemed
awful to take his money.

"No, you won't. How are you going to shop?"

"I have my Barclaycard."

"I'll send you a hundred quid, just in case."

"No, listen, Kevin. I have money of my own, Kitty's
legacy. Owen will advance me some money on my dividends. I'd rather do that."

"Why?"

And suddenly she was afraid. She mustn't make him suspicious. "Oh, all right then, send me a hundred pounds and I'll pay it back to you later, out of my dividends."

"Okay."

"Well, good night."

"Good night, Shee. And listen."

"Yes?"

"I love you."

Why had he said that? He almost never said it any more. She felt sick.

"I'll ring off," he said. "I hear the sounds of a Mrs. Milligan supper being served. Good night, Shee."

"Good night, Kevin."

"Ring me from Paris."

"I will."

When she went back to Les Terrasses, Tom was still asleep. She had to knock on his door to wake him.

"What time is it?"

"Ten past seven."

"Oh, God, I'm sorry. I'll hurry."

"There's no hurry," she said and sat in the chair by the window, watching as he stripped off the blue and white French sailor shirt he'd bought yesterday, stepped out of his shorts, and went into the tin shower. She looked at his narrow hips and waist, his long muscular legs, his hands with their attractive backing of black hair. She forgot what she had been going to say to him. As he turned the shower on, she stared at his penis. The shower was feeble and quickly ran cold, and he hopped out with a yelp. She got the towel and went to him. "Let me dry you off."

"Okay."

He stood, obedient, as she began to towel his chest and belly. For a moment, she thought of Danny, years ago, before he'd become too shy to let her dry him off. She found a second small towel and Tom used it to dry his hair as she toweled his back. And then, wearing her good chiffon, her hair done, her face made up to go out, she threw the towel aside and pulled his still-damp body against hers. "I love you," she said. "I love you, do you know that?"

"I love *you*."

After a moment, he released her. "I suppose if we're going to some big-deal place in Nice, I'd better put on a shirt and tie."

"Maybe you don't want to go all the way into Nice. We can eat here."

"Either way," he said. "Anyway, let's not make plans until you get that phone call."

She went to her purse and took out the telegram. "I got this."

"When?"

"Just before I came over here."

He read the telegram. "Sunday. That's tomorrow." "Yes."

She saw the skin grow taut over his cheeks. "What do you want to do, Sheila?"

"What do *you* want to do?"

"Me?" He grinned, throwing his head up in that startled way he had. "If it's up to me, let's pack our bags and get the hell out of here tonight."

"And then what?"

He stared at her, as though he did not understand the question.

"I mean, we can't just walk out on our lives, can we?"

"Why not?"

"Oh, Tom, be serious."

"I am serious. I'm not walking out on anything. You are. Or are you going to go back to him?"

She did not answer.

He waited, then said, "Okay, it's up to you. But if you decide not to go back to him, we can go up to Paris, get you a visa, and then go on to the States. We could be there in a couple of weeks."

"But I'd still be married."

"We'll get you a divorce. A Haitian divorce, it's easy. Then, if you want to, you can marry me."

"So you're proposing to me?" She laughed, it was relief, it was laughter that felt to her like tears. "You've known me only five days and you want to get married."

"I'm reckless," he said, smiling.

"It's all right, you don't have to plan anything so drastic. Kevin's not coming."

"He's not?"

"No. When I got this telegram I phoned him and told him I wanted to go to Paris and do some shopping. He never wanted to come here, anyway. So he's not coming at all."

"But why didn't you tell me right away?"

She shrugged.

"What was it, some sort of test? Did you think I was going to run off?"

"I'm sorry. I didn't know what you'd do. I'm sorry. I should have told you."

He stared at her. His anger died. He put his arms around her. "Listen, it's great news. But what if he calls you in Paris?"

"I thought of that, too. We'll have to go back to Paris. And, oh, God, I told him I'd be staying with Peg."

"You're not going to stay with Peg. We'll work something out. Let's stay at a hotel—the Balcons?"

"Good."

"And listen, I mean that about us going to the States. And about getting married."

"Don't you think you'd get tired of me?"

"No. Never."

She turned away. "Let's not go into Nice tonight. Let's just eat here some place."

"Mère Germaine's?"

"Or the Welcome. I'm paying for all those meals. We might as well eat there."

"Okay. When do we go to Paris?"

"Whenever you like."

"Tomorrow, then," he said. "Let's go tomorrow."

"You will leave tomorrow?" The night desk clerk, seemingly uninterested in his own question, pulled the ledger toward him, his finger tracing the booking, which was written in ink on a ruled page.

"Yes, I have to go home early. Is that all right?"

The desk clerk, the same dark young man who had called her to the telephone the other night, nodded impersonally. "Very good, *Madame*. I will make up the bill tomorrow. Do you leave before lunch?"

She hesitated, then looked at Tom. He nodded.

"Yes."

"Very well. Do you wish your key now?"

"No, we're going to the bar."

They went toward the lift. "There you are," Tom said. "No sweat. You just tell them and they do it."

"Still, I'm glad it was him and not Madame," Mrs. Redden said, and she *was* glad, it was impossible to explain: here she was deceiving her husband, taking all sorts of risks, and yet she had worried all through dinner about a simple thing like having to tell the hotel she was leaving early, when she had booked for two weeks. Now her mind moved to her next anxiety. "When we go to Paris, I'll have to tell Peg what's going on."

"I guess you will."

"I mean, in case Kevin rings her up to ask if I'm there. I hate telling her about us, though."

"Don't worry about it," he said. "I'll take care of you."

And it was true, from the moment she paid her bill next morning he seemed to take charge of things as never before, handling the luggage, making sure she got a window seat on the plane, ordering champagne from the stewardess, turning the airlines lunch into a celebration. But despite all that, when they landed in Paris, she was again filled with a sense of anxiety. In Villefranche they had been isolated, their universe narrowed to a backdrop of a few beaches, a quay, a restaurant terrace, and two hotel bedrooms. Anonymous among other holidaymakers, they had moved in the protection of a crowd. But now they were moving closer to that life she had left. Now, as they took the bus into Paris, they re-entered dangerous terrain, offering themselves again to the world, their enemy.

When they reached the town terminal it had begun to rain. He unlocked his duffel bag and pulled out a very rubbery Irish riding coat. She smiled when he put it on. He took a flat tweed cap from the raincoat pocket and stuck it, comically, on his head. "Perfect," she said. "I can see you holding up the end of the bar at O'Donoghue's."

They took a taxi from the Invalides, and by the time it let them down outside the worn façade of the Hôtel des Balcons, the rain had almost stopped. The wind blew strong, blustering their clothes against them, bringing her hair down into her eyes. As he went to pay the driver, she ran into the entrance hall of the hotel carrying her own suitcase, waiting there uncomfortably until he dismissed the taxi. They went together to the waxy wooden reception desk to ask for a double room. The

woman at the desk, after scrutinizing the ledger in a
doubting manner, tapped her finger on a page, turned to
check the keys, and, with a sudden smile, took down a
key and led them up two flights of stairs along a lino-
leum-covered corridor which smelled of cleaning fluid,
to unlock a door, switch on a light, and ask if this
suited them. And when they agreed that it did and the
woman handed over two passport forms and the key
and withdrew, they were alone in a high-ceilinged room
with a large double bed and a heavy wardrobe of dark
pine, a yellowed washbasin and bidet in a corner, and
shuttered balcony windows overlooking the street. She
caught him and hugged him, delighted with this dark
chamber of landlord browns and institution greens,
which, had either of them entered it alone, would have
seemed a place of purgatorial gloom. Here in this room,
shut in from the world, she regained her elation. This
was their home. In a few minutes they would go out and
walk together in Paris. Nothing else seemed to matter.

As he put his duffel bag down in a corner, she noticed
the stencil on its side. "Signal Corps? Were you in the
army?"

"No, that's just army-surplus junk."

"Tell me, is that all your luggage?"

"Right. All my worldly goods."

"You mean that's all you brought over from America
for three whole years?"

"Well, I had some books and papers, but I shipped
them home last month."

"Oh? When are you supposed to go back?"

"I have a charter flight on the twenty-eighth."

"Of *this* month?"

"Right."

She turned away from him, went to the window,
opened the shutters, and stepped out onto the balcony.

"Hey, isn't it raining out there?"

She did not answer. After a moment, she came back in, went to the bed, and picked up her raincoat. "Let's go for a coffee."

"In the rain?"

"Yes."

At once he knelt and began to pull sweaters, socks, and a sports jacket from his duffel bag. She thought of Danny, back from scout camp a few years ago, pulling clothes out of his rucksack, the good tweed jacket she had bought for him at Austin Reed's lying crumpled on the floor with a big oil stain on the back. She remembered the row about that jacket, her complaining about the money she'd wasted buying him good clothes. She watched Tom take out a small folding umbrella and open it to test it, its hood shooting up with a flat-sounding boom. *"Voilà, Madame."*

She put on her blue canvas hat. "Let's go."

But as they walked down toward the Carrefour Saint-Germain huddled under the umbrella, the rain increased to a soaking torrent, filling the gutters, spattering their clothes, sending them into the Saint-Claude for shelter. He ordered coffee and sat relaxed, making funny comments on the passersby. She laughed once or twice, but said little and, when the rain had stopped, asked if they could go out again. And so they strolled back to the Place de l'Odéon and up the winding street which led past the École de Médecine, there to meet and mingle with the great aimless crowd which drifted up and down the Boulevard Saint-Michel as though it were the central arcade of an amusement park, eyeing its shops stuffed with leather coats and blue jeans, its self-service cafeterias, bookshops, brasseries, souvenir stands, corner cafés, cinemas, and the sidewalk stalls which sold *croque monsieur,* hot dogs, and *crêpes Bretonnes*. As always on this boulevard, the faces were young, coming annually in an endless migration from every country, every continent, to alight here once in the long journey of their lives. Only the café waiters seemed native to the street: in their shiny black jackets and skirtlike white aprons, deftly flicking crumbs with their napkins, balancing trays, opening fat wallets stuffed with small notes for making change, they were the true custodians of this great thoroughfare, the guardians of its dens and entrances, wary yet confident, as different from their customers as sheepdogs from sheep.

When they reached the iron railings enclosing the medieval ruins of Cluny, he stopped and said, "Weren't you supposed to get in touch with Peg today?"

"I'll ring her tomorrow."

"But what if he calls today?"

"I know. I should get it over with."

"Otherwise, you'll worry."

She gave him a sad smile. "I see you know me."

"There are phones in that bar there. Or, we're quite close to her place. Do you want to drop in and see her?"

"No. That's the last thing I want."

"All right, then, it won't take a moment to phone. Just say you're back in Paris, staying at the Balcons, and tell her, if your husband phones, will she give him the hotel number. You don't have to mention me at all."

"What if she suggests I stay with her?"

"Say your husband might be joining you."

"Oh, you're very clever."

Then, taking charge again, he led her by the hand into the big corner brasserie, through a room full of customers to a flight of steps over which a neon sign read LAVABOS—TÉLÉPHONE. He told her to wait, bought a *jeton* from the woman at the cash desk, and led her down the steps to a tiled corridor. The phones were in the open, but partially enclosed by plastic bubbles which resembled giant football helmets. He ducked under one, found Peg's number, wrote it down, handed her the *jeton* disc, then moved off upstairs, going out of earshot.

That night when Peg Conway met Ivo Radic for dinner, she said, "Well, you were quite right."

"About what?"

"He did chase her down to Villefranche. And, would you believe it, they're back here in Paris. Together!"

"Eh bien."

"No, but Sheila Redden, of all people! I couldn't believe it. She tried to pretend she was on her own at first. But I said we'd heard that Tom had gone to Villefranche and asked if she'd run into him. And all of a sudden she spilled the beans. He's here with her at the Balcons. And if her husband rings up, I'm to say I'd no room to put her up and that she's staying at the hotel. Sheila! If you knew what a shock that is."

"Why not?" Ivo said. "These things happen, even to Irishwomen."

Mrs. Redden watched as he pulled the visa form from his pocket and held it out for her to take. She did not take it. He placed it, like a piece of evidence, on the bedspread. "I looked it over on the bus coming back," he said. "There's nothing to it, it's very simple."

"Why did you go there?"

"I don't know. When I came out of American Express, I just got the idea of going over to the embassy."

She sat in the only chair in the bedroom, wearing her raincoat as a dressing gown, the coat pulled low around her bare shoulders as she made up her face. It was an unseasonable fifty degrees and the hotel heat had been turned off until October. "What time is it?" she asked.

"Nearly twelve. What would you like to do today?"

She shrugged.

"Think of something. It's your holiday, after all."

"*What* holiday?" She threw her eyebrow pencil into the tray.

"I'm sorry. Did I say something wrong?"

She stood up, pulled the coat up around her shoulders, and went toward the unmade bed. She lay on it face down, sweeping the consular visa form to the floor. He knelt, picked it up, and threw it in the wastepaper basket.

"All right, forget it."

"No, don't throw it away."

"Why not? It seems to irritate you."

"It's not that. I don't want to think about it today."

He picked the form out of the wastepaper basket. "Look, Sheila, I don't want to do anything to make you angry."

"It's not your fault. A few days before my period, I'm not fit to live with. Wouldn't you know it would happen this week."

He went over to the bed and began to stroke her hair. "What about lunch, are you hungry?"

"Lie down. Just hold me for a while."

He lay beside her, putting his arms around her. He put his hand under her raincoat and, pulling down her pants, began to caress the insides of her thighs. She kissed him. "Waste of time putting on makeup," she said. But then, abruptly, she eased back and pulled up her pants. She got out of bed, dropped the raincoat, pulled a brown rollneck sweater over her head, and hooked a skirt about her waist. "Let's go out and have a sandwich, or something. I've got to phone Peg."

"Oh, did you arrange to phone her?"

"I was supposed to ring her up yesterday."

As they went down the winding staircase, he put his arm around her waist. "I'm glad you didn't call yesterday," he said. "We had a great lazy day, didn't we?"

"Today will be all right, too."

"Maybe it's not your period. Maybe it's just not knowing what's going to happen."

They had come into the lobby. She nodded and smiled mechanically to the old woman at the desk, but when they moved out into the street, she turned to him again, her face set and pale. "I thought we weren't going to talk about it!"

"I'm sorry."

She turned away, walking down the narrow street as though trying to get away from him. Rain started to spit as he hurried after her, overtaking her. They walked on, side by side, in silence, she staring ahead as though he were a beggar she was trying to ignore. Then, in a shift of mood, sudden as the shower which had stopped, she took his arm. "It *is* premenstrual. And thank God. Do you know, I was afraid I might be pregnant."

"What would we have called it?"

But she did not smile. "Do you know what I did this morning, after you left the hotel to go to American Express?"

"No, what?"

"I lay in bed telling myself to get up and get dressed and phone Peg. I lay there all morning. That's premenstrual. I had this feeling that something awful has happened to Danny and that Kevin is trying to get in touch with me. But I didn't do anything. When you're premenstrual you'd rather worry about not doing a thing than do it."

"Look, *I'll* phone Peg, if you like. You just want to know if your husband called, right?"

"No, I'll do it myself. Let's go to the Atrium. I can phone from there."

In the phone booth at the Atrium, she dialed Peg's office. A woman's voice asked, in French, who was calling. She gave her name and the woman said, "Sheila? Here's the two of us talking to each other in French. How are you?"

"Oh, Peg, hello. Is everything all right? I had this awful premonition last night."

"Where are you?" Peg asked.

"The Atrium."

"Listen, Sheila, I'm glad you rang. Something *has* come up. Could you come over to the Right Bank and we'll have a quick lunch together?"

"What? Did you hear from Kevin?"

"Yes. Listen, were you out this morning? I rang your hotel twice."

"No, I was in all morning."

"Oh, they're hopeless, these hotels. Look, can you meet me at a café called the Métropole in the rue Auber? Say, in half an hour. At one."

"All right."

Mrs. Redden went upstairs. He was waiting at the bar and had ordered two draught beers. "I'll come with you," he said, when she told him.

"No, I'd better go alone."

"Well, let's finish our beer and we'll take a Métro and I'll wait for you some place in the area."

"All right. But I can't drink any beer. I feel sick."

When Mrs. Redden walked into the Métropole, Peg Conway was drinking a Pernod in a booth at the back of the restaurant. "I know what you're thinking," Peg said as Mrs. Redden sat opposite her. "But, I need this drink. What about you?"

"No, thanks. I feel a bit sick."

"Sheila, I'm afraid I've made an awful bloody mess for you."

Mrs. Redden put her head down. "Are you all right?" Peg asked.

"Yes. Go on."

"Well, to cut a long story short, after you and I talked on the phone on Sunday I went out with Ivo, and the upshot of it is, I haven't been back at my flat since. I'm sorry. I forgot all about Kevin."

"Did he call?"

"Yes. Both nights."

Mrs. Redden lowered her head again. "I knew it."

"Anyway," Peg said. "I finally went home about eight this morning because I had to change before I went to the office. And the phone rang and it was him. So I said, very nicely, that you weren't here. I said I had other people staying with me and we didn't have a bed for you, worse luck, and that you were staying at this little hotel, and I gave him the number. And then he said, 'You have people staying with you, do you?' And I said yes, I had. And he said, 'That's funny, I rang six or seven times last night and the night before. I even phoned twice in the middle of the night.' Well, what could I say, it was stupid of me, but I got all flustered and I said, 'That's right, I wasn't here either night.' And then he said, 'I thought you said you have people staying with you.' I tell you, Sheila, it was like being in the witness box. So I said, 'Well, the truth is, these people were supposed to stay both nights, but actually they didn't show up.' So, he seemed to digest that for a minute or two and then he said, 'Peg, I'm very worried about Sheila. I've been worried sick the last forty-eight hours about not being able to get in touch with her. Tell me the truth. Is there something wrong?' So I said to him, of course not, you were in grand form. 'Look, Kevin,' I said, 'the truth is, Sheila wants to spend a few days on her own and she told me you'd be angry if you knew she was staying at a hotel, after her saying she could stay with me. That's the real truth.' Well. Dead silence on the other end of the line. And then he asked, 'What was that hotel number again?' So I gave him the number. And then—here's the part I'm worried about—when I got to my office I thought I'd ring you and warn you. So I phoned the Balcons. And wait till you hear. I asked for Madame Redden. And they said you weren't in."

"But I was. I was in all morning!"

"They said you were out. They said, *'Monsieur et Madame sont sortis.'* I asked if they were sure and they said yes. I asked if a gentleman had called a little earlier and they said yes. An Englishman? I said. And they said yes. And did you tell him Monsieur and Madame were both out? I asked them. And they said yes, they did. Does Kevin speak French?"

"Yes, a bit."

"Well, you see what I mean, don't you?"

"Monsieur et Madame."

"Exactly."

For a moment both women sat in silence. Behind them at the bar two Frenchmen began a loud discussion about the money made by the Brazilian soccer star Pelé. "Look," Peg said, "I'd better eat something. I have to get back to the office. Do you want something yourself?"

"No thanks."

Peg called the waitress and ordered a ham sandwich. "Listen," she said, "just tell Kevin the hotel made a mistake. They're always making mistakes in these little places."

"But, Peg, what if he went straight to the airport and got on a plane and is on his way here now? And what if he goes to the hotel?"

"I know," Peg said. "Why don't both of you move into my flat? You'd be safe there, you don't have to answer the door. And if he doesn't show up, next time you phone home tell him you've moved in with me. And I'll just move in with Ivo."

"Oh, but I couldn't do that to you."

"Why not? Go on. Here, take the key."

"But I couldn't put you out."

"You can and you will. Actually, I love staying at Ivo's place and you've given me a good excuse. Why don't you move into the flat right away."

Mrs. Redden took the key. "It's awfully good of you," she said. She began to cry.

"Ah, now, stop worrying," Peg said.

"I'm thirty-seven. And you know what age Tom is."

"So what? And today is Tuesday and tomorrow will be Wednesday."

The waitress brought Peg's sandwich and eyed Mrs. Redden, curious about her tears. Ravenous all of a sudden, Peg began to eat. "He's a very nice boy," she said. "Sensible too. And bright. Hugh Greer wrote to me that he was one of the best students he's ever had. Ah, Sheila, don't cry. This sort of thing happens all the time. Monogamy's a thing of the past. Relax and enjoy yourself."

"I know," Mrs. Redden said. "It's the only time I ever had."

What does she mean by that? Peg wondered, but as the tears were beginning to stop, she thought it better to let it pass. "Anyway," she said, "I'm sure it won't occur to Kevin that something like this could happen so fast. You've only been away a week."

"But I can't go on telling him lies."

"Why not? There are times in life when a lie is a kindness," Peg said. She looked at her friend. Do you ever really know another person? Sheila Deane, of all people, a big shy thing, always with her head in a book when I knew her, always worrying if she would find some man tall enough, and you just knew when she did she would let him boss her, turn her into a housewife, waste the hard work and the studying she did to get her degree.

Sheila Deane. Still, isn't it the quiet ones who surprise you?

"Madame Chicot, the concierge, has her own key," Peg said. "She lets herself in to clean. So if anyone else knocks, you don't have to answer. I'll come by for some clothes around six this evening and then you'll have the place to yourselves. I must run now. And stop worrying, promise me?"

"All right," Mrs. Redden said. She had dried her eyes. "You've been so good to us."

"Oh, don't be silly," Peg said and got up and went out, shaking her head to herself. The messes some people get into.

When Mrs. Redden came out of the Métropole a few minutes later, Tom Lowry was waiting for her across the street. They took a 95 bus back to the Left Bank and went straight to the hotel, where they spoke to the woman at the desk. The woman said there had been no telephone calls. "Are you sure?" Mrs. Redden asked. The woman said she was sure. But how could you believe her?

They checked out. At five o'clock they went around to Peg's flat with their belongings. The concierge said that Madame Conway had phoned to say if they were going out, they should leave the key under the carpet runner. She would come by at six for her clothes. On hearing this, Mrs. Redden said, "Let's go and shop. I'd just as soon not be here when she comes."

So they went out, exploring the narrow back streets of the *quartier*. They watched men cook exotic dishes in the front windows of Greek and Tunisian restaurants, inspected the stills outside small cinemas, then, having ordered a cooked chicken from the butcher, they bought vegetables and wine in a neighborhood market and

queued for fresh bread at a bakery. By the time they
picked up the chicken and got back to the flat, Peg had
been and gone, replacing the key under the carpet runner.

"Perfect," Mrs. Redden said. "Now, let me cook the
vegetables and get dinner on the table. I'll put the
chicken in the oven to keep warm, and you open the
wine, will you?"

As she went into the darkened kitchen to find the
light switch, she saw him enter the living room and
squat over a pile of Peg's records, his tight blue jeans
straining at his waist to reveal the bare skin of his back
down to the beginning of the cleft of his buttocks.
Peg's big tabby cat came up beside him, leaning
against him, rubbing its back along his leg. The music
came on: baroque. Kevin hated "classical" music. A
moment later she watched him get up, come into the
kitchen and pour the wine, hand her a glass, then
wander off toward the bedroom. She stood abstracted,
chopping carrots, her mind filled with him and with
the music until, at last, in sudden guilt, she turned to
look at the clock on the kitchen table. Kevin would
have had his supper by now and be watching the telly;
Danny would be lying on the floor of the den, doing
his homework with Tarzan, the dog, lying beside him.
Kevin she could imagine leaning back in the big wing-
tip chair, newspapers strewn about, the telly on full
blast. It would be rainy out, and beyond the brick wall
at the end of the garden the dark looming mountain
peak called Napoleon's Nose, rising in the night over
Belfast Lough. In the center of the city it would be
quiet, nobody about except the police and army patrols.
She put the carrots in a saucepan of water and turned
the gas on, hearing a slight explosion. It was a lie to
imagine that Kevin was sitting at home, content in

front of the telly. Who could be content after two days and nights of trying to get through to your wife in France, not knowing what she was up to? There's no excuse for not phoning him. And now is the time to do it.

She went into the dining room, searched the sideboard drawers, found cutlery and napkins, and set the table. In the living room the record ended, the needle making an ugly scraping noise. He came out of the bedroom and put on a new record. The music came up. Vivaldi, was it?

Her older brother Ned liked classical music. Tonight, Ned would be in Cork, alone in his bachelor digs. Her other brother Owen would be at home in Belfast with his family. Her sister, Eily, would be helping her sons with their homework in Dublin. All of them, back there in Ireland living their lives out as if nothing had changed. She wondered if Kevin had been in touch with Eily or Owen. She thought not.

I *must* phone Kevin. But first I'll serve the dinner. No, I must phone now, it's terrible not to do it. I'll phone him after dinner, when Danny's asleep.

A new record came on, a popular one, Françoise Hardy singing a song that everyone in Paris seemed to be singing this year. She went into the living room and he was standing by the window. He took her in his arms and, in time to the music, danced her around the room, the pair of them beginning to sing snatches of the lyrics. He had a nice tenor singing voice. I didn't know that. What else do I not know about him, this boy of mine? She stared up at his face with its high forehead framed by the dark lion's mane of hair, his eyes gleaming in the lamplight. Who did he make love with before me, what woman made him so skillful? Does he still think of her, whoever she is, or

does he forget, as I forget? Imagine if I could forget
my past forever. My past, that small story which is my
life. That story which began in my mother's big brass
bed on the top floor of 18 Chichester Terrace, November 7, 1937, and went on through First Communion and Verse-Speaking Contests and National
School and Convent Boarding at Glenarm and four
years at The Queen's University, Belfast. We always
seemed a crowd at home, we four children and Daddy
and Kitty and the two maiden aunts, the house always
lively, all of it gone now, quiet as a memory, its only
souvenir a few photo albums and old wedding an-
nouncements and examination certificates stuffed into
the top drawer of the little escritoire in the drawing
room of our house in the Somerton Road. And the
drawer gets fuller. I added Danny's baptismal record,
my strange baby born by Caesarian section, a fuzz of
black hair on his head, his tiny face white and com-
posed because, Dr. O'Neill said, he was cut neatly out
of my stomach, not dragged through my vagina. Remember that holiday in Connemara when Danny fell
off the pony in Clifden, the bone sticking up white out
of the broken skin of his little leg, how frightened I
was, worse than my two miscarriages. My son. He is
what I did in life. Apart from him, my life will disappear
like the lives of my parents, a few more documents
will be stuffed in that drawer, and someday the escritoire may be moved to some other house, maybe
Danny's, just as I remember it being moved to ours,
the day Kevin and I picked it up with the other pieces
from Kitty's place and brought them to our new house
in the Somerton Road. I remember the movers taking
it out of the van and leaving it on the pavement; it
looked so shabby I thought all the grand new neighbors would be looking through their windows at it. I

wanted the men to hurry up and bring it in off the street. Then it didn't fit with the other furniture in our drawing room, but I insisted it stay there. And there it is. My past. My past in a drawer.

At nine o'clock she served their dinner in Peg's dining room. He began to tell her funny stories about the summer he worked as a forest ranger in Maine, and she laughed and listened and did not think of anything else. She was offering him some fruit and cheese when suddenly, loud in the living room, the phone rang.

It rang again. She did not move.

"Shall I get it?" he asked.

"No."

"It could be Peg."

"It might be Kevin."

They listened, until it stopped ringing.

"Why could it be him?"

"Because," she said, "if that hotel said we've left, he has nowhere else to ring."

She turned and went into the living room. Danny, his broken leg, white bone sticking up through the skin. She put down her coffee cup. "Listen," she said, "would you mind going out for a little while?"

"You mean, now?"

"Yes. I'd better phone him."

"Sure," he said. He kissed her and went at once into the front hall. She heard the front door shut. She looked up instructions in the French telephone book and dialed Belfast direct. The phone rang just once before it was picked up.

"Hello," his voice said.

"Kevin, it's Sheila. Is everything all right?"

"Where are you?"

"In Paris."

"I mean, where are you staying?"

She did not answer.

"Look. I've been calling you since Sunday." She heard the familiar irritation in his voice. "Where the hell have you been?"

"I was in a hotel on Sunday and Monday nights. I believe you called me there. Peg said you did, but they're hopeless in that hotel, they never get anything right. I'm sorry."

"I thought you were going to stay with Peg."

"I wanted to stay in a hotel."

"Why?"

"I just wanted to, that's all. How's Danny?"

"Never mind Danny, Danny's all right, not that you seem to give a damn. Look, what's going on?" She heard his breathing, heavy and panting. "There's something funny going on. Either that, or somebody's playing a very dirty joke."

"What do you mean?"

"All right, I'll tell you. After I finally got through to your pal Peg Conway this morning and heard a whole rigmarole about people staying with her and then not staying with her, I can tell you I wasn't very reassured. So I rang this hotel number she gave me and the woman there said, *'Monsieur et Madame sont sortis.'* That's what she said. Well, of course, I thought there must be some mistake."

"Kevin, I keep telling you, I told you they get everything wrong in that hotel."

"Just a minute. I asked the woman *in French*. I spelled your name, I told her you were a lady traveling on a British passport and I said that she'd got the wrong room. And she said no, the only Redden she had was Madame Redden and she was with a gentleman and they were both out. She was quite definite. So you see what I mean, ha ha," he said, giving the false little laugh he gave when he was nervous. *"Monsieur et Madame.* I've been bloody well thinking I should get on a plane and come over. And bring a bloody gun, ha ha. You see what I mean, don't you?"

Suddenly she decided. "I'm sorry about this, Kevin. I should have told you sooner."

"What's that supposed to mean? Jesus, you're joking, aren't you?"

"Kevin, wait." She began to speak, the words badly phrased as though she improvised a lesson she had not prepared. "I was at the hotel, yes, and I wasn't on my own. I'm not on my own now."

"What in God's name are you talking about?"

"I should have rung you up before. But I didn't know what to say."

"Say what?" His voice had dropped to a whisper.

"I mean, I mean . . ." She stopped, catching her breath. "I'm not coming home."

"Now what? Wait a minute, Sheila. What's happened? What's *happened?*"

"I'm with someone else."

"Who?"

"You don't know him. That's not the point."

"Now wait," he said. His voice had become calm; it was the voice he used with patients, controlled, quiet, a voice which handed out verdicts of life and death. "Are you feeling all right? Are you upset about something? Tell me."

"It's not that."

"Who *is* this man?"

"I don't want to tell you."

"Sheila, do you know what you're saying?"

"Yes."

"All right, I'm going to get on a plane and come over. I'll be there in the morning."

"No, Kevin, I don't want you to. I'll call you in a few days. It won't help if you come now. It will just make things worse."

"Where are you staying?"

"I'm not going to tell you."

"And what if something happens to Danny in the meantime? How will I get in touch with you?"

"Please, Kevin, don't make things worse. I'll ring you the day after tomorrow."

"I suppose Peg Conway's mixed up in this."

"No, it's nothing to do with her."

"All right. I'm sorry. Listen, Sheila." She could imagine him standing in the hall at home pursing his lips as he did when talking to some patient who was going through a crisis. "I know I've made many a joke about your brother Owen. But he's a first-rate gynecologist, and, look, things like this happen to a lot of women. You're young for menopause, but we can't rule out any possibility. There's *something* wrong, do you understand? I know it's hard for you to realize it now, you're in the middle of it, but, as I say, it happens a lot. Now, listen. If I ask Owen to ring you up, would you talk to him? Would you do that as a favor to me?"

"No."

"Why not? You and Owen are close, and he's a good doctor. Just give me a number and a time he could ring you. Please, Shee?"

"I'm ringing off now. Good night."

"Shee, listen," he began, but she put the receiver down; she had to do it, he was treating her as a patient, it was the only way he knew to deal with trouble.

She went into Peg's bedroom, found Kleenex, and blew her nose to stop the tears she felt coming on again. Then, on an instinct, she went to the front door of the flat and unlocked it. He was sitting on the stairs, half a flight down. He turned to look up at her. "I didn't hear anything," he said.

"I know. Come on up."

"You reached him?"

"Yes."

He came up. She slid the chain across the inside lock of the door after admitting him. He put his finger on her cheek. A tear slid onto his fingernail.

"Oh, dear," she said. "I wonder, does Peg have any cognac?"

As she spoke, the phone rang. It rang. They stood facing each other, not moving.

It rang. It rang.

He lifted her chin, looked at her, then kissed her clumsily on the lips, and at his touch, she clung to him.

It rang. It stopped ringing. She kissed his cheek and his ear, stroking his long dark hair, fingering his face as though she were blind. And then, like survivors walking away from a crash, they went, clumsily, uncertainly, arms around each other, into Peg's bedroom.

The phone began to ring again.

He let go of her, turned, and ran out to the hall, snatching the phone off the stand, letting it dangle on its cord. He went back to her, kissed her hurriedly, and began to unbutton the neck of her dress. She stopped him. She went into the hall and picked up the phone, listening. The phone gave off a dial tone. She replaced it on its stand and went back to him. Gently he began to unbutton her dress again, she helping him as though both were children until, naked, they faced each other in the dark room, the blinds not drawn, the night traffic lights from far below on the Place Saint-Michel moving across the shadows of the high old ceiling like kaleidoscope flickers in a ballroom. Below, they heard the hum of traffic, the squealing of brakes, the faint far-off noise of car horns. Holding hands, they went to the big bed and lay down on it, her face still tearmarked, her sorrow and need for him quickly becoming desire, his tenderness changing to sudden, urgent lust. In the half darkness their bodies began to entwine and move.

The phone rang. It rang, it rang.

He raised her up, turning her around to kneel with her back to him, her face half buried in the soft pillow, naked to him, like a victim on a block, as he rose up behind her, his penis nudging and thrusting. The phone rang. It rang, but as he entered her, she no longer heard it. At last it stopped ringing, but she did not notice. In the half darkness their bodies continued to thrash and strain.

2

When the telephone rang that night, Dr. Deane and his family had already gone to bed. It was after the eleven o'clock news, and as he undressed he could hear his daughters playing the record player in their bedroom. Agnes, his wife, went along the corridor to the bathroom and stopped to knock on the girls' door in warning. "Anne and Imelda, turn that down, you'll wake the whole avenue up!"

The phone rang, just at the moment the record player was turned down. He lifted the receiver, expecting a patient. "Dr. Deane," he said.

"Owen, this is Kevin Redden."

"Oh, hello, Kevin, how are you?"

"Listen, Owen, I'm sorry to disturb you at this time of night, but I'm in a spot of trouble. Could I come over and see you? It's about Sheila."

"Sheila? Is she sick?"

"No, no, it's not that. It's something else."

Dr. Deane heard his wife inside the bathroom, turning on the water taps. He lowered his voice. "Kevin, let me come and see *you*. That might be better."

"Well, I hate to bring you out at this time of night."

"No bother," Dr. Deane said in a quiet voice. He tried to make a joke of it. "I'm used to night calls."

He had dressed himself again when he heard Agnes

leave the bathroom. She stopped by the girls' door, as she did most nights, to call: "Imelda and Anne, have you brushed your teeth?"

"Yes, Mummy."

"All right, then. Good night, dears."

" 'Night, Mummy."

He went out onto the landing, buttoning up his tweed jacket. "Don't switch the hall lights off," he said.

"You're not going out?"

"I'm afraid so."

"Where is it, this time?"

"Oh, it's just a case over on the Antrim Road," he lied. "I'll not be too long, I hope. Don't wait up for me."

"Take your scarf," she said.

It was raining out. In his car, he set the windshield wipers flicking and reminded himself that he had lied to her. He hated to do that. But she had the habit of telling everything to her sister and the sister told the mother, and so it was broadcast to all and sundry. And this did sound like a serious matter. It was not like Kevin Redden to ring up and ask for help. He and Redden were not at all close, a brother-in-law he saw perhaps twice a year at some family occasion, a large, handsome chap with an irritating nervous laugh that was very disconcerting and awkward when you first heard it. He wasn't at all the sort you'd expect Sheila to have married. She was fond of reading and the theater. Redden seemed just the opposite—never opened a book, liked his golf and fishing and so on. Still, he was clever enough, he had his F.R.C.S. and was on the staff of the Royal, the Protestant teaching hospital, which, when you considered that he was Catholic, meant he knew his stuff. Besides, Sheila had married very young, at a time when she was unsure of herself and her prospects. She was lazy about jobs, Dr. Deane remembered, and she had a restless side to her, too. He remembered their talks about religion and doing something worthwhile with your life. That restless side of her was something that perhaps she didn't understand too well herself.

When he drove into the driveway of Redden's big gazebo of a house in the Somerton Road, he noticed the front door opening before he stopped the car engine. Redden came out into the night, obviously nervous, shaking his hand, thanking him profusely for coming. No sign of Sheila, and when they went into the drawing room, he saw that a silver tray had already been laid out on a table, with whiskey, Waterford water jug, and glasses.

At first Redden said it all over again, about how sorry he was to bring him out at this time of night. He poured whiskey and both men sat, awkwardly, looking at the fire. And then, in a rush, Redden began to talk, and the whole story came out—how he had been held up by a series of accidents from joining Sheila on their holiday in the South of France, and how she had gone alone, and so on, and then, at last, about the telephone calls.

"I mean, Owen, I don't have to tell you I just couldn't believe my ears. There's only one conclusion in my mind and that is that she's not herself."

"Has she been ill, then?"

"Well, she has these premenstrual depressions."

"How bad are they?"

"Hard for me to say. You're a gynecologist. I'm not. I wonder—it couldn't be some sort of early menopause?"

"At her age? No, no," Dr. Deane said.

"I just don't understand it. I have no idea of who the man could be. She certainly wasn't running around with anybody from here, as far as I know."

"Mnn," Dr. Deane said.

"I wondered—I mean, I said to her on the phone that maybe if you could speak to her, Owen? Both as her brother and as a medical man, ha ha."

"And what did she say?"

"Oh, she was against it. I tell you the truth, Owen, I don't know what to do now."

"It's a rotten business," Dr. Deane said. He was shocked more than he would have guessed. The idea of Sheila taking up with some man abroad, then telling her husband about it over the telephone. It didn't sound normal. Anxiety filled him: this family thing again. He thought of Ned, his older brother. Another rotten business.

"Mind you, I could go over there and have it out with her," Redden said. "But that might not be the wisest thing to do at this point. I mean, if she's there with some man, it would be confronting her with her sin, so to speak. You know what I mean, ha ha. There would be no denying it later."

Unfortunate, that laugh, Dr. Deane thought, but gave his brother-in-law full marks for sense. If he wants her back, he's right not to force things. Besides, Sheila is not the sort to be bullied.

"Anyway, I don't even know where she's staying. I've been ringing Peg Conway's place, but I can't get any answer."

"You'll excuse my asking," Dr. Deane said. "But have you two been getting along all right?"

"Not one cross word."

"She's had no previous bother with men? Admirers and so forth?"

"No, no. Ah, she's a bit of a flirt, though. She doesn't even know she's doing it. But nothing serious."

"And before she went on her holiday, how did she seem?"

"Well, she was nervous. I noticed that. Worrying about every little thing, as though she was afraid the holiday would fall through. Of course, these times, as you know, who *isn't* nervous, living here in Ulster?"

"And the holiday did fall through, in a way."

"Yes. I suppose so. I know, it's partly my fault. To tell you the truth, I never was dead keen on holidays abroad."

"Tell me," Dr. Deane said, "has Sheila ever mentioned anything to you about my brother's illness?"

"You mean Ned. The dentist? No."

"Yes, you know him, surely?"

"Oh, of course, of course. But it's been years since I last ran into him. He never married, am I right?"

"That's right. He used to live in Dublin but now he's in Cork. Well, about three years ago, he had a nervous breakdown. None of us knew anything about it. I stumbled on it by accident when I went to a meeting in Dublin and went around to see him. It was a desperate thing. He wasn't looking after his practice. He was sitting in his rooms all day. Weeping spells. What had happened was he had fallen for some girl—late in life—and she threw him over. He was in a very bad way, poor chap. The upshot of it all was, I got him off to a hospital in Scotland. The psychiatrist there recommended electroshock."

Kevin Redden whistled.

"It was all done on the q.t., mind you. We arranged a story about him going on a cruise, winning a ticket and so forth. He had a couple of hospital appointments in Dublin. Any hint of mental illness would have affected his practice. Besides, Kitty, my mother, didn't want anyone to know about it."

"But he's all right now?"

"Oh, right as rain. He moved to Cork two years ago, and he's doing well. Still, the point is, he was diagnosed as depressive. And unfortunately he's not the only one in the family."

Redden took a stiff drink of whiskey. "Oh?" he said.

"My mother; between you and me, she had a similar episode. She was middle-aged at the time so it was put down to the menopause. But she was in Purtysburn Asylum for a few months. Ned and I knew about it, but the girls didn't. And, of course, on my father's side of the family, there are ulcers galore. I have them and so has Eily."

"I see," Kevin Redden said. "Listen, you'll have another drink?"

"No, no, I'm all right."

But Redden stood, took the glass from his hand, and insisted on pouring. "So you think in Sheila's case it could be something similar? A depressive cycle?"

"I don't know. So far, she's not had any symptoms of breakdown or whatever. But it's possible that, after this episode, she might find herself in trouble."

"You mean if this fellow, whoever he is, throws her over?"

"Look," Dr. Deane said. "There may be nothing wrong with her. I suppose I'd know better if I could see her."

"Yes. Oh, yes, Owen, I wish there was some way you could talk to her."

Dr. Deane drank a swallow of the whiskey and stared at a little escritoire in the corner, which he recognized as coming from his mother's house. Kitty's writing desk. "I wonder," he said. "Thursday's my day off. Maybe I could go to Paris and come back Thursday night. Oh, I suppose I *could* spend the night and get someone to cover for me on Friday. I'll see what I can fix up."

"Ah, if you could do that, Owen, it would be bloody marvelous. I'd stand the fare, of course. It's the least I can do."

The man had no tact or sense in some matters, Dr. Deane decided. But then remembered that his own Agnes might have made the same sort of offer. "No, no," Dr. Deane said, "I'm her brother."

"Ah, now, Owen, listen—"

"No, Kevin. I'll try to go over on Thursday. And I'll ring you as soon as I've talked to her."

"That's great. If she'll listen to anyone, she'll listen to you. She's always told me how fond she is of you."

"Well," said Dr. Deane. "Now I'll have a chance to find out."

On Wednesday morning Peg Conway woke in Ivo's bed. Last night, when she had gone to get her clothes from her flat, she had forgotten to pick up a letter which she needed in the office. So she breakfasted early and telephoned the Quai Saint-Michel. There was no answer. She decided Sheila wasn't answering the phone because of the husband and so, on her way to work, she made a detour to collect the letter.

When she arrived at the flat, it was about eight-fifteen. She rang, but there was no answer. She rang again, heard a noise inside, and the door opened to reveal Tom Lowry, his hair and shoulders wet, an inadequate hand towel draped around his middle. It was a sight which at once aroused her.

"Sorry to disturb you. I phoned earlier, but there was no answer."

"Right," he said. "We haven't been answering the phone."

"I came to pick up something."

"Sure. Go ahead."

She went into the bedroom, noticing the rumpled bed, and thought of him making love in it. She stood on a chair and, from the top of the wardrobe, took down the large cardboard box in which she kept her private correspondence. As she searched for the letter from Maître Saval, she heard Tom moving around in her bathroom. When she went outside again, he was waiting for her in the hall, dried and wearing just an old pair of blue jeans, which sat very low on his belly. She could see the line of his pubic hair.

"How are you getting on here?" she asked.

"Great. Hey, why don't you stay and have some breakfast with us?"

"No, I've had mine," she said, surprised at herself, for she could not take her eyes off his belly. He must certainly be an improvement on Kevin Redden.

"Let me at least make you some coffee. Sheila will be back in a minute."

"Tell me," Peg said, "when are you supposed to go back to the States? Ivo said you have a charter ticket."

"Right. For the twenty-eighth. If we go then."

"We?" She did not hide her surprise.

"Oh," he said. "I shouldn't have said that."

"I didn't know it was like that."

"Well, it is. Wish me luck."

Suddenly the new sexual attraction she felt for him turned to anger. "I don't know if I should."

"Why not?"

"Aren't you a bit young for Sheila? After all, she's married and has a teenage child."

"Oh, come on, Peg. Age isn't the problem."

Of course it is, you stupid young bastard, Peg wanted to say, but held her tongue, remembering that, in a way, she had started all this by introducing them to each other. "Listen, Tom," she said. "I'm a very old friend of Sheila's. I don't know what her life is like at home. I've no idea. But, my God, that's an awfully big step for her, going off with you to America. You hardly know each other."

He nodded. "I know. I'm not trying to make her do

anything she doesn't want to do. I think people should
be left free to make up their own minds. If she decides
to stay with her husband, I'll have to accept her decision. I won't try to do any con job on her, I promise
you. End of speech, I guess."

"All right," Peg said. "Sorry if I sounded cross. I'd
better run now. Say hello to Sheila for me, will you?"

"Okay. And thanks again for lending us the flat."

Peg went out and down the stairs, head filled with
this news. Was life in Belfast so desperate that people
wanted to run away from it, no matter when and with
whom? Was that it? Running away with a boy you'd met
only a week ago. As she reached the street door, it
opened and a woman carrying a small parcel came into
the lobby, a tall woman with a blue canvas hat pulled
down around her eyes, hurrying, almost bumping into
Peg before she looked up. It was Sheila Redden.

"Peg? Were you upstairs?"

"Yes, I had to get a letter."

"I've just bought croissants. Come up and have
breakfast with us."

Peg hesitated, then said, "Look, could we go around
the corner and have a quick coffee, just the two of us?
There's something I have to talk to you about."

"All right." They went into Le Départ and ordered
two *cafés crèmes*. Mrs. Redden took off her blue canvas hat.

"What's this about America?"

Mrs. Redden, startled, looked up, opened her mouth
as if to try to laugh it off, but decided not to. "Did
Tom tell you?"

Peg nodded.

"Well, nothing's been settled yet."

"I'm glad to hear it."

"Why are you glad?"

"Oh, for goodness' sake," Peg said. "You hardly know this boy. Tell me, are you having trouble at home?"

"No."

"Is it Belfast, then? Is it the life there, the bombs and all that? I can understand it would be enough to drive you into doing something drastic."

Mrs. Redden began to twist her blue hat nervously in her fingers. "No, it's not that," she said.

"Well then, what is it?"

"I don't know. We put up with our lives, we don't try to change them. I didn't realize it, until I fell in love. What I'm doing now is supposed to be selfish. It's what people used to call sinful. But I'm happy, in a way I never was before. Is that a sin?"

"No. But if you go off to America, you'll make other people unhappy. Kevin and Danny. And, in the end, maybe yourself."

The waiter brought the coffees. Across the river on the Quai des Orfèvres a police wagon started up its siren, badgering other traffic out of its way, squalling across the Pont Saint-Michel, stalled in a traffic glut outside Le Départ, then, dodging around a truck, set off loudly up the Boulevard Saint-Michel.

When it was quiet again, Peg said, "Sheila, I can't believe you're serious about this."

"But I am."

"You're really thinking of leaving Kevin for a boy you hardly know?"

"But I do feel I know him. I've never felt closer to anybody."

"You have a crush on him, that's all. He's handsome and sexy."

Mrs. Redden began to drink her coffee, as though in a hurry to finish it.

"I'm sorry," Peg said. "I shouldn't have said that. But you might feel very differently about all this a month from now. If you do it, you might regret it all your life."

"But I can't go back now. Not after this."

"Of course you can. Do you want to go back?"

"I don't want anything. I'm glad this happened. That's all I think about."

"But if it ends," Peg said. "Remember, I know about affairs. You think now you'll never get over this. You think if it ends you'll jump in the Seine. But life isn't like that. You *can* go back, you know. People do it all the time."

Mrs. Redden put the money on the waiter's chit. "Maybe so. Look, Peg, I must go. I must bring these croissants up to Tom."

"Let me pay that."

"No, it's paid."

"All right," Peg said. "Why don't you and Tom come around and have a drink with us tonight?"

"Would you mind awfully if I said no? We like to be alone."

Peg laughed. "Well, at least you're frank."

"And, Peg, can I ask you a great favor? Could we stay on in the flat until next week?"

"Yes, of course."

Suddenly, Mrs. Redden leaned across the table and kissed Peg on the cheek. "You and Ivo have been super about all this. You don't know how much it's meant to me."

"Oh, go on with you. Beat it," Peg said and smiled, watching her friend stand, put on the blue sun hat, and hurry off around the corner, wearing that red dress she probably thought was great but which Peg could have told her was already out of style. Next week, Peg said to herself, she wants the flat until next week. Isn't it next week that her holiday ends? Yes, that's it, next Monday. She'll go home then. She'll see the light.

Tom Lowry, on the balcony, looking down at the Seine and the street below, saw her for a moment on the sidewalk, directly beneath him, saw her red dress and blue sun hat, then lost her as she went in the street door to the building. A moment ago church bells had struck off the hour. The sky was a grimy fat mattress of cloud. Wind rattled the wooden shutters at his back and rain spattered on the gray balcony floor. He guessed she'd met Peg. He thought of what Peg had said about his being too young and wondered if she'd said the same thing to Sheila. Suddenly tense, he went back into the room and out to the front hall. He opened the front door and watched as she came up the flights of stairs.

"You ran into Peg?"

"Yes, alas."

"What did she say? Was it about us?"

"Mn, hm. Did the phone ring?"

"No."

"Good." She went into the kitchen and put the croissants on a plate. "Let's have our breakfast, then go out and look at pictures."

"I've got a better idea," he said. "Let's do something useful. Why don't we go and get your photographs taken and then go to the embassy and get you a tourist visa?"

"No, let's have fun."

"Can we really have fun?"

"Why not?"

"How can you have fun when you're sitting here scared that the phone will ring? Or that he'll take it into his head to come over here and raise hell?"

"He won't. If he hasn't phoned this morning, it means he's calmed down."

"Okay. But what *about* the visa? I mean, my charter flight is about two weeks from today. We don't have all that much time."

"No!" She got up from the table as though she would strike him. "I haven't decided anything. I'm not going to decide anything until this damn period starts. I can't."

"I'm sorry. Please, I'm sorry."

She came to him, standing over him, holding him, pressing his head against her thigh. He felt her tremble. "Oh, Tom," she said. "Come on, let's go to the Jeu de Paume and look at Impressionists. Let's not talk about anything until tomorrow, all right?"

"All right."

Next morning, from a dream in which he and his sister ran along Coast Guard beach in Amagansett, pursued by two men with knives who wanted to kill them, he woke alarmed to stare at a strange ceiling, his mind slowly restoring him to Paris, to Peg's big bed, and to Sheila beside him. But when he turned his head she was not there. For a while he listened, wondering if she were up and moving about in the flat. The only sound was the ticking of Peg's alarm clock. He pulled on his jeans and went out into the corridor, thinking she might have gone downstairs for the breakfast croissants. But two croissants were already on a plate in the kitchen. Beside them he found a note.

> Got up early and had breakfast. These are yours, and there's coffee on the stove. Have gone for a walk. Will be back about ten. Love, S.

He fingered the note. Alarm, the same unreasonable
alarm he had felt earlier in his dream, came back as he
stood staring out of the kitchen window at the shadows
of the courtyard below. It was raining. Until this morning she had never wanted to be separated from him.
Even yesterday, after their visit to the Jeu de Paume,
when she decided to do her hair and he to go for a
walk while she did it, she ran out after him, calling,
"No, no, come back, come back, I want to be with you,
I want to be with you," chanting the words as though
they were a mantra of her content. Yet today he was
alone. He poured coffee and sat down, disconsolate,
staring at the rain on the windowpane.

The Chapelle d'Accueil was in a side altar just off the
nave on the river side of the Cathedral of Notre-Dame.
There was a confession box in there and, in front of
the altar, a table with a lamp, lit while the priest was in
attendance. On the wall, to the left, was a placard:

C O N F E S S I O N S
Anglais—English
8–10   12–15 Horaires
M. Le Père Michel Brault

On the table in front of the priest were a large ledger
and a manila folder which contained sheets of ruled
notepaper. Mrs. Redden did not know the purpose of
the ledger, or what was written in the folder. She came
out of the shadows, going toward this chapel, which
sat like a small lighted stage off from the gloom of the
nave. The priest, the principal actor, looked up as she
made her entrance, gesturing her to sit on the chair
facing him across the table.

"Do you want me to hear your confession, *Madame?*"
he asked, in heavily accented English.

"No, I'd just like to talk to someone."

"Please," he said. He did not look like a priest. He
wore a gray cotton summer jacket, much like Protestant ministers wore at home. His stock was also gray,
frayed at the place where it was attached to his white
celluloid collar. She remembered her father, years ago,
talking about his first visit to France, saying the French
priests looked so poor it was a disgrace. But it was this
poverty which had attracted her when, entering the
cathedral, moving among the throngs of tourists who
milled, unprayerful, in the nave, she saw this fat, weary
old priest sitting at his table in a side altar, his cheap
spectacles askew on his nose, his worn gray jacket, his
baggy trousers. A priest should be poor. Irish priests
were not.

He looked at her. He was waiting for her to begin.

"It's about a friend of mine," she said. She had decided to say this. "A friend who tried to kill herself."

He nodded. He had the swollen, pitted nose of a
drinker. His hand, placed flat on the folder as though
he were swearing an oath, was large and white, unused
to any toil. I shouldn't have started this, she thought,
it's a mistake. "Father, do you know whether people
who kill themselves think much about it before they do
it?"

"Usually, yes."

"But sometimes not?"

He felt his large nose with forefinger and thumb,
pulling on it, preoccupied. "Possibly. Do you know of
such a case?"

"Well, this woman had never thought about it. But
last night she woke up and I think she wanted to kill
herself."

"She told you this?"

Mrs. Redden nodded.

"*Madame,* have you, yourself, ever thought about suicide?"

She looked at him sharply. "No," she said. "Why?"

"Because intelligent people often do think about it. After all, as Camus has pointed out, it is perhaps the only serious personal question."

An Irish priest would never say that. Suddenly she was able to tell him. "I'm sorry. I didn't tell you the truth. I am talking about myself. There isn't a friend."

He nodded, waiting for her to continue.

"Last night," she said, "I woke up. I hadn't had a nightmare or anything. The moment I woke up I felt drawn to go out on the balcony of the apartment I'm staying in. I felt I must climb up on the balcony railing and push myself out and jump. It was as though something were leading me on, making me do it."

"But you did not do it?"

"Obviously not."

He smiled apologetically. "Yes, of course. But did you try?"

"Do you mean, did I climb up on the rail? Yes, I did. But after a while I got hold of myself and went inside again."

Beyond, in the gloom of the cathedral, the organist struck a sudden practice chord, the sound immense and powerful like the roar of a God. The organist sounded a deep note, then a high, shrill one, then began to play the opening of a Bach fugue.

"Do you, perhaps, wish to punish someone?" the priest asked.

The organ, swelling, thundered to a stop, leaving behind a stillness in the vaulted roofs of stone.

"No."

"Sometimes people think of their own death as a punishment," the priest said. "A punishment of oneself. Or a punishment of others."

"Yes. But I don't want to punish anyone. Not even myself."

The priest rotated his head slowly, as though he suffered from a crick in his neck. "Sometimes such wishes are unconscious."

"Yes, I suppose. Perhaps I do wish to punish myself for what I've done. But I don't think so. I feel enormously happy, most of the time."

"Happy people do not wish to commit suicide, *Madame.*"

"But I am happy. Happier than I have ever been. I do have a difficult decision ahead of me. But I will make it."

"And after you have made it," the priest said, "will you still be happy?"

She turned away and looked at the wall to her right. On it hung a huge oil painting. The inscription read:

SAINT-PIERRE GUÉRISSANT
LES MALADES DE SON OMBRE
Laurent de La Hyre
Offert le premier Mai 1635 par
La Corporation des Orfèvres

"I don't know," she said. "Whatever I decide, my former life is over."

"Madame, are you a Catholic?"

"I was. I don't think I am any more."

"When you came into the cathedral this morning, did you take Holy Water on your fingers and make the Sign of the Cross?"

"Yes."

"And did you think, 'God is here'?"

"No, Father, I did it from habit. And from respect for other people who might be believers. I didn't come in to pray. I was walking along the Seine thinking of what happened to me last night. I felt I should talk to someone about it, a doctor, perhaps. And when I saw the cathedral I thought, Perhaps a priest has experience, people tell him things like this. So I came in. And then I saw you."

The priest smiled, showing a large gap between his upper front teeth. *"Eh bien,* I hope I will be able to help. Could you, perhaps, tell me what sort of decision it is that you must make?"

In the silence of the nave, there came a distant murmur of tourists, a shuffling of many feet, as a conducted tour group passed by the side altar, some looking in with curiosity at Mrs. Redden and the priest. The priest ignored the interruption. When the tourists had gone, Mrs. Redden looked at him and shook her head.

"Would it help you, perhaps, if you could talk about it?"

Mrs. Redden slid her chair back abruptly and stood up. "Thank you, Father. It's already helped me to talk to you."

"You should talk to *someone,*" the priest said. "Are you living alone?"

"No."

"Good. You should not be alone. Talk to a friend. Will you do that?"

She lowered her head.

"Or come and see me again. I am here every day except Sunday."

"Thank you, Father."

"God bless you, my child."

The organ gonged in clear tones as the organist again played the opening of the fugue. In the nave a group of Japanese tourists clustered in a circle, as though waiting to perform some complicated stage maneuver. Some stared around, robot-fashion, their ears plugged to plastic cords attached to boxes containing recorded lectures. Others held cameras aloft. Flashbulbs struck in ellipses in the gloom. Mrs. Redden came down from the side altar, going along the left center aisle, passing a field of empty chairs. She looked up at the great cruciform shape of the roof above her head and, hearing the deep organ tones again, she thought of the question asked by the priest: "Did you think, 'God is here'?" No, God is not here. Notre-Dame is a museum, its pieties are in the past. Once these aisles were filled with the power of faith, with prayer and pilgrimage, all heads bowed in reverence at the elevation of the Host. Once people knelt here, in God's house, offering the future conduct of their lives against a promise of heaven. But now we no longer believe in promises. What was it that priest said? Camus, suicide, the only serious personal question. She looked at the side altar and saw the priest open the large ledger in front of him and turn to a blank page. She watched him pick up an old-fashioned straight-nibbed pen and write something on the page. Is he entering my visit in that book? A small transaction of God's business. Debit or credit? I wonder which.

Outside a cold wind swept in an invisible puffball along the walls of the archbishop's garden, scattering a cluster of pigeons as though dispersing a street demonstration. Mrs. Redden caught her blue sun hat, holding it on her head. The clock on the Pont au Double said it was almost eleven. She began to hurry. Rain fell.

* * *

"Worried?" he said. "Of course I was. I thought for a while you might have gone back to Ireland."

"Without my suitcase?" she laughed. "You don't know me."

"Well, where *did* you go?"

"Oh, just for a walk. I'm sorry. You must be tired of sitting in all morning, waiting."

"I am," he said. "Let's go out now. Okay?"

"Of course."

As they went downstairs, she ran ahead of him, beginning to take the steps two at a time. He ran after her, turning the descent into a mock race, thinking that her mood was much better today. Perhaps he could bring it up at lunch.

"Which way will we go?" he asked.

"Depends on where you want to have lunch."

"Is Restaurant des Arts, okay?"

"Perfect."

Outside, the rain seemed to have stopped, but the sky was still gray, filled with shifting clouds. The winds whipped their bodies as they walked up the rue Danton.

"So, tell about this walk."

"Oh, I went along the Seine as far as the Pont d'Austerlitz. And on my way back, I wound up in Notre-Dame."

"What did you do, go to Mass or something?"

"I talked to a priest."

Suddenly he felt uneasy. In Villefranche she had said she was no longer a practicing Catholic. But he had lived long enough in Ireland to be wary of such protestations of freedom. A priest sounded like bad news. "And how did that go?" he asked.

"He quoted Camus. It surprised me."

"Camus on what? Religion?"

"No, on suicide."

"What did Camus say about suicide?"

"That it's perhaps the only important personal question."

"Camus was overrated."

"Do you think so?"

"Don't you know the only important personal question?"

"What?"

"Us. How are you feeling today, by the way?"

"Better."

"Feel up to talking?"

She shook her head.

"Sorry."

"No, you're right. I can't keep putting things off. But first I have to phone Kevin."

A *clochard* in a filthy blue cotton smock thrust himself in front of them, holding out a grimed hand, pink palm upward. *"Dis donc, tu veux me donner des sous, quoi?"*

Tom Lowry turned from the urgent hand, the dust-smeared face, the dulled, angry eyes. "Come on," he said and propelled her past the intrusion. But the *clochard,* running after them, muttering something unintelligible, pulled a wine bottle from under his smock and, staggering along a few paces to their rear, began to drink from it, red liquid, like watered blood, dribbling down his chin and neck. *"Dis donc, toi?"* Hurrying, they turned a corner, leaving him behind, coming out on the Boulevard Saint-Germain, where, slackening pace, Tom put his arm around her waist. "Tell me," he said. "If you phone your husband today, what will you say to him?"

"I don't know. I promised to phone him, that's all."

"But if he asks you to come home, what will you say?"

"No."

"Are you sure?"

"Yes, I can't go back. Not now."

"Then come to New York. Listen, I've worked it all out. I told you my charter leaves on the twenty-eighth. Well, yesterday, just on an impulse, I made a reservation for you on a TWA flight that leaves the same evening. It would get you into New York one hour after my flight arrives at Kennedy. I'd be waiting there for you. There's no problem about a tourist visa. We'll have plenty of time to get it. Usually, it seems, you can get it the same day you apply."

She stared at him. "You've already booked a ticket for me?"

"Yes. You can always cancel it. I hope you won't. Come with me. You don't have to marry me."

"I'm not going to marry you, don't you worry," she said, suddenly laughing.

"And if you get tired of the States—or of me—there'll be a thousand dollars in your name in a New York bank account. And a return ticket. Is it a deal?"

"You really are a crazy Yank."

"Say yes. It's a no-strings-attached offer."

"Well," she said. "We seem to be having our talk after all."

"It's not so hard, is it?"

Abruptly she put her head down. "I must phone home. I *must*."

"Okay, let's find a phone."

"No. You go and have a coffee and wait for me. There's a P.T.T. up the street. I'll join you in a minute."

He kissed her. "Okay, I'll be in that café over there."

At the nearby Bureau des Postes, Téléphones et Télégraphes, the telephone room was in the basement. There an urgent collection of people, including African and Arab students, German and English tourists, waited to call on the long-distance circuit. Mrs. Redden gave her number to a blonde, pregnant telephonist who sat at a desk at the end of the room. The telephonist wrote the number in a school copybook in front of her and told Mrs. Redden to sit down. On a bench, between an old man who smelled of carbolic disinfectant and a black student whose cheekbones bore the gray scars of tribal initiation, she waited, watching the movement of people in and out of the telephone kiosks, until the telephonist suddenly pointed to her and cried, *"Madame? Cabine Six!"*

She went into the kiosk. The phone rang. *"Parlez, Madame!"* the telephonist's voice cried when she picked up the receiver. Feeling like an actor in some foolish yet frightening drama, she obeyed the shrill command and said automatically, "Hello? Hello?"

"Who's that?" A woman's voice, far off, an Irish accent.

"Is Dr. Redden in?"

"No. Who's calling, please?"

"It's Mrs. Redden. Who is that?"

"Oh, Mrs. Redden, is it you? I can hardly hear you. This is Maureen. Dr. Redden is at the hospital. He said if you called to give you this number. Are you ready?"

"Wait," Mrs. Redden said, and then fumbled in her bag for her little address book, with its tiny pencil, the point almost worn to the wood. "All right, Maureen."

"Four-five-four-seven-seven."

"Four-five-four-seven-seven?"

"That's right. How is Paris, Mrs. Redden?"

"Fine, Maureen. I'll try that number now. Thank you."

And left the kiosk, going across to the telephonist's desk to queue, pay for her call, ask the telephonist to try the new number, and wait again on the bench beside two small Arab men who looked at her boldly, then eyed her legs with sidelong glances until the telephonist again signaled to her, crying, *"Madame?"* Again, in the booth, she picked up a ringing phone. *"Parlez, Madame!"*

"Hello."

"City Hospital surgical unit," a man's voice said.

"This is Dr. Redden's wife, calling from Paris. Is he there?"

"Hold on, Mrs. Redden, I'll see if I can get him," the voice said. And it was then, standing in a Paris telephone booth, the air heavy with the smell of stale tobacco smoke, that she faced the question at last. What would she say to him? What could she say to him?

"Hello, Sheila?" He sounded falsely cheerful.

"Kevin."

"How are you? I'm glad to hear from you. I was hoping, maybe, you'd phone yesterday."

"I said it would be a couple of days."

"That's right, I know you did. It's just that I haven't been able to sleep much at night, thinking of all this."

"I'm sorry."

"No, don't say that. I'm sure there've been mistakes on both sides. By the way, did you get that money I sent you?"

"What money?"

"Do you remember I told you when you rang up from Villefranche that I'd send you a hundred quid for shopping? Well, I sent it on to Peg Conway's address. Have you seen her?"

"Yes. But it isn't here yet."

"Well, it should have arrived by now."

"I'll ask Peg about it. Thank you. I'll pay you back."

"Never mind that. Are you staying with Peg, then?"

She did not answer.

"I'm just asking, because if neither you nor Peg are at her flat, the money could be there waiting for you."

"No, somebody's there."

"You'd never know it. I rang there the other night and got no answer."

"I took the phone off the hook."

"So you're there, then? At Peg's?"

"Yes."

"I see. And how are you? Or should I ask that?"

"I'm all right. How's Danny?"

"Oh, he's grand. I didn't say anything to him, by the way."

"Oh."

"I mean, I'm still hoping that he won't have to know about any of this."

She did not speak.

"Look, Shee, would it do any good if I come over and we could have a heart-to-heart chat? Maybe if we talk about this, we can find out what it is that went wrong."

"No."

"Shee, people go through these crises. I was talking to Owen the other night. He told me about your brother Ned. You knew about Ned, didn't you?"

Ned. Owen told him about Ned? Kitty said we were never to say. "You were talking to Owen? About me?"

"Yes."

"About this?"

"Well, I had to talk to somebody. I'm very worried about you."

"And what did Owen say?"

"Well, he mentioned Ned, he said Ned had a similar experience three years ago and that it ended in a nervous breakdown. He had to have electroshock, it seems."

"Oh, my God, Kevin," she said, suddenly furious. "What does Owen mean, 'a similar experience'? Ned was never married, he once studied for the priesthood, remember? And then he started courting some young girl and she wouldn't have him. It's as different from this as day from night."

"All right, all right, hold your horses. It was Owen who mentioned the possible connection."

"What possible connection?"

"Well, maybe you should talk to Owen about it."

"I don't want to talk to anybody." She couldn't just tell him, it's over, Kevin. There's no sense talking. Not now. Not today. "Look," she said. "I still have to think about things. I'm going to ring off now."

"When will I hear from you?"

"I'll call you on Saturday?"

"Not till then?"

"No."

"Well, I suppose I'll just have to wait. Is that it?"
She did not answer.

"All right. Take care of yourself, will you?"

"Goodbye. Say hello to Danny for me."

"I'll do that. Poor kid, he's still expecting you next Monday. He'll be very cut up if you're late."

"Goodbye," she said again. As she replaced the receiver, angry tears started in her eyes. Cut up! Danny, with his rugby and his bike team, Danny who hardly knows if I'm in the house or out, as long as his meals are on time.

She went upstairs and out onto the boulevard. The sky was the color of slate and a wintry wind whipped the pavement debris into a miniature sandstorm. As she put her hand up to shield her face, Ned, wearing his white dentist's coat, seemed to come before her, tall and awkward, stooping to conceal his height. She saw his sparse rusty hair, his long nose, sharp and red at the tip. In his hand he held a thin steel instrument and grinned when she pulled back, childishly, thinking it was a drill. "Come on, it's only a mirror," he said, showing her a small circle tilted at the instrument's end. "Now, let's just have a peek."

Owen said that when he visited Ned that time in his rooms in Leeson Street, he found him sitting in his dressing gown at twelve o'clock in the day. He burst into tears when Owen spoke to him. He was unable to stir out, unable to look after his simplest needs. "He was suffering from malnutrition, if you'll believe it," Owen said. But Ned was all right now. Eily saw him last summer: when she went to Cork he took her out for a drive in his car. They went down to Cobh and the sea. She said he was like his old self, but quieter, not so much fun as he used to be.

We were never to tell anyone about Ned. Kitty made that rule and we all agreed to it. I never even told Kevin. Because I'd made a promise. Yet the other night Owen told him, just like that.

"How did it go?" Tom Lowry said, rising to his feet as she came to the table.

"All right."

"You don't look all right."

"I'm all right."

"Do you want some coffee? Or some lunch?"

"No," she said. "You have something. And then let's go back to the flat."

* * *

"Il y a une lettre recommandée pour vous, Madame," the concierge said. *"Je l'ai mise en haut."*

The registered letter had been slipped under the apartment door. It lay on the polished wooden floor beside a circular and a newspaper. An English stamp, and her name and address written in Kevin's doctor's squiggle. "This must be the one," she said. She opened it and pulled out a money order on Barclays Bank, France, for one hundred pounds. Then found his note, written on surgery paper.

KEVIN REDDEN, M.B., F.R.C.S.
22 CLIFTON STREET,
BELFAST

Dear Shee
Here's the money I mentioned when you were in Villefranche. Am very upset but, understand me, it's *you* I worry about. Please think of us. Danny sends hellos.

Love
Kevin

She crumpled the note and stuck it in the mouth of her purse. She put the envelope with the money order on the hall table. "Tom?"

He came out of the kitchen. "Yes."

"Feel like lying down?"

He laughed and caught her at the waist, lifting her into the air.

"I'm too big, put me down."

"No, you're not." Quickly he carried her into the bedroom and dropped her on Peg's bed. "Oh, God," she called, as she bounced on the mattress. "You'll break it."

"Shut up," he said. "Strip!"

She stood up on the bed, running her panty hose as she pulled them down. She took off the rest of her clothes and, naked, stood above him as he bent over, his back to her, pulling down his trousers. She waited until he was naked, then, unsteadily, crossed the soft expanse of mattress and climbed onto him, piggyback, as she had done with her father when a child. Laughing, he caught her legs, holding his hands out like stirrups, and with her arms around his neck, both of them naked, raced into the living room, then, wheeling, ran down the corridor into the kitchen, as she spurred him, her stallion, with her naked heels. "Back to bed!" she cried. "Hup, there."

The doorbell rang.

He stopped, skidding, in the center of the hall. "The concierge?" she whispered.

He turned and, still carrying her piggyback, ran into the bedroom and kicked the door shut. He let her down and they stood, listening. It was not the concierge. The hall door did not open. Instead, after an interval, the doorbell rang again. He stared at her. "Who?"

She shrugged in puzzlement. He reached for his jeans. "Want me to open?"

She shook her head. The doorbell rang a third time. He put on his jeans. "I'll look through the peephole."

"No, they might see you do it."

She sat on the bed and he sat beside her. She seemed to be shivering. Again, the doorbell rang as they sat, prisoners of that sound, waiting. But the doorbell did not ring a fifth time. After a while she got up, put on her skirt and blouse, and, barefoot, wearing no underwear, went into the front hall. He joined her, just as she stooped to pick up the piece of paper which had been slipped under the door. It was a folded sheet of notepaper and on the back was written *Miss P. Conway*.

"For Peg," she said, but as she did, the paper opened on the fold. She saw the letterhead.

54 DUNDRUM ROAD
BELFAST

3:15 p.m.

Dear Peg,

I am in Paris for the night, staying at the Angle-terre Hotel. I am very anxious to get in touch with Sheila but don't know where to reach her. If you can help me, will you get in touch with me at my hotel? In the meantime, I will wait for a while in the café on the corner, in case you come home soon. Best wishes,

Owen Deane

P.S. Have tried your office number but they say you are off for the afternoon.

She handed him the note and watched him read it.

"Who's Owen Deane?"

"My brother."

She came up to the corner of the Place Saint-Michel as though she were at home and had been told there was a sniper in the next street. For a moment she wondered if he would be sitting there with Agnes, Agnes who might well force him to bring her along even on this painful journey. But when she came into the square, screened by the flow of people moving to and from the Métro entrance, she saw her brother alone, in Le Départ, down at the far end of the café, near the rue de la Huchette. He sat with a beer and a newspaper but he was not reading. Instead, he seemed interested in the antics of the guitar-playing youths and girls camped under the winged gorgons and green-slimed fountains in the center of the square.

He had not seen her. What an obvious tourist he looked in his fly-front raincoat and narrow-brimmed green hat. How old he looked, how failed. For one guilty moment she thought: If I have to introduce him to Tom, he's going to make *me* seem old. But then he pulled out his spectacles and picked up the newspaper in a studious, preoccupied way which instantly recalled his younger self. Poor Owen, he must be dreading this meeting.

She came out from her place of concealment near the newspaper kiosk and walked past him as though she had not seen him. But he did not notice her. At the corner of the rue de la Huchette she paused and looked back. He was staring in the opposite direction. She hurried into the café, came up behind him, and, bending over, said in his ear, "Excuse me, sir. Are you a private detective?"

He started, swiveled around, and jumped to his feet, whipping the spectacles off his nose, grabbing at her awkwardly, sweeping her into an embrace. His cheek felt unshaven although it was not. "Sheila. You scared the life out of me."

She held him, her arms tight about him, she had never understood it, but when they met, she and her sister and brothers, suddenly all of their wives, husbands, and children seemed members of another race, not part of the Family, that family whose allegiances antedated all others. Even with Ned, the brother she was no longer close to, her feeling was the same. It was as though they were survivors of another country, a tiny nation whose meaningless historical memories were of playing Snap in rainy, rented houses in Portrush in the summer, of being lined up two-by-two by Daddy to march to the Pool for an afternoon of swimming; of being made to compete for medals in embarrassing verse-speaking contests; of the day a maid called Annie killed a rat in the attic; of all of them keeping very quiet after supper in hopes that Kitty would forget to assemble them for the saying of the family rosary; of ice cream as a Sunday treat when one of the boys would be sent out to McCourt's for sliders and two siphons of lemonade; and of that famous family photograph when Daddy posed them on a ladder, against a tool shed in the garden, all dressed up in their good new overcoats, school caps and tams, four rungs of the ladder, the oldest at the top, while Kitty, cigarette dangling from her lips, raised the flash extension and Daddy, peering into his Rolleiflex, ordered everyone to smile.

Now, the second from the top of the ladder smiled at her with new caution. "Did Peg tell you I was down here?"

"No," she said. "I was in the flat when you came, but I didn't answer the door. Then I saw your note."

"Well," he said and, confused, made a gesture toward his table. "Sit down, won't you?"

"Did you just get in?"

"Yes, about an hour ago. Will you have a drink?"

"A coffee, maybe."

"Sure you won't have something stronger?"

"What's the plan? Get me drunk and shanghai me home?"

He smiled. "At least I've found you. I had an awful vision of coming all this way and *not* finding you. Or finding you and having you hit me over the head with your purse."

"I might do that yet."

"So." He looked around him. "Paris. It's beautiful, isn't it?"

"Yes."

"The family have all become awful sticks-in-the-mud about travel. All of us going off to Donegal and Galway and the like."

"I know."

"Mind you, Eily and Jim took their kids to Spain last year. They had a great time there, apparently."

She made a face. "Those awful British holiday villages on the Costa del Sol. They might as well never leave home."

"Still, I can't throw stones," Dr. Deane said. "Agnes

and I both love Kerry. The children do, too. It's almost
a second home to them."

"How are the girls?"

"Oh, very well. Imelda passed her O Levels, just
last week. Agnes and I were delighted. We went out
and bought a bottle of champagne to celebrate."

She smiled. "And how is Agnes?" she asked.

"She's in grand form. Did I tell you, she's now a
golf champion. She won the Ladies' Open at the club
last month."

"That's very good."

"Yes, and she's working on her poetry, too. She had
a poem published lately in some religious journal. *The
Messenger,* actually. Still, it's a start, what?"

She looked at him. Poor old Owen. "Indeed it is,"
she said. In the pause, he signaled a waiter.

"Do you want cream in your coffee?"

"No," she said. *"Un espress,"* she told the waiter.

"Bien, Madame."

"I always forget," he said. "You're quite at home
in France."

"Yes. I always was at home here. I don't feel at home
at home."

"Do you remember the time we were here together,
years ago, on our way to see Uncle Dan at The Hague?"

"Funny," she said, "I was thinking about that just
the other day."

"I remember how impressed I was at the way you
told the porter off in French. Using bad language, too."

She smiled and nodded. When would he get down
to it?

It was as though she had spoken aloud. Her brother
took off his ugly hat and put it down on the chair beside
him. How thin his hair is now: what is he? Eight years

older than me? He put his face up to the gray sky as though he were sunbathing. "Tell me, Sheila, how are you feeling?"

"What is it you doctors say? As well as can be expected."

He swiveled to look at her. There were brownish puffy sacs under his bright-blue eyes. "I saw Kevin the other night."

"So I gather. Who else has he told about this?"

"Nobody," Dr. Deane said. "Agnes knows, of course, but don't worry, she'll be like the grave, I promise you."

He saw the disbelief in her face. He could not blame her. He finished his beer.

"What, exactly, did Kevin tell you?"

"He said you told him you might not be coming home."

"Anything else?"

"He said you told him there was someone here. Another man."

"Did that surprise you, Owen?"

"Yes, it did. Although, I suppose these things happen. People go through a period of change. They want to change their lives. Believe me, I see it all the time in my practice."

"You mean with women."

"Well, I deal with women, of course, but it happens to men, too."

"And why do people try to change their lives, do you suppose?"

"Usually because they're getting on, reaching middle age. They feel dissatisfied. They want to achieve something."

"So you treat it as a medical problem?"

"I didn't say that."

"Kevin thinks it's a medical problem."

He looked at her out of the corner of his eye. "Did Kevin say that to you?"

"You and Kevin discussed me. You know it. You even told him about Ned's breakdown. I think that was rotten of you. One thing Kitty was right about is, what happened to Ned is his business and nobody else's."

"Kitty is dead," Dr. Deane said. "So I'm not going to criticize her. But I think she was quite wrong. It would have been easier for Ned if his friends and his family had openly acknowledged what was the matter with him."

"Maybe so. But we agreed not to tell anyone. I never even told Kevin about it."

The waiter came, putting down her cup of coffee, tucking a check under the saucer. Dr. Deane pointed to his beer glass and said awkwardly, *"Encore, s'il vous plaît."*

"So," she said. "What exactly has Ned's breakdown got to do with this?"

"Sheila, can I ask you a few questions?"

"What sort of questions?"

"How have you been? Have you had any loss of appetite, trouble sleeping, dizzy spells, trouble concentrating, irritability. Anything of that sort?"

"No. I'm very well, thank you."

"You haven't felt depressed?"

"No."

"The thought of leaving your husband and child doesn't upset you?"

"Of course it does. But that's not depression."

"All right, it's not depression, per se. But surely you can't feel happy about what you're doing?"

"I don't know, Owen. It's complicated. Most of the time I feel very happy. I feel alive in a way I never felt before. But the other night I woke up feeling suicidal. I think I know why. It was because I was still unwilling to face up to what's happened to me. I was still looking for some way out. Some way I could go on feeling like this but not having to pay for it. Now I know that's not possible. I'll have to pay. I've accepted that."

"And how will you pay, tell me?"

"I don't know. But I know that I can't go home again. That part of my life is over."

"It's *not* over," Dr. Deane said. "What nonsense! You can't just will your husband and child out of existence."

"I wonder. People escape from their lives. Did you ever read those newspaper stories about the man who walks out of his house saying he's going down to the corner to buy cigarettes? And he's never heard from again."

The waiter brought a fresh glass of beer. "The point is," Dr. Deane said, "you're not a man, and you haven't disappeared. In fact, you might find it pretty difficult."

"Women disappear, too."

"And what would you live on?"

"I have my Consuls and those other shares Kitty left us. They'd give me a start for a few months. My shares are still in your name, aren't they?"

"They are," Dr. Deane said. "Do you want me to sell them, is that it?"

"Yes, please. You could send me the money."

"So this new man of yours isn't able to support you?"

"I didn't say that."

"I'm sorry." Dr. Deane tasted his beer. "Sheila, what's wrong? Were you not happy at home?"

"Are you happy at home? Is anyone?"

"Do you mean because of the Troubles?"

"Oh, God, no. The Troubles, you can't blame the

Troubles for everything. That's become our big excuse. We have the Troubles. They're the only thing we believe in any more."

"I'm not sure I follow you, Sheila."

"The Protestants don't believe in Britain and the Catholics don't believe in God. And none of us believes in the future."

"That's a very gloomy prognosis, I must say."

"What do *you* believe in? Do you believe that if you live a good life here on earth you'll go to heaven? Do you believe in politics? Do you believe in trying to make this world a better place to live in? In Daddy's day, people believed in those things. The present made sense because they believed there would be a future. Nowadays, all we believe in is having a good time. Isn't that true?"

"Is that why you decided to do this? Because you want to have a good time?"

"No. It happened to me."

"But it won't last," Dr. Deane said. "You know that, don't you?"

"That's not the point."

"It is the point," Dr. Deane said. "Now, look, don't be cross, but Kevin could be right. This decision of yours could be a sign of mental illness."

"Like Ned? Oh, for goodness' sake, Owen!"

"All right, but the fact is, *his* trouble started with a love affair."

"Look, there's no comparison."

"Then let me say something else. Ned had a nervous breakdown. But he's not the only one. It's quite possible that we have a weakness of that sort in our family."

"Who had one? Who else?" Suddenly she was frightened.

"Kitty."

"Kitty?"

"It was just after you were born. She became suicidal, it seems. Anyway, she spent three months in Purtysburn Asylum."

"But isn't that something women have sometimes after a baby, a suicidal thing?"

"Postpartum depression. Yes. But I don't think it was that in her case."

She leaned forward and closed her eyes. The traffic noise seemed unnaturally loud. "Is that why you came?" she said. "To frighten me?"

"I came to help you, if I can. I'm worried about you."

"So you think I might be going through some sort of mental breakdown?"

"You may be doing what analysts call 'acting out.' "

"You don't think it's possible that I just fell in love?"

"Yes, of course," Dr. Deane said. "But that doesn't necessarily mean that you're all right. Look, who is this chap? Could I meet him?"

"No."

"Why not? Are you ashamed of him?"

"He's an American. He's ten years younger than I am. We've only known each other two weeks and we're living together. He wants to look after me. He wants me to come to America with him and marry him. Or not marry him. It's up to me. That's all. I'm sure this will just confirm your damn diagnosis."

"I didn't make any diagnosis."

"Well, anyway, that's the situation. I *am* like the man who went out to get cigarettes and didn't come back. Forget about me. Oh, yes. Sell my shares, will you? I'll write you a letter soon and let you know where to send the money. Will you do that?"

"I'll sell them as soon as I get your letter. All right?"

"Thanks. Now, I want you to go home, Owen. There's nothing you can do here. You think I may be mad. I know I'm not. So let's say goodbye. Nicely."

"Oh, come on. Let's at least have dinner together."

"I'm sorry. I have a date."

"Well, could I join you?"

"No."

And then, ashamed, she reached across the table and took his hand. She squeezed it. "I'm sorry, Owen." But at that moment she saw, fifty yards away, Tom Lowry, standing at the Métro entrance, watching them. How dare he spy on her. She had told him to wait for her in the flat. But, angry as she was, at the same time she felt an excitement at seeing him. She let go of her brother's hand and said, "All right, if you're not going till tomorrow, I'll have breakfast with you. I'll come around to your hotel about eight."

"Good. Sheila, I have to phone Kevin tonight. What will I say to him?"

"Tell him it's no use."

Dr. Deane bowed his head. "What about Peg, is she around?"

"Yes. Why?"

"Maybe she'll have dinner with me. You don't mind my getting in touch with her, do you?"

"She's your friend, too," Mrs. Redden said. She found Ivo's phone number and wrote it down for him, handing him the scrap of paper as she stood up. "All right. What's your hotel again?"

"The Angleterre."

She bent down and kissed him on the cheek. "See you in the morning," she said, and went quickly out into the street, mingling with the passersby. She walked to the curb, waited with the crowd, then, as the

light went green, hurried across the square to reach the
midway traffic island, where, as the second traffic light
went green, she went on to the safety of the pavement
on the far side of the square. Then turned and saw
that Tom, who had followed her, was stranded on the
traffic island by a red light. He glanced at the oncom-
ing automobiles and sprinted out inches ahead of the
traffic. She felt her heart jump in fear, until he reached
the safety of the pavement. When he ran up to join her,
she held him to her. "You might have been killed!"

And then, holding him, remembered her brother.
She turned and looked back across the expanse of square
to where he sat. As she did, her brother waved to her.
Slowly, she raised her arm and waved back.

Next morning, after breakfast with his sister, Dr. Deane took the bus to Orly. He had given up smoking three years ago, but when he arrived at Orly he went into the duty-free shop, bought a carton of Gauloises, and ripped open a package. The first puff made him dizzy. Inhaling, he went to another counter and, in penance, purchased bottles of Chanel toilet water for his wife and two daughters. Then, still smoking, he entered the bar and ordered a brandy-and-soda. He had thought of phoning Agnes from the airport to let her know he was on his way home, but after drinking the brandy, he ordered another and decided he would make the call when he stopped over in London. Halfway through the second brandy, he changed his mind and asked the barman where the telephones were. But as he started to walk to the phone booth, the flight to London was called.

So that was that. He would have to decide later just what to tell her. He was certainly not going to tell her that he had lost his temper and shouted at Sheila. That was just what Agnes would like to hear. But, still, that was what he had done. What sort of a way was that to try to help people, shouting at them? I should have gone off to the Louvre this morning, looked at some pictures, and gone back again this afternoon to apologize to her. A doctor should never try to treat his own family. It doesn't wash. If my father had been a medical man, what would he have done? What would he have said to her?

Dr. Deane walked out toward the waiting plane, thinking of his father and his father's great friends, Dr. Byrne and Chief Justice McGonigal, remembering their arguments about Shaw and Joyce, about Mussolini's policies vis-à-vis the Vatican, and the morality of Ireland's neutrality during the war. Not intellectuals, but men who read a lot, who loved discussion and despised golf, who never cared about the size of their house or the make of their motorcar. That older generation, passionate, literate, devout, still seemed to him more admirable and interesting in their enthusiasms and innocence than the later generation which claimed him as its own. His father would have made mincemeat of Sheila's arguments. His father would never put pleasure before principle as Sheila did, especially in an *affaire du coeur*. But then, as Sheila said, that older generation lived in the certainty of their beliefs. That was the point, exactly the point. If this were 1935 and Sheila were my father's younger sister, the whole discussion would have been conducted in the context of sin. I can talk about it only in the context of illness. My father would have talked of the moral obligations involved. I can only surmise the emotional risks.

And even then, wasn't I on thin ice? Do I know that she is ill? Of course not. In my opinion what she's doing could endanger her mental health and cause her grief and remorse. But do I know that for certain? All my opinions are reversible. They say that's a sign of intelligence, but is it? Fifteen years ago people like me read Freud as if we had found an answer. He seemed a genius. Today I am not so sure. Yet when I spoke to Sheila this morning my mouth was full of phrases from psychoanalytic textbooks, comfortable, because they offer an explanation which fits my prejudice. "Acting out" and "fugue state" and so on, and so forth. All out of books. Books have been my substitute for life. What do I know about a woman in love? Damn all. She looked happy, didn't she? I can tell myself till I'm blue in the face that she's in her manic phase, but I'm not a psychiatrist, I'm a gynecologist. Why did I get mixed up in this business?

I suppose because of Ned. The only hell I *do* know about is the hell of Ned's nervous breakdown. And how can you explain that hell to a person who believes she's happy? Who is—what was it she said?—"in a state of grace."

The stewardess waiting at the top of the ramp looked at his boarding pass, smiled at him, and said to sit anywhere in tourist. There were so few people traveling that he had a row of three seats all to himself. He removed his hat and placed it beside him, on top of his copy of the *Times*. Last night at dinner that Yugoslav said this American boy is head over heels in love with Sheila. What was it, he said? "Falling in love is a crime usually committed by innocent people. So they rarely get away with it." Very aphoristic, the French. Except that he is not French.

But Peg Conway thinks the whole thing will end next week when Sheila gives up her flat. I hope so, but I don't believe it. I think she's a bolter: she'll run off with this boy. There's that strain of oddness in our family, an instability. Ned and Kitty, and now Sheila. And don't forget Yours Truly. No, I am not forgetting Yours Truly.

When the plane took off he sat up, rigid, his hands gripping the sides of his seat. The cloud was thick all the way up and he was sure the left engine sounded as though it were out of whack. Once he would have been saying an Act of Contrition at this very moment. But now he remembered some remark of Agnes's about opening a dress shop if anything ever happened to him. Which was nonsense, she had no business sense at all, she could never run a shop. The plane began to shake. If I crash now, Agnes will blame Sheila for my death.

But then the plane came up to an empty blue sky and the seat-belt sign went off. That strain of oddness in our family. If Sheila had any sense she'd know there's nothing but trouble ahead for her. As the old women back in Donegal used to say of a pregnant unmarried girl, "Now, she's crying the laugh she had last year." And Sheila will do the same thing. I told her that. I said, "You're behaving like a selfish silly woman, how long do you think this will last? In ten years' time," I said, "you will look like this boy's mother."

Of course I was shouting at her by then. Home truths that should have stayed at home. Before that, damnit, we *were* having a reasonable discussion. Before the shouting I said to her, "You talk about being happy now. But I wonder. Are we supposed to be happy in this life?" And she laughed and accused me of still being a Catholic. But I said to her, "No, seriously, do you think it's possible for anyone to be more than intermittently happy in life? Continual happiness just isn't a possible state for anyone with a brain in their heads. If you were happy all the time, you'd have to be selfish and insensitive about all the unhappiness around you. You're happy now, I grant you. But I don't think it can last."

"Neither do I," she said. "Well, then," I said. "If it doesn't last and it leaves you more unhappy than you were before, is it really worth all you seem prepared to sacrifice for it?" And she said that it wasn't something you could put a value on. She said, "Kevin used to tell me that life wasn't all dancing in the dark. You know that old song. He said I was impractical, that I never faced facts. He was wrong. If I'd been impractical I'd never have married him. I'd have gone off to London or Paris and tried for a job, no matter how impractical that sounds. If I'd been romantic I would have tried for a different life."

"But you might not have found it," I said to her. "Yes, that's true," she said. "But I would have tried. That's what I blame myself for now. I didn't try."

And, damnit, that angered me and I said to her, "I think you're a bit late to try now." I never should have said that. That's when I told her she was a selfish, silly woman and about the boy being too young for her. I started shouting at her. What sort of way was that to try to help her?

The stewardess came around offering duty-free cigarettes. He pulled out his Gauloises and lit up. What will Agnes say when she sees me smoking again? What will I tell her when I get home today? She'll not keep it to herself. I might just as well say it's all settled, say it was a dustup between Sheila and Kevin and that Sheila will be back next week, as per schedule. That's what Peg thinks. I hope she's right. Yes, I'll tell Agnes that. Let's leave it at that.

She lay in semi-darkness, the window open to the noise of night traffic along the Seine. His arms were around her, her head rested on his shoulder, and he was talking about the future as she might have talked about it were she his age and unmarried. "At any rate," he said, "the next step, first thing Monday, is to go to the rue Saint-Florentin. You have your passport. It's a British one, right?"

When we make love he seems older and more experienced than me. Is that why he always plans our future after sex? Sex seems to give him authority. How does he know all those sex things that Kevin never knew? Do all Americans do them?

"Once we're in the States," he said, "there'll be no problem renewing the visa. We'll simply apply for you to stay on as an immigrant. It can be done."

He sees our lives in terms of movement, of having enough money to go some place, of getting visas and jobs, of making a new start together. Yet he always offers me a chance to back out. Money in a New York bank in my name, a return ticket and no recriminations, "if you change your mind, Sheila." Yesterday he said, "You never can force people, not really. In the end they do what they have to do." But do they? I can't bear to think of giving him up. If he felt the same way about

me, would he ever say the words "if you change your
mind, Sheila"? Maybe. He's young, he's American, he's
a man. He hasn't made the mistakes I have. He's not
afraid, as I am. If he worries about Kevin coming after
us, he never shows it.

"Are you asleep?" he said. "Are you listening?"

"Of course I'm listening. How much did you say it
will cost to pay my fare to New York?"

"Oh, about four hundred dollars."

"And the same to come back here?"

"Right."

"And how much money do you actually have?"

He laughed, and kissed her forehead. "So, you're
after my money."

"No, seriously. How much do you have? Two thousand dollars? Five thousand? Or what?"

He was silent for a moment, counting. "I suppose I
have about five thousand altogether. Somewhere in that
area. I have about two thousand in cash and traveler's
checks, and the rest is in a savings account at home."

"Then you can't afford to spend that much on me."

"What better way is there to spend it? Besides, I'm
going to make money in Vermont. You're speaking to
the next acting manager of Pine Lodge."

"I have some money, too. Shares. They're worth nearly two thousand pounds, I think."

"So we're rich," he said. "Turn around and let me
lie up to your back."

Obediently she turned and felt him move in behind
her, felt his penis stiffen. He kissed her on the nape of
her neck and then, as he began to fondle her breasts,
his fingers on her nipples, she heard a siren cry out,
far below in the night traffic. Excited, she turned to
him, taking his penis in her hand.

* * *

Later, in the middle of the night, the telephone rang. She woke, startled, as it pealed loud in the night quiet. She got up in a rush, grabbing her raincoat, pulling it on as she ran into the living room. As she groped for the table light, she felt her leg wet and, when she found the switch, saw a trickle of menstrual blood running down her inner thigh. She turned in panic, pulling a wad of Kleenex from the box on the table, then seized the receiver, as though it were her enemy. "Hello?" She heard the silence of an open line. "Hello?" she said again.

"Mum, is that you?"

"Danny? Are you all right? What's the matter? Is your father all right?"

"Yes."

"Danny, how did you get this number? Is your father there?"

"He's asleep."

"Well, what is it? Danno, what *is* it?"

"Nothing. I want to talk to you."

"But it's the middle of the night."

"Is it true you're not coming home?"

"Who told you that?"

"Uncle Owen was here tonight. I heard him telling Dad."

"What did he say?"

"He said you told him you're not coming back. And that you're going to New York to live with an American."

"Does your father know you heard this?"

"Yes, he does. I asked him about it."

"Oh, my God," she said. "And how did you get my number?"

"I found it right here beside the phone. Dad's been ringing you for days. Don't you even know that?"

"Danny, listen to me. This is not something I'm going to talk to you about on the phone."

"Why not? Are you going to leave us, or aren't you?"

"Look, Danny, this is a grownup matter. I'm sorry but it's too hard to explain. Now, I'm going to say good night."

"So, you *are* going to run away. I think that stinks. It stinks, do you hear me, Mum? It stinks."

He was crying, she could hear him. "Oh, Danno," she said, "listen, don't cry. Don't worry, please. Listen, I'll ring you up tomorrow or Monday, all right?"

"What do you want to go to America for?" He was bawling now, childishly. "It's not fair to Dad, so it isn't."

"Now, stop that, Danny. Stop it. Stop that crying. Be a big boy. Go on back to bed."

"It stinks. You stink!"

He hung up the receiver there, far away. She could imagine him, barefoot, in his pajamas, his cheeks apple red with angry rubbing, smeared with the oil of his tears. Her child, the child she remembered always that day he was photographed in his first suit of clothes, in a tiny gray flannel jacket and short trousers, standing at the top of the stairs at home, waiting to come down when Kevin said he was ready, a smile on his fat little face, drunk in his baby pride. She waiting at the bottom of the stairs. Kevin snapping pictures. And at the last step Danno ran to her, hugging her, her only son, his little arms tight about her neck. She turned from the phone and found Tom Lowry waiting in the darkened entrance to the living room.

"Was that your kid?"

"Yes."

He came to her. "Poor Sheila."

"It's all right."

"Did your husband get him to phone?"

"No, it was his own idea."

Again she felt the blood trickle down her inner thigh. She turned from him and went alone into the bathroom. But later, when she came back to bed, he was waiting. In bed he held her, his arms around her, holding her until he believed she was asleep.

She was asked to put her handbag on the table. The United States Marine guard inspected its contents and then she and Tom went out across a very French courtyard to enter a room marked PASSPORT OFFICE. The office, like the building, seemed French rather than American, but beyond the waiting area she saw a large American flag, impeccably clean, impressively displayed, so that it seemed more like the symbol of a religion than a national banner. For a moment she was caught up in a premonition of what America would be like, a clean, flag-waving country whose people spoke in voices foreign yet familiar, people whose habits seemed strange but who were, in an odd way, like relatives, for they were the true denizens of that Other Place she had gone into dark picture houses to watch all her life. And there was something of this strange dichotomy in the manner of the consular officer who called her to the desk and questioned her, something avuncular yet ominous in this pleasant-faced man with his aviator-style glasses who went over the visa application form, asked her about her husband's occupation and if she was going on a regular or charter flight. She had made out a statement, saying she was visiting a friend who had invited her, giving Tom's sister's name and address, and explaining how she had a son and a husband in Ireland

and would return in two weeks. The consular officer read it carefully, as she waited, sure in her heart that his disturbingly friendly manner would soon turn to cold dismissal. But nothing of the sort occurred. After a few more questions, her form and photograph were put in a folder and she was told to take a seat. Shortly afterward she was called back to the desk. Her visa application had been processed and her passport was stamped with the visa. It was after two o'clock when they walked out of the office in the rue Saint-Florentin, and suddenly Tom whooped like a madman.

"We did it, we did it!" he said. "Man, was I scared there'd be some foul-up."

"But you said it would be easy."

"And it was. Wow, it was great. But, Jesus, supposing they'd said they had to check with your husband. That's what scared me. But never mind. We got it. That's a good omen."

She kissed him.

"Okay," he said. "Now we're going to celebrate. We're going to go up to Le Drugstore and I'll buy you an American lunch. Hamburgers and beer."

"All right. I've never seen you so happy."

"Well, why not. It's happening, isn't it. I was so scared when I watched you at that counter. Still, I guess your being married and with a husband and child, that helped."

He flushed as he said it. "Sorry. Well, you know what I mean."

"Yes, of course," she said. "I saw the consul look at my wedding ring. I'm sure it helped."

But he was still embarrassed, still flushing. "It's just— look, I know what you've had to go through. Your kid phoning you Saturday night. I get scared sometimes that all of that will get to you. And then, today, I saw you apply for the visa. Oh, Sheila, it's going to be great. You're going to love it in Vermont. Look, I don't know how to say this, but I'm grateful that you decided for me."

She kissed him. "Shut up."

But half an hour later, as they sat in the glassed-in terrace of Le Drugstore, he seemed to want to talk about it again. "You know, I don't feel *guilty* about taking you away. I suppose I should. But I don't. I just feel so grateful—to you, to the embassy, to everyone. It's as if this is my birthday."

She stared through the glass at the Arc de Triomphe up ahead. On top of the monument, tiny as toys, people were parading about, peering down at the city below them.

"What I mean is," he said, "I don't know what I'd have done this week if you'd said you wouldn't come away with me."

"Look at those people."

"Where?"

"Up on top there."

"I was up there once. There's a fantastic view of Paris."

"How do you get up?" she said. "Climb steps or what?"

"No, there's an elevator."

She pushed aside her hamburger. He noticed she had hardly touched it. "Can we go up there now?" she asked.

"Why not?"

"All right, then. Let's go as soon as you're ready."

Four tourists talking Dutch with the loud confidence of people who know their conversation is not understood crowded into the small elevator with them, for the trip to the top of the Arc de Triomphe. When they emerged on a surface of white stone and walked to the edge of the plinth, she saw that there was no safety rail. Below, like the spokes of a wheel, the avenues spread out from this central hub.

"Isn't it great?" he said.

She looked down the Avenue de la Grande-Armée and then over at Sacré-Coeur and the Eiffel Tower. "It's like a cemetery. The buildings are like gravestones."

But he did not seem to hear. "In New York the great view is from the Empire State Building. Imagine. Next week you and I could be standing up there, looking down at Central Park and the Hudson River and the U.N. and all of it. Let's do that, okay?"

"I'll miss Paris."

"If you get homesick for Paris, would you settle for Montreal? It's only about an hour from where we'll be in Vermont."

She moved closer to the edge of the parapet, leaning over, looking down. She sensed him come up behind her.

"I wonder, do many people jump?" she said.

"It wouldn't be hard. Why in hell don't they put up a guard rail?"

She sat down on the stone plinth, dangling her legs over the parapet. Her hands gripping the edge of the plinth, she leaned out, staring at the tiny figures far below. She leaned farther.

"Sheila? That's scary. Come on back."

She leaned out, her vision blurring. She felt his hands grasp her shoulders. She caught her breath and leaned back against his legs. "Aren't you scared of heights?" he asked.

"I used to be. Terribly."

"Come on. Get up."

She eased her legs back and stood, dusting her skirt. "I'm sorry. Let's go down, then."

Mrs. Milligan put a slice of rhubarb pie on a plate, placed a small silver cream jug beside it, then took the tray into the den. He had hardly touched his pork chop and potatoes.

"Ah, Doctor, have you not eaten your chop? It was a lovely one, too. The butcher kept it for me special."

"Is Danny asleep?"

"Yes, he went right off."

"He took the pill?"

"Aye, I gave it to him myself. Now, ate your dinner. Go on."

"No, I've had enough."

"I'm just going to have to give it to Tarzan."

Tarzan, hearing his name, rose up from the rug, his ears forward, his thick bushy tail clumping against the coffee table.

"Well, Tarzan looks hungry enough, don't you, boy?" his master said.

"Oh, he'd ate till he burst, that dog," Mrs. Milligan said, picking up the dinner plate. She put the rhubarb pie down in its place. "Now, try a bit of this. I made it myself."

"All right. And what about coffee?"

"I'll be in with it in a minute, Doctor."

Tarzan's eager Alsatian eyes went from Mrs. Milligan

to his master and, suddenly, received the sign. Making token jumps at the tray, he followed Mrs. Milligan down the back passage to the kitchen.

Kevin Redden listened to her go. Does she know anything? Did Danny say anything to her? He had warned him to hold his tongue. He looked at the television set. On the screen contestants in a ballroom-dancing contest: an English plumber in white tie and tails swept his evening-gowned partner across a sprung, polished floor to the strains of the Anniversary Waltz. Mrs. Milligan came back in and put down a tray with his coffee. Except that it was not coffee, it was a coffee pot filled with hot water, and instant in a coffee jar. Sheila would not have allowed that: instant served in the jar. "Will that be all, Doctor?"

He nodded, but she did not notice. "Will you be wanting anything else?" she repeated.

"No thanks, Mrs. Milligan. Good night, now."

"Don't forget to eat up that bit of sweet."

"All right. Good night."

He heard her leave the room. In a few minutes she would finish the dishes and go upstairs. She was living in for the two weeks of Sheila's holiday and they had rented a telly for her room. Once up there she would not stir down again tonight. He pulled a prescription pad from his pocket and looked again at the notes he had jotted down:

> Say about how D overheard.
> And Owen's visit here.
> Will go Wed.
> Want talk now.

He put a fork in the pie and, for Mrs. Milligan's sake, ate two bites of it. He made instant coffee and turned the television sound off, listening for the housekeeper's footsteps on the stairs. Ghostly ballroom dancers whirled and twisted on the screen. When he heard her go up, he put the prescription pad in his pocket and went into the front hall where the phone sat on a monk's bench, under large elephant tusks, which supported a brass dinner gong. When he was a little boy, he remembered the gong being rung for dinner in his father's house. And in his grandfather's day it had been used to summon to meals as many as fifteen people, parents, children, and spinster relatives. Now it was never used. He dialed France, then Peg Conway's number. Anger heated in him as he let the phone ring for a full two minutes. He replaced the receiver and put the prescription pad back in his pocket. He might as well lock up. He went to the front door, first opening the inside door and then the heavy outer door. It was raining. On the rim of light around the porch lamp, he saw the shadows of the driveway and the front gate, beyond which were the street lamps of the Somerton Road. He locked and bolted the front door, then the inside door. From habit, as he came back into the front hall, he tapped the glass of the barometer on the wall. The barometer had never worked properly. Now the needle moved to *Fair*. He went back into the den, passing the television set and its swirling, ghostly dancers, going through to the kitchen to lock the back door. When he switched off the kitchen light and looked through the glass door panel he saw that McCusker, the gardener, had left the wheelbarrow out in the rain. In the scullery Tarzan rose up, tail wagging, from his bed of potato sacks. He patted the dog, shut him in again, then, returning to the front hall, went upstairs to the first-floor landing and looked into his son's room. The light was on and Danny was asleep, his mouth open.

Redden turned off the light, then went into the master
bedroom, where, facing him, was the extra-large bed
they had bought when they moved into this house.
The right side of the bed was his: for almost two weeks
now the left side had not been disturbed. He turned
away, abruptly, as though he had seen something that
displeased him, and went out again to the landing.
From Mrs. Milligan's room on the third floor he heard
taped laughter from the television set. He went down
the landing toward the rear of the house and entered
a doorway, groping for an unfamiliar switch. Finding
it, he flooded the small space in a harsh, unshaded
light.

This was her room: her sewing room, the room in
which she paid household bills, read sometimes, and
did God knows what else he knew nothing at all about.
It was untidy: there was an ironing board set up in
the middle, a dressmaker's dummy with a pattern pinned
on it stood in the far corner, and there was a small
Singer sewing machine on an old-fashioned tabletop,
next to a large, irregular pile of women's magazines.
Floor to ceiling, two walls of the room were books,
arranged in old, dark-painted bookshelves she had
brought from the Deane house when her mother died.
He went now to the shelves, staring at book spines, as
though he might find hidden in them some proclamation
of who she really was. Those large volumes on the bottom shelves had been her father's: sets of blue Shake-
speare, Milton, Dryden, Pope; green and gold volumes of the works of George Bernard Shaw. There
were two shelves of Everyman editions, faded and
worn; then Penguins, and some French books, Gide
and Valéry and Anatole France: they must be the
books she used when she studied French at Queen's.
There were small books of poetry, mostly in French—

Rimbaud, Baudelaire, and other writers whose names were unfamiliar to him. And Hemingway and Saki, and Joyce's *Ulysses,* which he remembered dipping into years ago as a dirty book. He wondered if she had other dirty books hidden away somewhere on these shelves. On the top row were schoolgirl romances and such. He pulled out an odd-looking red clothbound book from this row, but, opening it, found it was an atlas, with her name in schoolgirl copperplate. Sheila Mary Deane, Jun IV, Sisters of Mercy Convent, Glenarm. N. Ireland. He put the book back on the shelf. Always stuck into books: poetry, plays, and novels. A lot of rot. He remembered her chatting with Brian Boland about "modern writers." Rubbish. As if reading some bloody novels makes her better than me.

He sat in the small old wicker chair beside the sewing table. On the wall calender nearby she had circled a date. It was, he realized, the date she left for France. Below the calendar was an old chest of drawers with framed photographs on top of it. He got up and went to look at them: maybe they were the clue? Of course, in pride of place was her Uncle Dan, the ambassador, the cause of a lot of her silly notions. He picked up the uncle's photograph: a big fat twit of a man in a morning coat, presenting his credentials to Queen Juliana of the Netherlands; ambassador smiling at Queen, two fatties the pair of them. He put the photograph down and looked to see who else she had up here on her private altar. Her two brothers, Owen and Ned, long ago in some seaside place. And one of her father, old Professor Deane, she a little girl getting a piggyback ride on her daddy's back. And that photo I took of Danny on the stairs in his first suit of clothes, when he was a wee boy. And where am I? I ask you.

But then he saw, behind the other photographs, a

large framed picture of himself and Sheila in their wedding clothes, cutting the cake at the Imperial Hotel, his hand on hers, guiding the knife, both of them smiling at the photographer. He peered closely at the bride's face, oh, she was pretty, her smile a bit silly that day, for she was a little tight on champagne, wearing a tulle headdress which made her even taller, so that she towered over both mothers, his and hers, who stood behind them puffing on cigarettes, rival chieftains briefly joined. And then, with pain, remembered how, after the wedding reception, he and she had flown to London and on to Villefranche, where, in that hotel room, he first saw her with all her clothes off. The same place she was last week with some Yank, maybe in the very same bed we were in for our honeymoon. You bitch, you dirty, bloody bitch.

Downstairs, the phone began to ring. He hurried out, running down to the front hall, wanting to get to it before it woke Danny. It was not her, of course, it was the British Army at Lisburn, calling about the case he had for surgery tomorrow morning. He listened to the English voice and told it what he wanted done. "Would you hold on a moment, sir?" the sergeant said, and then the duty officer came on to apologize for ringing up so late. He said, "Not to worry," and hung up. If he went to Paris on Wednesday he would miss his army surgical round. He had better explain that to the colonel tomorrow. This army job was a terrible grind. Well, she didn't want me to take it, she complained about it. I should have heeded her.

He turned restlessly and went into the big front drawing room, which, lately, they used only when people came. He put on a reading lamp and drew the blinds. It was still raining. He sat on the big sofa, that same sofa she sat on talking about books to Brian Boland

the time I taxed her with making up to other men. She
cried then. I always thought she was an innocent, that
she didn't know men and what they were up to. Dancing in the dark and all that. I suppose *I* was the innocent. There she was, pretending to be shy, pretending to be a good wife, Danny's mother, and, all the
time, what was she thinking? It was that bloody uncle
of hers that ruined her, that big fat twit of an ambassador. Spends her whole bloody life dreaming about living in some place like Paris, the very place where she
ended up last week, on her only-oh, and there, made
to measure for her, waiting in the wings, is some young
Yank just out of Trinity, with his Ph.D. in James
Joyce's Laundry List. That's what Owen said: He's just
out of Trinity. Aye, nattering away, the pair of them,
about Camus and Yeats and what have you, and she
so bloody happy that she's not with me, having to talk
about patients and the Troubles at home. Aye, Paree
and the young Yank, and the next thing you know, she's
leading him on until he's mad for her and thinks she's
mad for him, just the way Brian Boland did. That's just
what happened, I'll bet.

He sat down at the grand piano in the drawing
room, opened the lid, and struck a note, then shut the
lid again clumsily, so that it closed with a loud slam
of wood on wood. When people find out your wife has
run off with another man, they'll be sorry for you, or
make fun of you, I don't know which is worse. Twenty
years ago I'd have put the priest on her. But nobody
heeds the priests nowadays.

He looked at his wristwatch, a gold-cased Longines,
a graduation present from his father. Decided, he got
up, went into the front hall, and dialed Peg Conway's
number once again. The phone rang and rang. So she

wasn't going to answer, was she? All right. I can keep this up all night.

But after eight rings someone picked up the receiver.

"Hello?" he said.

There was no answer. Maybe he had a wrong number.

"Kevin?" It was her voice.

"Yes, it's me."

"How's Danny?"

"What do you care?" (By God, I'm going to give it to her this time.)

"How is he?"

"He's upset. I've had to dose him with sleeping pills."

"Oh, no."

"Is it any wonder? Do you know what happened? On Saturday night your brother Owen came to see me, and when we'd finished talking we found Danny outside, listening on the staircase. Poor bloody kid, he's destroyed."

"Yes. He rang me up about it in the middle of the night."

"He *what?*"

"He rang me up here. In Paris."

"Danny did? How did he get the number?"

"He said it was by the phone in the hall."

He caught his breath, trying to control his anger. "Jesus, Sheila, have you any idea of what you're doing to us?"

She did not answer.

"Look, I'm coming to Paris. We've got to settle this."

"No, Kevin."

"I'll be there tomorrow afternoon. I have to operate at eight, but I'll come right after."

"Kevin, it's not going to help for you to come here. Not at all."

"I see. So you're planning to run off to New York without even bothering to say goodbye to us, is that it?"

"Who told you I was going to New York?"

"Your pal Peg Conway told Owen the other night. Oh yes, and she said that this Yank is ten years younger than you are. That's nice, ha ha. That's very nice. Yes, I can just see it. When you're fifty, this bucko will be thirty-nine. Five years younger than I am now. And can you see me in bed with a woman of fifty? Can you?"

She did not speak.

"Sheila, are you listening? Does what I'm saying make any sense to you at all? Or is it dancing-in-the-dark time again?"

She did not answer.

"All right," he said, "let's try to talk like friends. I'll tell you what. If you come to your senses and come home now, I'll give you my word, nothing will be said by me. Nothing. Because I want you home. I want you for Danny's sake. Do you hear me, Sheila? And I want you for my own sake, too. Please, Sheila?"

He listened. She was still there.

"Point number two," he said. "If you come back now, nobody will be any the wiser. Only Owen and I, and poor wee Danny know about this. And Agnes knows something's up, but not to worry, Owen will keep her quiet, ha ha. And if you'd rather have a couple more weeks there before you come home, that's all right, too. Quite all right. We miss you, but it's all right. Do you hear me, Sheila?"

"Kevin, I'm very sorry about what's happened. I am."

"Wait now, I've not finished. There's something else. I thought we were happily married, but maybe I was wrong. *I* was happy, but maybe you weren't. Maybe I haven't paid as much attention to you as I should have. I know I shouldn't have taken on this army job, because that annoyed you. I'm sorry about that. But these are bad times here, and people don't always do the things they should do. Now I'm going to say something I've not said before. I've been sitting thinking about all this, do you see? And I've decided that, no matter what happens in Ulster now, things will never be any good here. Not any more. Not in our time. We'll be paying for this mess as long as we live. Don't you agree?"

She did not speak.

"Now, do you remember, Shee, you talked about us emigrating? That was about two years ago, wasn't it? And I said no. Well, I've changed my mind. I think we *should* emigrate. We'll go to Canada, or Australia, whichever you like. With my qualifications I can get a job anywhere, and, abroad, I'll make twice as much money as at home, ha ha. So just tell me where you fancy. Toronto, Sydney, or wherever, and I promise you we'll be out of here by next spring. Or even by Christmas, if you want it. And don't worry about Danny. He'll just switch rugby for ice hockey, ha ha. He'll be all right. What do you say, Shee?"

He waited.

"No reaction at all? All right. You don't have to make up your mind at once. I just mentioned it. Now, another thing. I've looked up the flights for Wednesday. I can drive down to Dublin, park at Collinstown airport, and catch a direct flight that gets into Paris at ten past twelve. We could have lunch together, just the two of us."

"No, Kevin."

"Just lunch. Just a talk?"

"No."

"I'll go back right after lunch and we won't even

discuss this other matter, if you don't want to. I just want to see you. Just for an hour or two?"

"I have to move tomorrow. I'm going to a hotel."

"I'm not talking about tomorrow," he said. "I'm talking about Wednesday. You'll be moved by then."

"No, Kevin. Please, don't. If you come you won't find me."

It was his worst fear. He had one more card, and now he played it. "Well," he said, "maybe I couldn't have come, anyway. I didn't want to tell you this, but Danny is not well. He has a temperature of a hundred and three. Unless the fever goes down, I suppose I'd better stay close to home."

"Oh, God, what's wrong with him?"

"He got sick last night. Listen, what did you say to him when he rang you up?"

"Nothing. I told him I wouldn't discuss it with him. I said I'd give him a ring in a day or two."

"Well, I think you'd better do that, then."

"All right. When will I ring?"

"Tomorrow, around suppertime. All right?"

"All right," she said.

"And listen, Shee, do you have a number I could reach you at? In case of an emergency?"

"Wait," she said. He heard her put down the phone. After a while she came back. "It's Odéon eight-eight-oh-five."

He wrote it down. "All right. Is that a hotel?"

"Yes. What do you think he has? Could it be an infection?"

"You know kids. It could be anything."

"So I'll ring you at suppertime tomorrow," she said.

"All right. Good night, Shee."

"Good night."

He picked up the prescription pad, tore off the number, and went back into the den. He had forgotten to switch the television set off and now, mouthing soundlessly, some Protestant minister stared at him from the set, delivering the late-evening prayer. He sat down in the dark of the den, in front of the dying coals of the fire, staring at the minister's image. *Somebody has to stop her. Somebody has to protect her from herself. She's mad. Yes, mad. I'll say nothing to her when she rings up tomorrow. I'll tell her Danny's a lot better. Not to worry.*

The minister, smiling, bowed his head. The screen went to blackness. Then the sign-off pattern appeared. The Queen. Kevin Redden stared at the Queen. He got up, shut off the set, and went out into the hall. He looked in the address book beside the telephone, then rang a number.

"Dr. Deane speaking."

"Owen, this is Kevin. I know it's late, but could I come over and see you for a minute? It's urgent, I'm afraid."

"Of course, Kevin. I'll be expecting you."

Dr. Deane, waiting for his visitor, had been about to answer the front doorbell when he heard Agnes moving about in the bedroom. He went back in to look and found her at her dressing table, making up her face, wearing her good floral quilted robe over her nightgown. She turned and smiled at him. "I'll just come down for a minute, just to say hello to him. It's only polite."

"Please, dear, don't."

"What do you mean?" Her voice rose to a shout.

"Shhh. You'll wake the children. I just think it would be better if you didn't come down, dear."

He might have guessed when she heard that Redden

had phoned she would not rest until she was in on it. Now she began to wheedle: "Listen, you go down, and I'll make a cup of tea and bring it in to you. He'd probably like a cup of tea."

The doorbell rang again.

"I'll give him a whiskey."

"Do you not want me to hear, is that it?" He could tell she was going to start a shouting match. Just this once he must stand his ground. "Stay here!" he said and shut the bedroom door.

"So that's the way of it. I'm not allowed to go down and welcome a visitor in my own house!" Her voice came through the shut door as he turned to find his younger daughter, Imelda, standing out on the landing in her nightdress. "Daddy, the doorbell."

"Yes, I know. Go back to bed, pet. It's about a patient."

She nodded, acquiescent, her plump features framed in the horrible hair curlers he hated so much. As he started downstairs, the doorbell rang a third time. Didn't Redden realize how late it was? He looked up to be sure Imelda was back in her room before switching on the hall light and unlocking the front door. His visitor was hatless and coatless, although it was pouring rain out. He saw Redden's big Humber parked in the driveway, saw that Redden had left the gate open to the road outside.

"Come in, Kevin, come in," he said, and led the way into the sitting room, seeing it, suddenly, as a stranger might, shabbily untidy, with the furniture hidden by those awful yellow chintz covers made from material Agnes had picked up at a Parish Sale of Work. There were records on the floor, scattered by the children and their friends. He went through to the dining room and opened the sideboard, coming back with a bottle of

Paddy, two glasses, and a siphon of soda water. "You'll take something, won't you, Kevin?"

Redden nodded distractedly, going to stand at the fireplace, warming his rear at the embers, throwing his head up like a man about to make a public speech. "I'm sorry, barging in on you at this hour. You were probably off to bed, were you?"

"Agnes was. But I'm a late stayer-upper," Dr. Deane lied. "She's asleep, as a matter of fact." He held up the bottle. "Say when."

Whiskey was poured. Redden asked for a splash of soda, then stared into his glass. "I talked to your sister again tonight," he began, using the words "your sister" as though he were some sort of outside agent beginning a report.

"And?"

"I offered her anything she wanted. I even offered to emigrate. I wasn't cross with her, I did everything I could to reason with her. But it's hopeless. I think she's going to fly the coop to America any day now."

"You do?" Dr. Deane took a stiff peg at his drink. His stomach seared him. He had forgotten to take his Gelusil and now he felt in his jacket pocket for the little roll of pills.

"It looks like it."

"That's bad news."

"I've got to stop her," Redden said. "For her own sake, if not for Danny's."

"How would you do that, Kevin?"

"Well, I talked to the American Embassy in Dublin today. I have a patient who has a pal there. It seems the Americans have all sorts of regulations about who they let in. No Communists, no moral turpitude, no insanity in the family, and so on. This chap said she may have applied for a tourist visa in Paris. It's something she can get without much difficulty. But if they find out she's running away from her husband and child—and, in particular, if there's any history of mental instability in her family—I think I can put a stop to it. That's why I came around here tonight."

"Oh?" Dr. Deane said. He sat in his old armchair and stared at the dying fire, the pain ebbing as the Gelusil took effect.

"She'll be angry at me, of course," Redden said. "But I think she'll thank me in the end. I'm trying to help her, you know."

"Mnn."

"You could help, too," Redden said.

"Me?"

"Well, on this question of her family history," Redden said, then stopped and looked toward the door. Dr. Deane turned in his armchair and, he knew it, she had come down after all. She stood in the opened doorway in her floral robe, her black hair all done up, feigning total surprise. "Owen?" she said, and then, pretending, "Oh, Kevin, is it you? I saw the light. I thought this man of mine had fallen asleep again over a book. Kevin, how *are* you? Owen told me your news, of course. I'm *awfully* sorry."

"Hello, Agnes," Redden said, standing up.

She smiled. "Would you like a cup of tea?"

"Oh, no," Redden said hurriedly. "We're just having a nightcap."

Dr. Deane knew he must do something, and at once. He got up, went to her, and kissed her on the cheek, for she set great store by public demonstrations of affection. "You go on up, dear," he said. "I'll be up shortly."

But she looked past him, toward Redden. "Any word from Sheila?"

Redden flushed, then shook his head. Dr. Deane, foreseeing more questions, touched her gently on the shoulder. It was the merest suggestion of easing her on her way, but it made her turn on him, her face a cartoon image of rage. "Good night, dear," he said gently.

"Good night, Kevin," she said, turning to give Redden a strained smile.

"Good night, Agnes," Redden said. Dr. Deane closed the door, shutting her out. "Sorry," he said. "You were saying?"

"Well, I could go over to Paris and talk to the American Embassy there. If I had a note from you outlining the family history, it would be a great help."

"Ah, damnit, Kevin, I'd rather not do that," Dr. Deane said. "My own sister. It just seems unethical."

"But I'd use it only as a last resort. Only if they insist on some corroborating evidence. I mean, if I tell my own story, it will probably be enough."

Dr. Deane finished his whiskey in a gulp. "It probably will," he said. "Besides, I've no real evidence that there's anything the matter with her."

"I don't want you to say anything about her," Redden said. "I want you to give me a note about Ned and your mother."

"Honestly, I'd rather not. It's something you don't do."

"And what *do* you do?" Redden asked loudly. "What do *I* do? Do I stand on principle and see my marriage destroyed and my wife risk a breakdown—if she's not in that state already? Damnit, Owen," Redden said, and Dr. Deane saw now how overwrought he was, his eyes glistening, his voice high in an emotional tremor. "I'm asking you to help all of us. I'm asking you to write a simple statement of fact which I promise I won't use with the consul unless it's absolutely the last card I can play. And I give you my word of honor it will stay between you and me. Sheila will never get wind of it. I promise you that."

"That's not it," Dr. Deane said, his own voice now emotional.

"I'm asking you to help me, because I'm at the end of my rope," Redden said, and now there was a terrible new sound in his voice, the faltering of a man who has never wept but is just about to begin. "Of course, it's a last resort. Of course, I'm going over there to talk to her, to reason with her, to tell her I love her, to try to make her see sense. I'll do all that before I try to block her, do you see? I mean, blocking her is the last thing I want to do, because she'll not forgive me for it. I know that. But if our marriage and our son won't bring her to her senses, then I have to do something. I thought of writing to this boy's family in America, if I could find their address. I thought of killing the young bastard. I thought of everything, Owen. The last few days have been bloody hell."

"I know," Dr. Deane said. He rose and poured himself a very large drink.

Redden leaned forward, staring at the fire. He had begun to weep. He wiped his eyes with the knuckles of his hand. "As I say, I'm still hoping. I love her. I want her back."

Dr. Deane stared at his whiskey, then drank it. Pain from his ulcer hit him in a wave. Kevin Redden was trying to use him. It was wrong, but what was right? She probably *will* have a breakdown if that boy throws her over later on. Imagine her sitting paralyzed, like Ned, in some room in New York.

"All I'm asking you to do is write a note to me confirming what you told me in our conversation, about your brother and your mother. Not about her. As you say, we have no evidence of her being ill. But if you said in your note that you wonder if it's wise, under the circumstances, for her to go to America at this time. Just a letter to me. That's all."

Just a letter to Kevin. Dr. Deane drank the rest of the whiskey. His head seemed to expand in a wave of intoxication. Just a letter to my brother-in-law, a letter that will probably never be needed. Just to give him a little help to face the American consul.

He rose, went to his desk, sat down a trifle unsteadily, and unscrewed his old-fashioned fountain pen. And, at that moment, saw the sepia-brown photograph of his father in academic robes which he had placed in an honored position on the mantelpiece. His father, the photograph, was stern, his mouth down at the corners, his hand clutching his sheepskin. His father's eye, grave, hooded, stared at him in familiar, hurt reproof. Stop feeling sorry for yourself, his father would have said. Do something. It's for her own good, isn't is? Well, is it, or isn't it? Make up your mind.

He began to write:

> Dr. Kevin Redden, M.B., F.R.C.S.
> Merrymount
> 408 Somerton Road
> Belfast
>
> Dear Kevin,
> This is to confirm the facts I outlined to you in our recent conversation in regard to my younger sister, Sheila. As I told you

He paused and raised his head. Pain came, the familiar ulcer pain. "Kevin," he said, "get yourself a refill, will you? And pour me a little, too, like a decent man."

She was in the shower stall in Peg's bathroom with an ugly plastic shower cap on her head when she heard him open the shower door behind her. "Oh, don't come in," she called out, ashamed of his seeing her in the ugly cap. But he joined her under the water jet and, wet, embraced her from behind, then took the soap bar and began to lather her back, soaping her thighs, his hand caressing her bottom. Suds sliding over her skin, making her slippery to his touch, as smiling, she turned, the silly cap forgotten, and took the soap from him, soaping him all over until he was dripping with lather: she looked at his penis, which stood out throbbing, then soaped it and squeezed it so that it stood even more urgently. Laughing, they embraced under the jet, sluicing the soap off, until she stepped out of the shower, pulling her cap from her head. He came after her, drying her back and bottom and, half-dry, running, laughing like children, they went into the bedroom and there, at eight o'clock on a gray, rainy Paris morning, he fondled her breasts until, filled with an urgent intoxication, she felt his left hand touch her there, exciting her clitoris, and then his right hand guided his thick, stiff penis inside her. Only ten minutes earlier she had been standing in the shower, her mind gloomy with last night's phone call from Kevin, thinking of Danny's illness and how she must phone home tonight, knowing today was their last day in this flat because Peg had phoned to say she was moving back in; it was Tuesday, the date they had arranged. Peg had said they could stay on in the spare room, but Tom said they must move to a hotel for the rest of the week. And now, all of those gloomy responsibilities she had faced in the shower seemed insubstantial as a dream. They made love, then lay for a while, and made love again, and dozed. At last, he roused himself. "What time should we move to the hotel?"

"Let's wait till after lunch," she said.

"All right. What would you like to do this morning?"

"I want to tidy this place. And we should leave some little present for Peg, flowers perhaps, and a bottle of cognac."

"All right."

She moved closer and lay with her head on his bare stomach. "I have to phone home at six."

"Don't worry, Danny will be all right. It's probably just a cold."

"I know. But I suppose I'll have to explain to him soon."

He was silent for a moment. "Well," he said, "don't tell them definitely that you're going to New York. Not yet."

"Why?"

"Because your husband might come over here and make a scene. Or he might phone the embassy and try to screw up your visa."

"I thought of that, too," she said.

"So don't say anything."

"All right. But I'll have to do it *sometime*."

"Don't do it today."

* * *

That afternoon they moved back into a room on the
top floor of the Grand Hôtel des Balcons. It was larger
than the room they had occupied there seven days ago,
and this time, the balcony looked out on an inner courtyard and a hodgepodge of the roofs of surrounding
buildings. At five-thirty they walked over to the Atrium,
and at ten minutes to six, she went downstairs to the
telephone and called Belfast.

"Kevin?"

"Hello, Shee."

"How is he?"

"Oh, he's grand. His temperature is down and he's
sitting up and taking nourishment. It was probably some
little virus. He's better."

"Would you like me to speak to him?"

"Well, I don't know. You're not exactly a great fa-
vorite in this house at the moment."

"Maybe I should say hello to him, at least."

"All right. Hold on, I'll ask him."

He went away. She stood in the plastic phone bubble,
looking down the corridor to where the lavatory attendant, a stout woman in a white smock, sat knitting
a pullover. In front of the woman was a tray with three
one-franc pieces attached to it by cellophane tape. Mrs.
Redden looked at the woman, and at the plate, and felt
herself begin to tremble. If I go away on the plane and
never tell him, never tell my only child, what will he
think about me, what will he feel about me the rest of
his life? Will I ever see him again?

"Hello?" It was not Danny, it was Kevin.

"Yes."

"Look, Shee, he doesn't want to talk to you."

"Oh."

"Maybe it's just as well. I mean, for now."

"Yes," she said. Her trembling diminished.

"Have you thought about what I said to you last night? About emigrating."

"Yes."

"Well, and have you any good news for me, I hope? Ha ha?"

"Kevin, it wouldn't make any difference if we emigrated."

"I see. So you're off to America, is that it?"

"I didn't say that."

"Well, are you or aren't you going to America? Or are you planning to slip off without even telling us?"

"Kevin, I've already left home. I told you that."

"So you don't care if you never see Danny again?"

"That will be up to you."

"All right. You *won't* see him again. He won't want to see you. Especially after what he'll have to go through when the whole world knows his mother ran off and left him. When he's known as the kid whose mother became a whore."

"There's not much point in us talking, is there?"

"Wait a minute," he said. "Ah, Shee, I'm sorry I lost my temper. When am I going to hear from you again?"

"I don't know. Goodbye, Kevin."

She put the receiver down. She felt the trembling increase and at the same time felt nauseated, as though she would vomit. She stood for a moment, then went shakily up the steps to the main floor of the café, where a handsome gray-haired man was sitting talking to Tom. For a moment she did not recognize him but, as she went closer, remembered he was Peg's friend, Ivo. As she came up, the gray-haired man stood, bowing to her in an exaggerated manner. *"Bonsoir, Madame.* How nice to see you again." He drew out a chair for her. She turned toward Tom, who looked worried.

"All right?" he asked.

"Yes, he's much better."

"Great."

He signaled a waiter, then put his hand on hers. "You look as though you need a drink. A Pernod, okay?"

"So you are off to America?" the Yugoslav said.

She looked at Tom.

"I would very much like to go to America," the Yugoslav said. "France is not a country for a foreigner. Very undemocratical, especially for *refugiés* from the socialist countries. I envy you, *Madame.* Of course, you will have to live with this fellow." He slapped Tom on the back. "And I know, from my own experience, that will not be easy." His laugh showed even white teeth, but at the back of his mouth she saw the steel clip of a bridge.

"Sheila's not as fussy a housekeeper as you are," Tom said. "So we get on fine."

At that moment the waiter put her Pernod on the table. When she poured water in it, she saw the tremor in her hand. *"A vôtre santé,"* the Yugoslav said, raising his glass of vermouth.

"A la vôtre," she said. The Yugoslav smiled at her flirtatiously. *"Madame,* you have created a monster. This fellow. He's a different man since he met you. Jealous. If I smile at you—*regarde sa gueule!"*

She turned to Tom. She wished this bloody idiot would go away. But Tom laughed, embarrassed.

"Peg and I had the pleasure of meeting your brother the doctor," the Yugoslav said. "A most charming man."

"Where *is* Peg?" she asked.

"You didn't see her downstairs?"

"No."

"Wait." He swiveled in his chair and peered toward the rear of the café. "Ah, here she is."

Peg, coming up the stairs from the lavabos, dressed in a green coat and gray slacks, her satchel purse swinging from her hip as she strode toward the table with a look on her face which did not seem entirely friendly. "So here you are," Peg said. "The hideaways. I thought we might track you down here."

Mrs. Redden rose and, guiltily, bent over to kiss her small friend on the cheek.

"I thought you and I were supposed to get in touch," Peg said.

"I'm sorry."

Peg turned to Tom. "By the way, thank you both for the flowers and the cognac. You shouldn't have done it."

"What will you drink?" Tom asked.

"Nothing, thanks. How are you getting on?"

"Great. We've got Sheila's visa."

"Before you go to America," the Yugoslav said, "I want to cook dinner for you. My special turkey. *Cǔrka na Podvarku.*"

"It's terrific," Tom told Mrs. Redden.

"And champagne," the Yugoslav said. "We will have champagne. We must fix a night."

"Sheila, I wonder if I could have a word with you," Peg said quietly.

"Maybe we will have a glass of champagne now," the Yugoslav said. "To celebrate you getting your visa."

"No," Peg said. "At least, not for me. Sheila and I have a little errand to do. Why don't you and Tom finish your drink and wait for us here. We won't be long."

"What's this, what errand?" the Yugoslav asked.

"We'll be only ten minutes," Peg said.

"Le donne, le donne," the Yugoslav said, smiling.

Tom Lowry looked across the table. "Are you okay, Sheila?"

"Yes, of course." She stood, taking up her purse. "We won't be long."

Peg, going with her, turned as they reached the street and waved back, smiling falsely at the two men. Outside, she took hold of Mrs. Redden's arm. "I came here specially to see if I could find you."

"Where do you want to go?"

"Oh, let's just walk."

Peg's hand, holding Mrs. Redden's arm, seemed the hand of a jailer. The sky was dark with a hint of rain: the wind cold, the day dying. "You know, of course, that I saw Owen the other night?"

"Yes, I'm sorry about that. It must have been awkward for you."

Peg did not answer, but guided Mrs. Redden into the rue de Seine. "Poor Owen," she said. "It must be ten years since I last saw him."

"He's got very old, hasn't he?" Mrs. Redden said.

"We're none of us getting any younger."

"I know."

"He's worried about you, Sheila. Did he tell you he's afraid you might be risking a nervous breakdown?"

"That's a lot of rubbish."

"Is it?"

"Yes, it is. Now that they can't put the fear of God into you any more, they put the fear of going mad instead."

"It worried me, though. All that stuff about depression and mental crisis."

"Falling in love *is* a mental crisis."

"Oh, Sheila!" Peg said.

Mrs. Redden turned away, looking into a shop window filled with handbags, seeing not the display but a pale reflection of her own face. "Anyway, if it doesn't work out, I can always come back," she said.

"And what about your child?"

"Danny's fifteen. He's not a child. In three or four years he'll be leaving me, anyway."

Peg lit a cigarette after two tries with her book matches. Puffing on it, she turned back to Mrs. Redden as though she had made up her mind. "The thing that worries me, though," she said, "is that people Tom's age fall in and out of love very easily. Don't you remember what it was like when you were twenty-six?"

"When I was twenty-six I was married and had a child. Now, shall we go back to the Atrium?"

"None of my business, right?"

"I suppose so."

"I'm sorry."

"No, *I'm* sorry," Mrs. Redden said and put her arm around her friend. "Look, you've been awfully good to us, lending us the flat and helping us. I'm the one who landed Owen on you. I'm sorry."

"All right, then," Peg said. "I've said my piece. Listen, Ivo and I are going to the new Godard film at seven. Would you like to join us?"

"No, thanks. You go ahead."

"All right. But Ivo wants to cook dinner for you some night before you go. When are you leaving?"

"Friday night."

"What about Thursday, then?"

"Thursday. That would be nice."

As they re-entered the café, both men stood up. *"Les voici,"* the Yugoslav said. "Where are your parcels?"

"We didn't buy anything," Peg said. "Ivo, we're going to give them dinner at my flat on Thursday. Will you do your turkey?"

"A pleasure. *Cŭrka na Podvarku.*"

"I'll bring the champagne," Tom said.

Peg kissed Mrs. Redden on the cheek. "Thursday, then. Let's say at seven."

When Peg and Ivo went out, Mrs. Redden sat down at the table and finished her Pernod very quickly.

"What did she want? A heart-to-heart talk?"

"Something like that."

"Ivo too."

"What did he say?"

"Oh, that I'm ruining your life. Breaking up your happy home. By the way, how was the phone call to Belfast?"

"So so."

"And your husband? You didn't tell him anything?"

"No. But he told me that if I go to America he'll never let me see Danny again."

"The bastard." He reached across the table and took her hand. "Are you upset?"

She shook her head and looked through the glass at the flow of traffic scooting out of the rue du Four like Dodg'em cars in a fairground. Suddenly, inexplicably, she felt herself tumble from the mental tightrope on which she had balanced for the past two weeks.

"What's wrong, Sheila?"

She looked at him. "Supposing you were told you would never see *me* again. What would you do?"

"I wouldn't listen."

"But supposing I told you."

He stared at her. "Is this some game?"

"It's a question."

"Is it Danny? Has that changed your mind?"

"No, I just asked what you would do."

"Do you mean, would I let you go?"

"Yes, I suppose."

"If it's what you want, then you have to do it. Are you going to give me up?"

"Oh, darling," she said, "it's much more likely to be the other way around."

"What do you mean?"

"Nothing. Let's stop this awful conversation. I started it. I'm sorry. What will we do tonight?"

"Whatever you like."

"Why don't we walk along the river, take a bus over to the Bourse, and eat in that place we were in last Friday?"

"The noisy place?"

"Yes," she said. "I feel like a noisy place."

In Belfast, that Wednesday morning, Kevin Redden rose at first light. He shaved and dressed himself as for his wedding, picking out his best dark suit and the shirt and tie she had chosen for him last Christmas but which he had never worn. He tried and discarded two silk handkerchiefs for his breast pocket before settling on a plain white linen. He stared at himself in the mirror, then recombed his hair so that it did not lie too flat on his head. He drank a cup of tea, packed a small bag with overnight things, and, thinking of her, added Valium and a strong sedative. Then he said goodbye to Mrs. Milligan and Danny (who thought he was only going to Dublin) and by 8 a.m. was in his new Audi, driving south. His car was stopped and searched at a British Army roadblock near the border, but, even with this delay, he arrived at Collinstown airport outside Dublin at ten-fifteen. He made arrangements for parking his car overnight, and was ticketed and in the airport lounge half an hour before the flight was due to be called. There was low-lying fog on the Continent. Flights to Zurich and Brussels were delayed, an announcement which produced in him an intense feeling of anxiety.

But the Paris flight was called on time. Two hours

later, when he had landed at Orly and cleared French customs, he went to a telephone and rang the number she had given him. It was, as he suspected, the same hotel to which he had telephoned previously. He took down the address and, later, on the bus going into town, lettered it carefully on one of his prescription pads.

GRAND HÔTEL DES BALCONS
6, RUE CASIMIR-DELAVIGNE

This pad he showed to a driver in the taxi rank at the Invalides, searching the man's face to see if he understood. When the man nodded, Redden climbed into the back seat and sat, oblivious of the passing streets until the taxi came up toward the Place de l'Odéon and stopped before the unprepossessing entrance to the hotel. He paid off the driver and went into the lobby, carrying his raincoat and overnight bag. He had rehearsed his questions as though preparing for an oral examination and now, in his indifferent French, he began his inquisition.

"*Pardon, Madame. Quel numéro de chambre, Madame Redden?*"

The middle-aged woman at the desk looked at him, then answered in an English as accented as his French, "*Madame* Red-on. Fortay-eight."

"Is she in?"

"No, *Monsieur*. She go out."

"Do you know when she will come back?"

"No. Most days, after lunch, they come back to the room."

"What time?"

"Two, three o'clock."

He looked at his watch. It was one-thirty. He looked behind him and saw a small table and two easy chairs in an alcove. "Maybe I'll wait a while."

"As you wish."

He crossed the lobby and sat in one of the chairs. Most days, after lunch, they come back to the room. He thought of his honeymoon, long ago, in Villefranche. We used to do it then, after lunch, with the wine in us. Well, she won't get any fucking done today. He did not go beyond that thought. He sat in his best dark suit in a hotel lobby in a foreign city, waiting for his wife to come in with her lover. All at once he felt like a man knocked down in an accident and brought into the emergency ward of a hospital. He knew where he was, and what had happened. He did not know what would happen next.

But when he had been sitting there for half an hour a new anxiety took him. What if she came in, saw him, and ran out again, forcing him to chase after her? He got up, smiled at the woman behind the desk, who did not notice him, then went outside and looked up and down the narrow street. He crossed the street and stood in the doorway of a neglected shop which seemed to sell orthopedic shoes. He pretended to examine the plaster foot casts in the window, but kept an eye on the hotel entrance. The important thing was to let them go upstairs, then knock on the door and confront them. He would tell the Yank he had to talk to his wife alone and then stay with her in the room. That way, he would have her some place where she could not walk away from him. At home she always broke up rows by running upstairs and going to her sewing room.

The sky darkened. It began to rain. He buttoned up his raincoat and shifted restlessly in the doorway, looking up and down the street. He realized that, suddenly, he was shaking. It was as though, unknown to himself, he had worked into a rage. *You mustn't lose your temper.* Yet as he tapped out this warning, it became a code, not understood by his other self, that stranger who trembled and wet his dry lips, who stared up and down the street like a criminal awaiting his prey.

Shortly after two o'clock, a sudden thunderclap sounded its warning in the Luxembourg Gardens, where, arm-in-arm among a small group of spectators, Mrs. Redden and Tom Lowry watched an Algerian, a Ghanaian, and an Indian who squatted on the steps of a deserted *belle époque* military band shell, playing two flutes and a sitar for their own pleasure. Lightning blazed above the trees, leaving the sky darker for its passing. Almost at once, rain sheeted down, bringing the music to a stop as performers and audience hurried up the steps of the band shell to shelter under its hexagonal roof. There, looking out at the downpour, Mrs. Redden thought of Ireland, of holidays long ago, when rain, implacable, inevitable, would end the picnic, the game of tennis, the afternoon on the strand, banishing the holidaymakers to the prison of a seaside boardinghouse lounge. She shivered and tightened her hold on Tom's waist. On the last morning of those summer holidays, she and the other children would wake to see their father already loading the car and know they would sleep that same night in their own beds at home. Inevitable, implacable, the rainstorm wept itself out. She saw Tom look at his watch.

"What time is it?"

"Twenty past two. Want to go back to the hotel for a while?"

"All right."

They walked out of the gardens and down the rue de

Vaugirard. This holiday, unlike those holidays long ago, would not end with her sleeping at home. Two nights from now I will be high over the Atlantic Ocean and on Saturday I will be walking around in the Other Place. I am going to America. I am starting my life over again. But as she said these words to herself, she found it hard to imagine what the new life would be like. And, again, she was afraid.

As they came through the Place de l'Odéon and into the rue Casimir-Delavigne, she stopped and looked at him. "Tom, supposing you go on to New York alone this week?"

"What do you mean?"

"Wait. Supposing I follow you, say two weeks from today? That would give you time to think about things. And if you still want me to join you then, I promise I'll come."

"Do you know what that plan is?" he said.

"What?"

"It's fear of flying," he said, and laughed. "You're afraid of flying, that's it, isn't it?"

"No, no."

"Oh yes, it is," he said and laughed, and looking at him, she did not want to leave him, she did not want to spoil things now, so she laughed, too.

"Maybe so," she said.

He took her hand and they went into the hotel.

When Kevin Redden saw his wife coming down the street hand-in-hand with a stranger, his first instinct was to retreat farther into the doorway of the orthopedic shop because it would be shameful if he were seen spying on them. This shame, which he did not understand, was counterbalanced by an insatiable, eye-glaring curiosity about the Yank who had stolen his wife. And so, dodging about, peering through the glass of the window, he discerned that the stranger was much younger than he, about the same height, and not at all the sort of caricature American his fantasies had created. He looked like someone from home, an intern off duty, perhaps even a med student.

They were laughing. Oh yes, the heartless bitch getting ready to abandon her only child was laughing! For one disquieting moment she seemed to look across the street directly at him, hiding in the doorway. Then, hand-in-hand, she and the man went into the hotel. He stepped out from his place of concealment, his breathing shallow as though he had run up the street. *I must calm down.* He turned back to the shop window and tried to mirror himself in its reflection, but the window was dull and the sky gray, and all he caught of himself was that he was standing there in his raincoat, carrying a small bag like some door-to-door salesman. He waited for a moment, then crossed the street and went into the hotel. The middle-age woman was still behind the desk. He did not go directly to the desk but walked into the little alcove and took off his raincoat, because he did not think he looked well dressed in it. He put it and the overnight bag down behind one of the easy chairs. If they were stolen, what matter: he did not want to knock on her door and be opened to, standing there with a bag in his hand. When he had straightened his tie and patted his handkerchief to make sure it was in place, he went over to the desk.

"Is Mrs. Redden back yet?"

"Yes, sir, she just came in."

"Forty-eight, you said?"

"Yes, sir. Do you want I telephone?"

"No, no, I'll go on up. She's expecting me," he said, and hurried to the stairs before the woman had a chance to reply. He took the stairs two at a time. On the top step he stumbled, catching his heel in the carpet runner. As he went down the corridor, searching for the number, he took his second handkerchief from his trouser pocket and wiped his palms, which were clammy. When he got to the door marked 48, he knocked gently. Two knocks.

"*Allo, oui,*" a man's voice said. "*Entrez.*"

They must be expecting a maid. He opened the door and, as he did, saw her standing by the window, her back to him, closing her raincoat about her. He saw why. She had already taken her dress off, the dirty bitch. There it was, lying on the chair. The boy friend had his coat off. She turned around. "Kevin!"

He did not answer her. He looked at the man. "Do you mind?" he said. "I'd like to have a word with my wife."

The man looked over at Sheila.

"Tom, I wonder, would you wait for me downstairs?"

"Are you sure?" the man said. He was a Yank all right, a bloody Yank with a flat, twangy American accent.

"Yes, please," she said. The Yank nodded, then looked angrily at Redden. "Excuse me," he said, making Redden give ground in the doorway. Redden shut the door and, as he did, saw the hotel key in the lock, a wooden ball hanging from it. He turned the key, locking the door, then put the key in his pocket.

"What do you think you're doing?"

"Making sure you don't walk out."

"Give me that key."

"Shut up," he said. "And sit down."

You mustn't talk like that, don't lose your temper, he warned the unpredictable person who was now in control of him, but it was too late, he *had* lost his tem-

per. He had already made an enemy of her. "I'm sorry,"
he said. "I didn't mean to sound cross."

"You have every right to be cross," she said. She sat
on the bed and looked at him. "Kevin, I told you not
to come. It's no use."

"But it's got to be some use," he said. At home,
lying awake these past nights, he had planned to say
this, to be both sensible and kind, yet threatening in a
quiet, professional manner. But she was not one of his
patients: she did not even seem to be his wife any
longer, and so, in his panic and anger, that unpredictable
person took over inside him, and that person, that
bloody fool, spread out his hands like a peddler and
smiled, and tried to get a bit of a laugh into his voice,
as he said, "I'm wearing my good suit. Did you notice
that?"

"Yes, I did."

"Do you know why I'm wearing my good suit,
Sheila?"

She shook her head.

"I'm wearing it because I want you to come home.
I've been hoping that maybe when you see me you'll
think I'm not so bad, ha ha. I thought to myself, This
boy friend, this Yank, must be stiff competition. He
probably looks like a film star, ha ha."

"Kevin, don't."

"Mind you, he *is* a good-looking chap. And he's a lot
younger than me, ha ha. I hear he has a degree from
Trinity. You and he can natter away about modern
writers, and other matters of interest, ha ha. I can't
compete there, I'm afraid."

"Kevin, stop it."

"I'm sorry. I *am* sorry. I was hoping to be very nice
about all this. I thought, you see, that I'd come here
today and talk to you and then maybe go away and

spend the night some place, and then come back and
talk to you again tomorrow morning before I go home.
Of course, it was a bit of a shock to see you here with
your dress off and another man in the room, ha ha. But
that's all right. I'm over that now. I realize I've lost the
battle. When are you going to America?"

"Soon."

"Then you've already got your American visa?"

"Yes."

He whistled. "So nothing I can say or do would
change your mind, is that it?"

"Yes. I'm sorry, Kevin. I've treated you—I've been
rotten to you and to Danny. But it happened. I fell in
love with somebody else."

And now the unpredictable person inside of him
could no longer smile and try to win her over. "Indeed.
Just like they do in books. Yes, exactly. It's books, of
course, that you got all your notions from. Not from
real life. All those novels and trash that's up there in
your room at home. I wonder sometimes if some of
these authors who write that stuff shouldn't be prose-
cuted. Or maybe we should hand out prescriptions for
books the way we do for drugs. Not to be taken by
mouth. Not for people who can't read right from wrong.
Yes. Because you're not the heroine of some bloody
book. And that wee boy back in Belfast is not just something in a book. He's sitting there in the den in the
Somerton Road this minute, expecting his mummy to
come home. And I'm not the buck stupid husband
in some bloody novel. No more than you and this Yank
fucking each other blind for the past two weeks is some
great romantic love story."

"Don't say 'fuck.' We can talk without that."

"Ah yes. Listen to the Child of Mary, will you? Don't
say 'fuck,' but do it. But I say 'fuck' because that's all it

is. Sex and nothing but sex. Young Yankee Stud Meets Lonely Married Lady in Secret Riviera Affair. Abandons Family to Elope to America. I can just see the headlines in the *News of the World*."

"All right," she said. "It's true, sex is a big part of it."

Suddenly he hit her. He did not know he was going to do it until he had knocked her back with a slap on the jaw. Her raincoat fell open and he saw her panty hose and her bare breasts. "Sex, is it?" he heard himself shouting. "Is that what you want, is it sex you want?" And as he did, to his shock, he felt an erection. He caught her and pushed her down on the bed, spread-eagling himself over her, beginning with his left hand to pull down her panty hose.

"Kevin, will you stop it. Get off me!"

But now that unpredictable person inside of him saw a strange woman who had been in bed screwing some young Yank for the past two weeks, a woman he did not know any more, a woman who wanted sex, and a good bloody beating into the bargain. Sex, he'd give her sex, if that's what she needed, he'd fuck the living daylights out of her. He stared moonstruck at her long white thighs and belly and the dark pubic hair as he pulled down her panty hose, struggling with her, tearing the panty hose, staring at her white, milky skin, which used to make him think of sin.

"Kevin, are you mad, will you stop it!"

She wrestled with him. She hit him in the face with her fist as he backed off and stood up, unzipping his trousers, pulling out his penis, which he held like a club in his fist, staring at its red tip, then staring at her. "So you want fucking, that's what you want, eh? Fucking!"

"Kevin, don't! Stop it." She tried to get up, but he hit her hard, knocking her back on the bedspread, spreading himself over her, pinning her down. "Shut up!" he said. "I'm going to fuck you, do you hear me? Just like the bloody whore you are."

And then, as though realizing that she could not push him off, she began to sob, but the sight of her tears only excited him further, and now he had her naked, and he kicked free of his trousers and forced her legs apart, pushing his penis in, beginning to pump and strain, holding back an orgasm which in his terrible new excitement he could barely control: this was not his wife, it was some strange woman in a French hotel, and her weeping, her fear and loathing of him, made his excitement greater. And then, as he worked his hands underneath her, grasping the cheeks of her bottom, pulling her toward him, it seemed to him that she responded, and with a rush of satisfaction, his orgasm began. He heard himself utter a loud, uncharacteristic groan of pleasure.

Then lay panting, the bed disarranged, the woman moving away from him, getting off the bed, going to put on her dress while he watched her, then going behind him to the other corner of the room. He heard water running in the washbasin. He was no longer angry. He felt curiously at peace. He felt that he was in charge. He sat up and put on his trousers, buckling his belt, pulling down the peaks of his waistcoat, straightening the handkerchief in his suit jacket pocket, using a pocket comb to tidy his thick curly hair. She was at the little washbasin, doing something to her face, just as if they were in their bedroom at home.

"You're coming with me," he said.

She went on putting stuff on her eyes.

"Right, Sheila?"

She took a comb from her purse and began to brush her hair.

"When you're ready," he said, "I'll take your suitcase and we'll go downstairs and I'll tell your friend
that you're going home. We'll take a taxi to the airport
and get the next plane to London. We should be able to
get a connecting flight to Dublin tonight. I have the car
waiting at Dublin airport. You can be home with
Danny before midnight. And nothing will be said. We'll
not mention this again, either one of us. We'll just treat
it as—as if it were something we read about in a book,
ha ha. And close the book."

She went on brushing her hair.

"Besides," he said, "you have no chance of living in
America, you know. You won't be allowed to stay."

He watched her as he said it, and saw her look at
him through the mirror.

"Oh, you might be able to go off there now, on a
tourist visa. I might, or might not, be able to stop you.
But once you're there, that's another matter. I've already
spoken to the American Embassy in Dublin. I know
the drill. I simply report the truth to the Americans—
that you're no tourist, that you have no notion of coming back to Ireland, that you're living in America with
a man who isn't your husband. And, also, I have a letter here from Owen, with information about your
mother and brother and their breakdowns. Two breakdowns already in your family. Mental illness is something the Yanks are dead set against. That's what they
told me at the embassy in Dublin. I have a good con-
tact there."

He waited. She went on combing her hair.

"I know what you're thinking," he said. "You think
I'm doing this to get back at you. But that's not true,
Sheila. I was angry, I'll admit it. But I'm not any more.
Because, just look at the facts. Two and a half weeks
ago you'd never heard of this kid. You were going on

a holiday with me. That's not *normal,* Sheila. Surely you must know that?"

She did not answer.

"No, I suppose you don't. You're in what they call the manic phase. They tell me it doesn't last long, that phase. In a few weeks, you'll be in stage number two— the depths of depression. And God help that boy downstairs when *that* starts."

She put her comb in the purse and shut the purse. She did not look at him. "Do you have Owen's letter on you?" she asked.

"Yes." He took the letter from the inside pocket of his jacket and held it up so that she could read it. "But don't touch," he warned.

She came closer and read the letter. "It's not to the American Embassy. It's only a letter to you."

"It will corroborate the statement I plan to make to the embassy."

She turned away again and went to the window, looking out at the hodgepodge of roofs in the courtyard beyond. He did not speak. Let her think about it. She turned, went to the bed, and straightened out the bedspread. He was silent. Yes, let it sink in. Give her time to come around.

When she had finished straightening the bed, she went to the wardrobe, opened a drawer, and took out a fresh pair of panty hose. Turning her back on him, she put them on. He watched her. She put on her shoes and picked up her purse. She went to the mirror, put on her blue sun hat, pulling it down over her eyes. She turned to him.

"Are you ready?" he said. "Where's your suitcase?"

"I'm going downstairs now," she said. "I'd advise you to go home."

"What?" Anger reddened his face.

"Let me finish. No matter what happens to me, Kevin, I'm never going back to you. That's final."

"Oh, one other thing," he said. "This kid downstairs must have family over in America. I can trace them through the records at Trinity. I can let them know just what their son is letting himself in for. A runaway wife and mother, with a chance of mental illness, ha ha."

"Unlock the door, Kevin."

"Not until you tell me you're coming home with me."

She screamed. He ran around the bed to stop her, but she ran from him, screaming, a terrible sound, a sound that frightened him. For the first time he believed she *was* mad. He turned back and, fumbling, unlocked the door. She stopped screaming only when he opened the door and held it open. "Jesus Christ, you *are* mad," he said.

She went past him and, again, that unpredictable person began to shout inside his head, someone foul with rage, calling after her, "All right, go! But I'm going to have you deported, do you hear? And when you're sent back to Belfast I'll divorce you. And you've seen Danny for the last time. And you'll wind up in an asylum, it's where you bloody well belong."

She ran down the stairs and he ran after her, shouting, both of them coming into the lobby, where the woman at the desk was staring up at them, alarmed and disapproving, and where the Yank stood in the middle of the room, looking ready to hit someone. She went to him at once, and he put his arms around her. "Are you all right?" he said.

"Yes."

The boy turned, staring at Redden. The woman behind the desk said something in French, very cross, but

Redden did not understand it. He shut his fists and stood staring at the boy, ready to fight. But Sheila linked her arm in the boy's. "Come on, Tom," she said.

He saw them move toward the front entrance. He ran after them, caught her wrist, and said, "If you walk out that door with him, you're finished. I promise you that."

"I believe you," she said. "Now, let me go."

And then he could not bear to look at her any longer. He let go of her wrist and ran into the alcove, grabbing his raincoat and bag. She and the boy were going out through the doorway, but he pushed past them. He was going to be the one to walk out on *her*. In the street he met a downpour, but did not stop. He ran down the street, the raincoat over his arm, his best dark suit getting soaked. When he reached the junction of the rue Casimir-Delavigne and the rue Monsieur-le-Prince, the taxi rank was deserted. In pelting rain he hurried on, going toward the big boulevards. He did not look back.

When Mrs. Redden saw him run out of the hotel door like a lunatic, she stopped short. "Wait," she said. "Let him go." They stood in the vestibule and watched the rain outside. After a moment she went forward and peered out, looking up and down the street.

"Has he gone?"

"Yes," she said.

"What happened up there? Why did you scream?"

"He wouldn't unlock the door to let me out."

"The bastard. What did he say? What's he going to do?"

"Nothing. Just talk. Don't worry about him."

"Are you sure?"

"Yes."

"Do you think he'll be back?"

"No."

It had seemed a pleasant idea when Ivo proposed it over champagne on Thursday night, after serving them his special Yugoslav dinner. Peg and he were to come with them to the Gare des Invalides for one last farewell drink before they took the airport bus. But, in fact, at five minutes past seven on Friday evening, when the taxi turned into a tree-lined avenue outside the Invalides and stopped at a door marked DÉPART, Mrs. Redden, looking very nervous, turned to Peg and said, "I hate these goodbyes. Couldn't we just say goodbye here in the taxi? Just leave us here?" And Peg, seeing the strain in her friend's face, agreed, kissed her sentimentally, clung to her, and said, "Oh, Sheila, I wish you luck."

"What's this?" Ivo said. He and Tom were taking the bags out of the taxi's trunk.

"They want us to go," Peg said. "To say goodbye now."

"Ah," said Ivo. "Then I must read my beautiful poem here on the street?"

"Yes, darling."

And so, with the taxi man waiting, Ivo pulled from his pocket a slip of paper which he said was a translation of a Yugoslav classic and, to everyone's embarrassment, read out a maudlin verse about lovers embarking on the long journey of life. And then there were more embraces and promises to write and Ivo and Peg got back into the taxi and the taxi pulled away from the curb, Peg's hand waving farewell through the open window. They were alone now, the two of them, leaving Paris at last, she going to wait in the great hall of the *aerogare* while he hurried off to a window to purchase tickets for the bus.

Behind her, in the departure hall, clerks consulted schedules, punched computer keys, and filled out tickets. A long line of travelers moved in two queues toward the windows of the *bureau de change*. A tour group identified by identical yellow flight bags picked over souvenirs in the gift shops and lined up at the news stall to flick through the pages of glossy magazines. Two small boys, inventing ways to kill the boredom of waiting, swooped past Mrs. Redden, arms outstretched, imitating the flight of aircraft. She thought of Danny when he was their age, and turned away, unable to look at them. And then saw Tom coming toward her, his duffel bag over one shoulder, her suitcase in his left hand.

"All set," he said. "Let's get the next bus out."

"Let me carry my suitcase."

"No, it's fine."

At the TWA counter at de Gaulle airport the clerk inspected her ticket, then asked to see her passport. He returned the passport, tore part of her ticket off, asked how many pieces of baggage she wished to check and whether she wanted a seat in the smoking or non-smoking section. Tom then put her suitcase on the weighing scale. The clerk put a baggage-check ticket on it and lifted it onto a conveyor belt. She watched her suitcase move along the belt and disappear through some rubber matting which opened, like a mouth, to admit it. "Boarding at nine-fifteen, Gate 9," the clerk said. "Thank you, Mrs. Redden. Have a pleasant flight."

They had already checked Tom's duffel bag at the charter airline counter. Now, to leave France and fly away to a new life, they must first be shut in. Their passports were examined by a French police official, their hand luggage and their persons were searched for weapons, and they entered a limbo of lounges, bars, news stalls, and duty-free shops to wait for their separate planes. They sat on a red plastic sofa, his hand in hers. "So it's happening," he said. "Are you nervous?"

"No."

"Your hand feels cold."

"I'm all right."

He took a card from his pocket. "Now, in case there's any delay in my flight, here's what you do. You'll land in New York at the TWA terminal. Just go to the TWA lounge and ask them to check on the arrival time of my flight. Wait in the lounge until I show up. Here, it's all on this card, the charter firm name, flight number, and phone number to call. Put it in your purse."

On the electronic board facing them, a sudden clicking sound signaled a change. Her flight information did not alter, but his now registered a gate number and the notation that the flight was leaving on time. At eight-twenty his flight was called. He smiled at her, and they stood up together, walking toward the glass doors where a stewardess waited to check the boarding passes. "At least, my flight being first means it's pretty sure I'll be waiting for you when you get in," he said.

"That's true."

"You've got your visa and your passport. There'll be no problems, right?"

She nodded.

"Still," he said. "Isn't it lousy to be separated, even for a few hours?"

They joined the queue of passengers going through the gate. When it came his turn to show his boarding pass to the stewardess, Mrs. Redden put her arms around his neck. "I love you," she said. "Imagine if we'd never met. I love you."

He kissed her. "See you in New York. Listen, why don't you go over to the bar now and have a drink and a sandwich? You won't be eating dinner much before midnight, our time."

"Yes, all right." But she held him and kissed him again, holding him until all the other passengers had gone through and the stewardess, waiting, said sympathetically, "Excuse me. Time to go."

"I love you," she said a last time, and watched as he showed his boarding pass and went past the stewardess down the corridor. At the end of the corridor he turned and waved to her. A uniformed attendant came up and the stewardess handed him the boarding passes. *"Quarante-huit,"* the stewardess said. *"Quarante-huit,"* the attendant agreed.

Tears, uncontrollable, started in her eyes. She waved to him. He waved a last time, then turned away. But she waved and kept on waving until he was out of sight.

The priest came along the side aisle of the Cathedral of Notre-Dame shortly after 11 a.m. and went up the steps of the Chapelle d'Accueil. He went to the table which was placed in the center of the chapel and switched on the reading lamp. He glanced at the confessional on his right, and at the empty altar in the rear, then took off his shabby plastic raincoat and put it away in a small cupboard. In his baggy trousers and worn gray cotton jacket, spectacles askew on his nose, he seemed a comic figure, God's comedian, preparing some strange theatrical skit. He sat at the table, opened the large ledger, and wrote something in it, using a fine-nibbed pen which he dipped in a bottle of Quink.

He was still writing when he became aware that a woman had come up the chapel steps and was waiting to speak to him. He looked at her, peering over his spectacles, as she tucked in her auburn hair, which escaped in soft untidy tendrils from under a blue hat. The sun hat was pulled forward to conceal the fact that her eyes were swollen by recent weeping. He noticed such things. He recognized the woman.

"Good morning, *Madame*," he said, raising his large white hand as in benediction, gesturing, splay-fingered, to the seat opposite him. She sat facing him across the lamp's pool of light.

"Do you remember me, Father?" Her voice was so low he could hardly hear it.

"Excuse me," he said. "My ear is a little deaf."

"Do you remember me?"

"Yes, *Madame*. You were the lady who said she must make a difficult decision."

"Yes, that's right."

"And have you made it?"

"Yes." Her voice broke as she spoke, and the priest, understanding, leaned a little forward into the pool of light, putting his hand up, his broad stubby fingers covering his eyes as though he were in the confessional, listening to, but not looking at, the penitent. "Would you like to talk about it?"

"I don't know," she said. "I was supposed to go to America. But I didn't because . . ."

She did not finish, but he was accustomed to these things. He knew to wait.

"I couldn't," she said at last.

"You were going to live in America?"

"Yes. With someone. I even used the ticket. That's why I came to see you. I have to get some money. I must pay back that ticket I wasted."

"I don't understand," the priest said. "You didn't go, but you used the ticket?"

"I let the airlines people take the ticket. I went to the airport." Suddenly she laughed, but the priest did not look up. He knew it was laughter which disguised tears. "I even sent my suitcase on to New York. Every stitch of clothes I have."

"Why did you do that, *Madame*?"

"Because I didn't want the other person to know I wasn't going. If he'd known, he wouldn't have gone himself. But I don't want to bother you with that. I came about the money. You see, there's some money which is due to me. I'd like to have it sent to me in care of you. Could you help me?"

The priest nodded, his fingers still spread to conceal his eyes. "I think so, yes. Someone will send money here. And I will keep it until you come for it. Is that what you want?"

"No. I'm going to London. The person who's to send the money is my brother. He may ask you where I am, but I don't want him to know. He may tell you I'm ill, mentally ill. But I'm not. So you mustn't give him my address. I mean, this address I'll send you from London."

"You don't have a London address yet. Is that it?"

"Yes. As soon as I find a place to stay, I'll let you know."

"Tell me," the priest said, "last week we talked about Camus. Do you remember?"

"Yes, Father."

"You said, when we talked, that you felt a desire to kill yourself. Do you still feel that way?"

"No."

"Are you quite sure?"

"Oh yes," she said and laughed again, that laughter which was like weeping.

"Can you tell me why you changed?"

"I don't know, Father. Last night I stayed in an awful cheap hotel. And it was the night I'd decided not to go to America. So, you see . . . Anyway, when I went to the window of the room, I no longer felt I wanted to jump. Not at all. So that's over." She opened her purse, found a tissue, and blew her nose.

The priest joined his large white hands together, as though in prayer. "You said your brother believes you may be ill. Why does he believe that?"

"Because he's a doctor and because there's some history of mental illness in our family. But I'm all right. I am, Father. I won't ask you to help me unless you believe it."

The priest looked at her left hand. "You are married?"

"Yes."

"Have you left your husband?"

"Yes, I have."

The priest separated his hands, turning them palms down on the ledger. "I see. And now you are going to start a new life?"

"Yes."

"I remember the last time we talked," the priest said. "You said then that you are not religious."

"Yes."

The priest looked beyond the pool of light, out into the darkness of the nave. "You do not believe in God?"

"I did once. But I don't now."

"Why not, *Madame?*"

"Because it doesn't make sense. You can't go on believing, once you think the idea of God is ridiculous."

The priest smiled, showing the gap between his teeth. "I can," he said. "And I do."

She looked at him through swollen eyelids. "That's a funny thing for a priest to say."

"I know," the priest said. "It doesn't make sense. But believing in God is like being in love. You don't have to have reasons, or proofs, or justifications. You are in love, *voilà tout.* You know it."

The woman began to weep.

"I'm sorry," the priest said. "You want me to help you about this money. I will be glad to do what you say. Just give me the instructions."

"And you won't tell anyone the address. No matter what?"

"No matter what," the priest said.

He felt for and opened a drawer under the tabletop and took out a sheet of cheap, graph-lined paper. "Write your name so that I will know if a letter comes for you." He dipped his pen in the bottle of Quink and handed it to her. She wrote her name, then added a second name to the sheet. "That's my brother," she said. "He's the one who will be sending the money. I'll write you my new address as soon as I get settled. And thank you, Father. You're very kind."

She pushed the sheet of paper across the table. The priest looked at it. "Very well, Mrs. Redden. Now, if I were you, I would get some rest."

"I'll be all right. Thank you again."

"God bless you, then," the priest said.

She went down the steps, going from the small lighted area of the chapel into the shadows of the huge nave, where, day after day, tourists moved like restless, mindless birds up and down the aisles. The priest sat again and opened the right-hand drawer of his table. He pulled out a fat shabby cardboard folder, secured by a large paper clip. He placed the slip of paper with her name in a small rectangular envelope and inserted it under the edge of the clip. He took up his pen and, as an aide-mémoire, wrote across the envelope,

Irlandaise—argent faire suivre

He paused and looked over his spectacles. Then added,

Tentative de suicide?

3

After two days in Paris, Dr. Deane decided he might as well go home. He was a doctor, not a detective, and he had found out what he could. From now on, it seemed likely that his investigations would be reduced to following after every tall young woman he saw in the street, in hopes that if she turned around she would reveal herself to be his sister. Besides, his tachycardia was worse, and last night, in his hotel room, his mind had begun to prey again on the most gloomy possibilities. So he phoned Peg Conway to say he was leaving and to thank her for her help, then wired Belfast to give his flight-arrival time. He had hoped that Anne, his older daughter, might drive out to the airport to pick him up. But when he landed in Belfast, the person who met him was Agnes.

"Well," she said, after he had kissed her. "Welcome back, Sherlock Holmes. I was right, wasn't I? It was a complete wild-goose chase."

"Yes, in a way," he said, for it was never wise to contradict her. "But, on the whole, I think it was worthwhile."

"How's that?"

"Well, I'll tell you, dear," he said and, taking her arm, led her out of the building. It was raining, and so cold it was hard to believe this was summer. "Actually," he said, "I found out quite a bit. She's not in America at all. She's probably still in France."

This was to have been his bombshell, but he might as well have said it was a rainy day for all the notice Agnes took. She found the car-park ticket and he put up the umbrella she had brought. Under its shelter they went out toward the car. "Remember the letter the boy friend sent in care of Peg? Well, there was an American address on the envelope. So I took the bull by the horns and rang up, asking for her. She wasn't there. Then I asked for him, and got him. He was very hostile, as a matter of fact, but I had a definite impression that he doesn't know any more than we do about where she is. In fact, I think there's a good chance she's still in France. I'll tell you why."

"You rang up America? How much did that cost?"

"Oh, it wasn't bad. Peg wouldn't let me pay but I forced a few pounds on her."

"Why didn't you open the letter?"

"Ah, no, I couldn't do that. I have it with me, though. I thought I'd send it on to Sheila when I hear where she wants her money sent. Don't you think that's the best idea?"

"You forgot to fasten your seat belt," Agnes said.

"So I did. Thanks, dear." He buckled up, and they drove out of the car park. "Yesterday," he said, "I went to see that priest."

"The French priest?"

"Yes, the one she wrote me to send the money to. A nice man. He hears confessions in English. Anyway, I played the innocent with him, didn't say a word about her mental state. I just said that I was worried I might have trouble getting the money to her in America because of foreign-exchange regulations. So he said, 'Your sister is *not* in America.'"

" 'So, where is she?' said I. He said he couldn't say, but that there wouldn't be any necessity to send the money to her in dollars. So I asked him, 'Where should I send it and in what currency?' He said he didn't know yet, but that he would let me know as soon as he could. Of course, that worried me, do you see? I mean, if he hasn't heard from Sheila yet. You see what I mean, dear? I hope she's all right."

"Don't you worry your head," Agnes said, and laughed. "Sherlock Holmes. Going to Paris and ringing up New York. And do you know all you had to do? Sit tight at home at 54 Dundrum Road."

"What are you talking about, dear?"

"I'm talking about Sheila. She rang you up this morning. She's going to call back at nine o'clock tonight."

"Where did she ring from? Did she tell you where she is?"

"She didn't tell *me* anything, she didn't even have the manners to ask for me. She spoke to Imelda, and when the child asked if she wanted to speak to me, she said no, she'd call back."

"And did Imelda not say I was in Paris?"

"Yes, she told her."

"And did Imelda say how she sounded?"

"How would Imelda know?" .

"Yes, I suppose. Anyway, that's great news, isn't it? I can't tell you the terrible gloomy thoughts I had in Paris last night. I'd never forgive myself if anything happened to her now."

"Don't worry, nothing's going to happen to her. Didn't I tell you she'd be all right? Any woman who'll walk out on her husband and child after a three-week fling is not going to kill herself. Didn't I say that?"

"So you did, dear," Dr. Deane said. "So you did."

* * *

His daughters were making supper when he and Agnes got back to the house. He kissed them, gave them presents of silk scarves from the Paris duty-free shop, and then went into the den, shutting the door, saying he wanted to look over his post. What he wanted was a large whiskey. He poured it and lit the fire. He supposed he should phone Kevin Redden, but, honestly, he didn't feel up to it. He had barely been able to be civil to the man ever since Redden let slip that he had showed Sheila that letter. And, in his most recent conversation, Redden said that he'd made a full report to the American Embassy in Dublin and that, furthermore, he was suing for divorce on the grounds of desertion. So why phone him to tell him the news? What does he care?

Instead of phoning, therefore, Dr. Deane downed a second whiskey. As he finished it, the girls came to the door and said supper was on the dining-room table. Food was the last thing he wanted, but there was still an hour to kill before Sheila's phone call was due and so he went in and managed a few bites of the ham and cauliflower. Imelda had made a chocolate cake with a cream filling and Agnes was very pleased with it and praised it and so nothing would do them but that he try it. "That piece is far too big for me," he protested, and as he did, the telephone rang. He stood up precipitately and hurried into the den, shutting the door behind him before he picked up the receiver. But he was too late. Agnes had already run to the hall and picked up the phone out there.

"It's Agnes, Sheila," he heard her say.

"Hello, Agnes. Is Owen back yet?"

"Yes. How are you? Where are you?"

"Hello," he said, cutting in. "Sheila?"

"Yes."

"Agnes, I'd like to speak to Sheila alone, if you don't mind."

He'd pay for that later, no doubt, but still, it had to be done. "All right, I'll hang up," Agnes said and clicked the receiver, but he was not deceived. He knew she was still on the line. At least, now she would be quiet.

"Hello, Sheila?" he said. "Did you know I was over there in Paris looking for you? I've been terribly worried. How are you?"

"I'm all right."

"And where are you?"

"Owen, I'm ringing you about those shares. Did you get my letter?"

"Yes, I did. And I've sold the lot and there's about sixteen hundred pounds out of it."

He heard Agnes's intake of breath on the other line. She had had no idea it was that much.

"It could have been more," he said. "But the market's down just now. How do you want it paid? Into a bank would be best, I suppose?"

"Can you pay it into a post-office savings account?"

"I suppose so, yes. Do they have that sort of thing in France?"

"I don't want it paid in France. I want it paid in London."

"Then you're in London, are you?"

She did not answer. "Can you pay it into a post office in London? I can open an account at the Belsize Park post office on Haverstock Hill."

"That's in Hampstead," he said. "I know that part. John Devaney used to live near there. On Parkhill Road, I believe."

"How long will it take for the money to get to London?"

"Oh, I don't know. A few days, a week, I'm not sure."

"Well, there's some of it I want paid out at once," she said. "I owe it. It's whatever the equivalent is of four hundred and fifteen dollars. I wonder if you could send that directly to someone in the United States."

"Of course I could. Who will I send it to?"

"Have you got a pencil?"

"Yes, fire away."

"It's to go to a Mr. Tom Lowry, Pine Lodge, Rutland, Vermont."

"Yes, I spoke to him the other day."

"Where?" Her voice faltered.

"I rang him up in Vermont. He wrote you a letter in care of Peg in Paris. It gave his address. I rang him, hoping to get some news of you."

"How is he?" Her voice was now a whisper.

"He seems all right. I have his letter here, I can send it on. But, Sheila, I think you did the right thing, not going with him. The only thing. By the way, what are you living on now?"

"I'm all right."

"I feel bloody terrible about Kevin showing you that letter I wrote him. I shouldn't have written it, and he shouldn't have shown it. I only wanted to help you. Will you believe that?"

"It doesn't matter now," she said. "And thanks for cashing in my shares."

"Listen, Sheila, I'd love to see you. What if I flew over and put the money in your hand? I have this letter for you, too. Just let me talk to you for half an hour. And I promise there'll be no preaching."

She hesitated. "You'd bring the money, and the letter?"

"Yes, I'll go to my bank first thing in the morning. Just tell me where."

"Could you come tomorrow? Say late tomorrow afternoon."

"Come where?"

"London," she said. "Meet me at six o'clock at the Primrose Hill Park gate opposite Regent's Park zoo on Prince Albert Road. Do you know where that is?"

"I'm writing it down. I can find it. At six, you said?"

"Yes. And we'll only talk for half an hour. You can be back home tomorrow night. Is that all right?"

"Yes. All right."

"See you at six, then. And thanks, Owen."

"Take care of yourself," he said. He heard her hang up, then Agnes hung up. He sat down in the den and stared at the fire, waiting for her.

"Well, aren't you the soft one," she said, coming in. "Did you hear the way she ordered you around? Just like a messenger boy. And sixteen hundred pounds you're going to hand over to her."

"It's her own money, dear."

"And the letter. It was the minute you mentioned you had a letter from her boy friend that her ladyship changed her mind about seeing you. If you go, Owen, you're making a real fool of yourself."

"I want to see her," he said. "I thought I told you to get off the phone."

"Oh, I'm glad you brought *that* up. You were so rude, I couldn't believe my ears. I felt as if I was going to cry. You and that family of yours, I declare you're married to them, not to me. I mean, here's your own wife in her own house being told to get off the phone as if she's some outsider."

Anne and Imelda were in the doorway. They had heard her.

"Was that Aunt Sheila, Daddy?"

"Yes," he said.

"And where is she?"

"London. Did you make any tea or coffee?"

"Coffee," Anne said. "Do you want it in here?"

"Yes, thanks."

"So you're going, then?" Agnes began. "Cupid, love's messenger, bringing her the boy friend's letter. Well, I never heard the like."

"Agnes," he said. "Please?"

"What's the matter? I just asked you a question. I just want to know how many more fares you're going to pay, running after her. Why don't you ask her at least to pay your expenses, out of her sixteen hundred quid?"

"Mummy," Anne said. She took her mother's arm. "Come on, Mum," Imelda said, taking the other arm. And somehow they did what he never could do. Got her out. Got him some peace.

The manageress in charge of all of the Hampstead branches of Fastkleen Laundries was a stout, awkward person in her fifties, with a face empty as an actor's after the curtain comes down. Every customer, irrespective of age or sex, was addressed as "Dear." She worried about mistakes in making change and counted everything twice; yet, in a crisis, when a customer's laundry had been mislaid, she was a model of patience, turning over docket after docket and almost always coming up with the missing item. On the first day of Mrs. Redden's employment, the manageress spent the morning with her, then left her on her own for the afternoon, returning just before closing to collect the day's takings. "All right, dear? Everything all right? Good. Tomorrow, you can run the shop yourself."

On the afternoon of the third day, the manageress came in about four and saw that Mrs. Redden had been weeping. "Anything wrong, dear? Customers making a fuss?" Mrs. Redden said, no, she was all right, it was all going very well, really. "That's good, dear," the manageress said and reached under the counter for a sign which read BACK IN 15 MINS. She put the sign in the window. "Let's go across the street for a minute."

"Been in England long, dear?" the manageress asked,

when, settled in the back of the pub, they had ordered a ruby port and a dry sherry.

"No, just about a week."

"Got a place to stay?"

"I have a bed-sitter. It's off Haverstock Hill."

"Bit pricey, I'll bet?"

"Yes."

"Have any friends in London, dear?"

"No, not really."

"You want to join one of these social clubs. There's an Irish club over in Camden Town. We have some Irish girls working for us up in Hampstead Village branch, they took me there last week. We had a nice time. I like the Irish songs. You're not going to keep this job, are you?"

"What do you mean?"

"I should imagine you could do better, dear. You've been to the university, haven't you? I saw it on your application form. You'll get a better-paying job soon, I should think."

"Oh, but this job suits me. I mean, for now. I don't want a job I can't do, you see."

"Yes, you get your bearings. Yes, that's right. You married, dear?"

"I was, yes."

"Well, here's to us that was. By the way, dear, if you ever have to leave the shop, better give me a ring first, so that I can cover for you. We have inspectors, you know. I know sometimes the girls like a little time off to nip out to shop or something. It's hard getting settled, especially when you're new, like."

"Thank you. That's very nice of you."

"Yes. Oh, we had to laugh, that night at the Irish Club. There was a fellow sang these songs. Laugh! It can be a bit lonely, I should imagine, when you first

come over. Listen, maybe you'd better run on back
now, dear. See you tomorrow, half past five. All right?"

The room was in the attic of a Victorian terrace house
at the unfashionable end of Gloucester Gardens. The
roof sloped so that, when she was in bed, it seemed
that the ceiling was sliding down on top of her. There
was a large wardrobe, its drawers and compartments
empty as she had no change of clothing. There was also
an easy chair and a desk facing the window, which
looked out on a view of four long narrow back gardens.
In the evenings, when she came home from the laundry,
she ate sitting at this desk, and, later, moved the easy
chair to the window and read books from the local
library until the long summer light had faded. At night
she dreamed a lot. Her dreams were erotic and often
jealous, in particular a recurring dream where she stood
on the balcony of the room in the Hôtel Welcome while
he made love to some young girl on the bed inside. She
dreamed often of accidents, of being with him in a
crashing airplane, or holding him as their car plunged
over a cliff. Sometimes these dreams would waken her
and she would lie sleepless, wondering what he was doing today, wondering if he was thinking of her, as she
was thinking of him. And often she would think of
money: she had never thought of money in the old days.
Now she would think of how she used to spend six
pounds having her hair done and never even notice
when she paid it out. She remembered her first three
days here in London, when she had only two pounds
left in her purse after paying a week's rent on the room.
She would wonder why Owen had not written to Father
Brault in Paris, or why Father Brault had not sent the
money on. Kitty's little nest egg. Now it seemed such an
awful lot. She earned twenty-five pounds a week and

paid ten pounds of it for this room. Far too much. But all the other rooms she had looked at had been so dirty.

And then, while she lay under the sloping wall, the light would come in, a morning light, and soon it would be time to rise and hurry through half-deserted streets to open the laundry shop at eight.

At work, she would start to think of him again. It had been this way ever since she had walked out of the airport, two weeks ago. Even when she was busy, making change or finding a customer's shirts, she would look up each time the shop bell rang, as though he might be the next person to walk in. She knew that this could not happen. She knew there was no way in which he could trace her. She did not want him to walk in. And yet she could not help it. She thought of him constantly. She knew that some day she would no longer think of him all the time. But it had not happened yet.

And so, when at last she got up the courage to phone Owen and was told there was a letter from him, she felt a sudden terrible urgency to know what he had done and what he had written to her. That was why she agreed to Owen's coming. It was foolish.

Or so she now thought. Mrs. Dixon had come by at five-thirty as usual, to pick up the day's receipts, and had agreed to let her go a few minutes early and to close up the shop for her. And so at ten minutes to six she walked up Regent's Park Road to Primrose Hill, entering the park. It was a warm summer's evening. Ahead of her, coming in off the street, a girl and a young man let loose their dogs, which, released from their leashes, ran in absurd galumphing circles, barking, tongues lolling with joy. To her left, on a broad lawn of grass now yellowing from the summer heat, four young men kicked a football, aiming at impromptu goalposts made by their jackets, while two older men walked slowly along a path, their loud voices deep in argument, oblivious to the pastoral sweep of the hill, the lawns, the panorama of London, distant and still in a summer's evening haze. She had told Owen she would meet him at the entrance nearest the zoo. As she went toward that gate, she realized that he would expect her to come from the street and not from the park. She would probably see him before he saw her. For one frightening moment she wondered if Owen had told Kevin about this meeting and if, by any chance, Kevin might come with him. There was no trusting Owen any more. But somehow she did not think Kevin would come, and so she walked on, her pace a little slower now, her mind going again to that which obsessed her: Tom's letter and what he had said in it. And so, as a church clock, somewhere, began to toll six times, she came down past the children's playground, past the mothers, the sandbox, the swings, going toward the gate where Owen would be. She saw him, and as she came closer, she watched to see if he was alone. He was. He stood underneath the park notice board, tall and ill at ease, wearing the same green suit he had worn when she spoke to him last month. He carried a small attaché case and turned this way and that, looking up and down the road as though she might pass by and he would miss her.

She hesitated, wanting to go back, afraid to touch again that world she had left. But there was the letter, the last word not yet said. Suddenly she quickened her step.

Dr. Deane had arrived early. He did not realize how nervous he was about this meeting until the taxi put him down at the park gate across from the zoo. He waited half an hour, smoked two cigarettes, and ran out. To-morrow he must stop smoking.

At first he watched the street, expecting to see her come along Prince Albert Road. But as it grew closer to six, he glanced back into the park and, to his surprise, saw her walking down Primrose Hill. She was a good distance away and was wearing a blue suit which looked heavy for this heat. As she came along the path, some dogs, playing in the grass, bounded out in front of her, causing her to halt. He waved to her. She waved back.

He began to walk toward her. As she came closer, he saw her face more clearly. Something had changed. He could not say, exactly, but she looked older.

"Hello, Sheila," he said, going up to her, his kiss tentative, uncertain as to his welcome. But she hugged him, just as in the old days when they had been the Family.

"I'm delighted to see you're all right," he told her. "I was worried about you, you know."

"There's a bench over there," she said. "Let's go and sit on it."

He took her arm as they walked along the path. Hard to see if she was depressed or not. Somehow he thought not. At least, not like Ned.

"How was the flight?"

"Bumpy," he said.

"Are you still afraid of flying?"

"Always. I have your money, by the way. I also sent off that money to America this morning."

He felt her stiffen.

"That's what you wanted, wasn't it?"

"Yes. What did you say? Did you put in a note?"

"I wired it. I just said in the wire it was from you."

She sat on the bench. She seemed distracted. "I wonder, will he know what it's for?"

"Oh, I imagine so," Dr. Deane said. He sat beside her and opened his attaché case. "Here's the rest of your share. Fourteen hundred and twenty-two pounds, made out on a draft on Barclays Bank, Leicester Square branch. It's not as much as I'd hoped, I'm afraid."

She took the envelope, did not look at it, and stuffed it into her purse. "Thanks. Did you bring my letter?"

"Yes." He took it from the attaché case, the airmail envelope with its American stamps looking a bit dog-eared by now. She took the letter, looked at the address, then put it carefully in her purse. She bent forward, her head down as though she were faint. He touched her arm. "Are you all right?"

"Yes," she said. She raised her head and stared off across the park. "How is Danny, have you heard?"

"Agnes phoned your house a few days ago. He's upset, of course. It's to be expected. By the way, Sheila, there's something I want to say to you. Would you like to come back and stay with us for a while? We have plenty of room."

"No thanks."

"Or I could find you a flat. I think if you were living in Belfast, Kevin wouldn't stop you seeing Danny from time to time. He might even let him stay with you, off and on."

"I have a job here."

"What sort of job?"

"In a shop."

Now he was angry with her. "I see. Working in a shop. Living alone in London. Is that what you're going to do with your life?"

She did not answer him. She opened her purse again

and looked at the American's letter. "Go on," he said angrily. "Go ahead and read it, if that's what you want to do."

A young man, bearded, wearing blue jeans, went past them, pushing a high English pram in which there were twin children. A listless Irish setter trailed the pram, turning to stick its nose up Mrs. Redden's skirt. She moved the dog's head away, then stood up. "I'd better go," she said. "Thanks very much for coming, and for bringing the money."

His anger left him. Instead, absurdly, he felt he was going to cry. "Stay a minute, won't you? I want to say I'm sorry about writing that letter for Kevin. I didn't think he'd use it that way."

She looked away up the hill. "Did he take it to the embassy?"

"I'm afraid so."

"So, if I wanted to go to America now, I'd be stopped?"

"Probably. But you don't want to go to America, do you? I think you made the right decision. You were too old for that boy, Sheila."

"I think I'd better say goodbye now."

"So soon?"

"Yes. Thanks for all you've done."

Clumsily, they approached each other. Clumsily, she kissed him.

"Will you write to me?" he asked. "Let me know how you're getting on."

"Maybe. Goodbye, Owen." She let go of him and, turning, went quickly back along the path, catching up with and passing the young man with the pram. Dr. Deane watched her go, his sister, come here to meet him like a spy, going back now to enemy country, to that unknown world across the park. His sister, that tall woman in a blue suit, walking away up the broad sweep of hill as though hurrying to some urgent assignation, becoming smaller and smaller in the hazy evening sunlight until she reached a stand of trees where the path wound around, hiding her from view. He had been waiting for her to turn, to wave, to give one last look back. But she left him as she had left all the rest, Danny, Kevin, home. No look back. He stood for a moment, then went out of the park gate.

She walked on. She walked over Primrose Hill and down through the trees, along the path which led to the gate at Elsworthy Terrace. Families were eating picnic suppers on the grass, children playing communally between the picnicking groups. She did not open the letter until she turned into the quiet tree-lined walk which ran along the edge of the park.

PINE LODGE
RUTLAND, VERMONT 05701

Tuesday

Darling,

I came here after waiting all of Friday night at Kennedy. My plane arrived on time and I went to TWA to wait for yours, which also came in on time. I thought at first you might have been delayed in immigration because of that letter your brother wrote, but then they told me you hadn't boarded the plane. I just couldn't believe it. I pointed out your bag to them, sitting there unclaimed in the baggage area. Then I decided that you must have panicked and changed your mind at the last minute. Did you? And why? Are you afraid your husband will try to have you deported? Or was it that nonsense about your age, or your son, or what? Now, I'm beginning to wonder. Did you plan this all along? Did you let them take the ticket and check your bag, just so I wouldn't suspect anything? I'm beginning to think that's pretty close to the truth. I remember you never did anything about coming here, until I pushed you into it.

Well, that was my mistake. I told you before, people do what they have to do. I didn't want to force you to come. If you've decided to go back to your husband, then good luck, I can't stop you. I don't even know your home address. I suppose I could phone your husband, but I think I've made a big enough fool of myself already.

At any rate I'm here, working in the hotel. I'm sending this to you in care of Peg in the hope that she'll forward it. If you change your mind, phone me collect and I'll fix another ticket and help you with the visa and be there to meet you when you land. If not, if all the things you said were lies and it was just an affair for you and now it's over, well, so be it. But I want you to know this. I meant it, and I mean it.

> I love you,
> Tom

There was a wooden bench at the end of the tree walk. She sat on it and read the letter again. She sat for a long time. The picnicking families began to pack their baskets and fold their blankets. After a while, she was the only person in that part of the park. The sun began to go down behind a summer's haze of golden cloud, and the park keeper came up over the hill, his gate keys in his hand. She read the letter a third time and then, as she went toward the gate, tore letter and envelope into small rectangles, dropping them into a wire rubbish basket. The park keeper was waiting to lock up. She went through the gates and walked off down the street like an ordinary woman on her way to the corner to buy cigarettes.